W9-BRY-722

THE MIDDLE OF SOMEWHERE

Center Point
Large Print

Also by Sonja Yoerg and available from Center Point Large Print:

House Broken

This Large Print Book carries the Seal of Approval of N.A.V.H.

THE
MIDDLE OF
SOMEWHERE

SONJA
YOERG

CENTER POINT LARGE PRINT
THORNDIKE, MAINE

This Center Point Large Print edition is published in the year 2016 by arrangement with New American Library, an imprint of Penguin Publishing Group, a division of Penguin Random House LLC.

The text of this Large Print edition is unabridged. In other aspects, this book may vary from the original edition. Printed in the United States of America on permanent paper. Set in 16-point Times New Roman type.

ISBN: 978-1-62899-855-9

Library of Congress Cataloging-in-Publication Data

Names: Yoerg, Sonja Ingrid, 1959– author.
Title: The middle of somewhere / Sonya Yoerg.
Description: Center Point Large Print edition. | Thorndike, Maine : Center Point Large Print, 2016. | ©2015
Identifiers: LCCN 2015046528 | ISBN 9781628998559 (hardcover : alk. paper)
Subjects: LCSH: Hikers—Fiction. | Interpersonal relations—Fiction. | Large type books.
Classification: LCC PS3625.O37 M53 2016 | DDC 813/.6—dc23
LC record available at http://lccn.loc.gov/2015046528

To Richard

Acknowledgments

I owe my agent, Maria Carvainis, a huge debt for help with this book. I sure needed it. I also thank Elizabeth Copps for her keen insight.

I'm grateful to my editor, Claire Zion, who saw before I could what Liz's story was really about. Thank you, Claire, for pointing the way. I'm also grateful to Jennifer Fisher, Caitlin Valenziano, and the rest of the team at Penguin.

Helga Immerfall, Julie Lawson Timmer, and Jerry Smith read earlier versions; I value your advice, time, and friendship. My wise and wonderful daughters, Rachel and Rebecca Frank, read numerous versions, putting aside their college texts to give me a hand. I wouldn't dream of submitting a manuscript without first running your gauntlets.

I also acknowledge a group of writers, most of whom I've never laid eyes on, but who are, nevertheless, my friends and dear to me. Eileen Goudge, Samantha Bailey, Richard Kramer, and Melissa Cryzter Fry—thank you for your wisdom and open hearts. The same goes for Ann Garvin and the other fabulous members of the Tall Poppy Writer collective, whose advice and support is my new drug. Oh, and thanks to all of you for the laughs.

Richard Gill walked with me the two hundred twenty miles of the John Muir Trail, and walked them again and again in draft after draft of this story. His photographs of the Sierra inspired my writing daily and kept me true to the Trail. Our shared love of this landscape is inscribed on every page. Thank you for taking that journey with me, and all the others as well, especially this longer one, where in my heart we are forever walking along a mountain trail under a blue sky filled with invisible stars.

I only went out for a walk,
and finally concluded to stay out till sundown,
for going out, I found, was really going in.

—John Muir, from *John of the Mountains*,
the unpublished journals of John Muir,
edited by Linnie Marsh Wolfe.
Boston: Houghton Mifflin Co,
1938, p. 439.

Chapter One

Liz hopped from foot to foot and hugged herself against the cold. She glanced at the porch of the Yosemite Valley Wilderness Office, where Dante stood with his back to her, chatting with some other hikers. His shoulders shrugged and dropped, and his hands danced this way and that. He was telling a story—a funny one, judging by the faces of his audience—but not a backpacking story because he didn't have any. His idea of a wilderness adventure was staring out the window during spin class at the gym. Not that it mattered. He could have been describing the self-contradictory worldview of the guy who changes his oil, or the merits of homemade tamales, or even acting out the latest viral cat video. Liz had known him for over two years and still couldn't decipher how he captured strangers' attention without apparent effort. Dante was black velvet and other people were lint.

Their backpacks sat nearby on a wooden bench like stiff-backed strangers waiting for a bus. The impulse to grab hers and take off without him shot through her. She quelled it with the reminder that his pack contained essential gear for completing the three-week hike. The John Muir Trail. Her hike. At least that had been the plan.

She propped her left hiking boot on the bench, retied it, folded down the top of her sock and paced a few steps along the sidewalk to see if she'd gotten them even. It wasn't yet nine a.m., and Yosemite Village already had a tentative, waking buzz. Two teenage girls in pajama pants and oversize sweatshirts walked past, dragging their Uggs on the concrete. Bleary-eyed dads pushed strollers, and Patagonia types with day packs marched purposefully among the buildings: restaurants, a grocery store, a medical clinic, a visitor's center, gift shops, a fire station, even a four-star hotel. What a shame the trail had to begin in the middle of this circus. Liz couldn't wait to get the hell out of there.

She fished Dante's iPhone out of the zippered compartment on top of his pack and called Valerie. They'd been best friends for eleven years, since freshman year in college, when life had come with happiness the way a phone plan came with minutes.

Valerie answered. "Dante?"

"No. It's me."

"Where's your phone?"

"Asleep in the car. No service most of the way. Even here I've only got one bar."

"Dante's going to go nuts if he can't use his phone."

"You think? How's Muesli?" Valerie was cat-sitting for her.

"Does he ever look at you like he thinks you're an idiot?"

"All the time."

"Then he's fine."

"How's the slipper commute?" Valerie worked as a Web designer, mostly from home, and had twenty sets of pajamas hanging in her closet as if they were business suits.

"Just firing up the machine. You get your permits?"

"Uh-huh."

"Try to sound more psyched."

How could she be psyched when this wasn't the trip she'd planned? She was supposed to hike the John Muir Trail—the JMT—alone. With a few thousand square miles of open territory surrounding her, she hoped to find a way to a truer life. She sure didn't know the way now. Each turn she'd taken, each decision she'd made—including moving in with Dante six months ago—had seemed right at the time, yet none *were* right, based as they were on a series of unchallenged assumptions and quiet lies, one weak moral link attached to the next, with the truth at the tail end, whipping away from her again and again.

Maybe, she'd whispered to herself, she could have a relationship with Dante and share a home if she pretended there was no reason she couldn't. She loved him enough to almost believe it could work. But she'd hardly finished unpacking before her doubts had mushroomed. She became desperate for time away—from the constant stream of friends in Dante's wake, from the sense of sliding down inside a funnel that led to marriage, from becoming an indeterminate portion of something called "us"—and could not tell Dante why. Not then or since. That was the crux of it. Instead, she told Dante that years ago she'd abandoned a plan to hike the JMT and now wanted to strike it off her list before she turned thirty in November. She had no list, but he accepted her explanation, and her true motivation wriggled free.

The Park Service issued only a few permits for each trailhead. She'd faxed in her application as soon as she decided to go. When she received e-mail confirmation, a crosscurrent of relief and dread flooded her. In two months' time, she would have her solitude, her bitter medicine.

Then two weeks before her start date, Dante announced he was joining her.

"You've never been backpacking, and now you want to go two hundred and twenty miles?"

"I would miss you." He opened his hands as if that were the simple truth.

There had to be more to it than that. Why else would he suggest embarking on a journey they both knew would make him miserable? She tried to talk him out of it. He didn't like nature, the cold or energy bars. It made no sense. But he was adamant, and brushed her concerns aside. She'd had no choice but to capitulate.

Now she told Valerie, "I am psyched. In fact, I want to hit the trail right now, but Dante's holding court in the Wilderness Office."

"I can't believe you'll be out of touch for three weeks. What am I going to do without you? Who am I going to talk to?"

"Yourself, I guess. Put an earbud in and walk around holding your phone like a Geiger counter. You could be an incognito schizophrenic."

"I'll be reduced to that." She dropped her voice a notch. "Listen. I have to ask you again. You sure you feel up to this?"

Liz reflexively placed her hand on her lower abdomen. "I'm fine. I swear. It's just a hike."

"When I have to park a block from Trader Joe's, that's a hike. Two hundred miles is something else. And your miscarriage was less than three weeks ago."

As if Dante could have overheard, she turned and walked a few more steps down the sidewalk. "I feel great."

"And you're going to tell Dante soon and not wait for the absolute perfect moment."

Despite the cold, Liz's palms were slick with sweat. Her boyfriend knew nothing of her preg-nancy, but her friend didn't have the whole story either. Valerie had made her daily call to Liz and learned she was home sick, but she'd been vague about the reason. Knowing Dante was out of town, Valerie had stopped by and found Liz lying on the couch, a heating pad on her belly.

"Cramps?"

"No," Liz had said, staring at the rug. "Worse."

Valerie had assumed she'd had a miscarriage, not an abortion, and Liz hadn't corrected her. Next to her deceit of Dante, it seemed minor. Valerie had made her promise she would tell him, but when Liz ran the conversation through her mind, she panicked. If she revealed this bit of information, the whole monstrous truth might tumble out, and she would lose him for certain.

"I will tell him. And I'll make sure I've got room to run when I do."

"He'll understand. It's not like it was your fault."

Liz's chest tightened. "Val, listen—"

"Crap! I just noticed the time. I've got a call in two minutes, so this is good-bye."

" 'Bye."

"Don't get lost."

"Impossible."

"Don't fall off a cliff."

"I'll try not to."

"Watch out for bears."

"I love bears! And they love me."

"Of course they do. So do I."

"And me you. 'Bye."

" 'Bye."

Liz put the phone away. She checked the zippers

and tightened the straps on both backpacks. On a trip this long, they couldn't afford to lose anything. Besides, a pack with loose straps tended to creak, and she didn't like creaking.

Dante was still chatting. He glanced over his shoulder and flashed her a boyish smile. She pointed at her watch. He twitched in mock alarm, shook hands with his new friends and hurried to her.

"Leez!" He placed his hands on her cheeks and tucked her short brown hair behind her ears with his fingers. "You're waiting. I'm sorry."

She was no more immune to his charm than the rest of the world. The way he pronounced her name amused her, and she suspected he laid it on thick deliberately. He had studied English in the best schools in Mexico City and spent seven years in the States, so he had little reason for sounding like the Taco Bell Chihuahua.

"It's okay." She rose onto her toes and kissed his cheek. "We should get going though. Did you get the forecast?"

"I did." He threw his arms wide. "It's going to be beautiful!"

"That's a quote from the ranger?"

"*Más o menos*. Look for yourself." He swept his hand to indicate the sky above the pines, an unbroken Delft blue.

Things can change, she thought, especially this late in the season. Her original permit had been for the Thursday before Labor Day. It could snow or hail or thunderstorm on any given day in the Sierras, but early September was usually dry. She'd had to surrender that start date when Dante insisted on tagging along, because he didn't have a permit. They were forced to take their chances with the weather, two weeks closer to winter.

And here it was, September fifteenth. A picture-perfect day. Dante's beaming face looked like a guarantee of twenty more like it.

When he'd first seen the elevation profile of the John Muir Trail, Dante said it resembled the ECG tracing of someone having a heart attack. Up thousands of feet, down thousands of feet, up thousands of feet, down thousands of feet, day after day.

"You're going to love Day One in particular," she'd said, pointing out Yosemite Valley at four thousand feet, then, twelve miles along the trail, their first night's destination at ninety-six hundred feet.

He'd shaken his head. "Impossible."

"Difficult, yes. But entirely possible."

He'd argued that since they would arrive at Tuolumne Meadows the second day, and could easily drive through the park and pick up the trail there, they should skip that nasty climb.

"That would be cheating," she'd said.

"It could be our little secret."

18

"I'm doing the *whole* John Muir Trail."

He'd sent her a doleful look, but didn't bring it up again.

At least not until they'd been climbing for two hours. Panting, he undid his hip belt and slid his pack to the ground. Dark patches of sweat stood out on his green T-shirt. Liz stepped aside to let a group of day hikers pass. She leaned forward on her trekking poles, but did not take off her pack. They'd already taken two breaks and hadn't yet reached the top of Nevada Falls, two and a half miles from the start.

He plunked himself onto a boulder, took off his cap and wiped his forehead with his sleeve. "It's not too late to turn around and drive to Tuolumne."

She stared out across the valley. "Breathtaking" didn't begin to describe it. A mile away, the falls shot out of the granite cliff like milk spilling from a pitcher and crashed onto a boulder pile before being funneled into a foaming river. She could make out the tiny colored forms of people at the falls' edge. The tightness in her chest loosened slightly at this first hint of vast space. Above the falls was Liberty Cap, an enormous granite tooth, and beyond that, Half Dome. Its two-thousand-foot sheer vertical wall and rounded crown made it appear to once have been a sphere split abruptly by an unimaginable force, but Liz knew better. A glacier had erased it, bit by bit.

Her back to Dante, she said, "Let's keep going to the top of the falls. Then we can have lunch, okay?"

The trail leveled out after Nevada Falls, no longer as steep as a staircase. After a set of switchbacks, they passed the turnoff for Half Dome, where all but a few of the day hikers left the main route. The early-afternoon sun was a heat lamp on their backs, and by two o'clock they'd finished the three liters of water they'd carried from the valley floor. At the first crossing of Sunrise Creek, Liz unpacked the water filtration kit. She'd shown Dante how it worked at home—for safety's sake—but gadgets weren't his strong suit. He might be inclined to coax bacteria, viruses and parasites out of the water with a wink and a smile, but she was the professional gizmologist. She designed prosthetic limbs, myoelectric ones that interfaced with living muscle. He worked for the same company, on the sales side.

Crouching on the grassy bank, she attached the tubes to the manual pump and dropped the float into a small current. It took five minutes to filter three liters. She handed Dante a bottle. He took a long drink.

"So cold and delicious!"

She disassembled the filter and carefully placed the intake tube in a plastic bag she'd labeled "DIRTY!" "And what's strange is that every stream and lake tastes different. Some are flinty, some are sweet, some are just . . . pure."

She zipped the pouch closed and looked up. Dante had that expression he reserved for her. His dark brown eyes were soft and a smile teased at the corner of his mouth, as if someone were poised to give him a gift he'd been wanting forever. She held his gaze for a moment—his love for her running liquid through her limbs—and got up to stow everything in her pack.

Liz had consulted the map when they'd stopped and knew they had to climb more than five miles and fifteen hundred vertical feet before making camp. Her feet were sore and her thighs complained as she hoisted herself—and her thirty-pound pack, nearly a quarter of her body weight—ever upward. She was fit, as was Dante, but this first day was asking far more of her body than it was accustomed to. Hiking would get easier as they got stronger, but there was no getting around it: today was a bitch.

They walked in silence, kicking up small clouds of dust. The creek stayed with them, then disappeared, and they were left with only pines, boulders and trail. After an hour or more, they came over a rise. The trail followed the crest for a short stretch, then dipped toward a creek bubbling down a seam between steep slopes. On the near bank two hikers were resting—the first they'd seen since the Half Dome turnoff. Each man sat leaning against a pine tree. The nearer man was large, and imposing even while seated. He'd taken off his boots and socks, and his long legs were crossed at the ankle. His head was tipped back, and his eyes were closed. When the other, smaller, man swiveled in their direction and lifted his hand in greeting, Liz immediately noticed their resemblance. The same lank, sandy hair, the same square jaw and full mouth. Brothers. They even had identical cobalt blue packs.

"Hey," she said.

The big one opened his eyes and massaged his jaw. "Hello."

Closer now, she judged they were both in their twenties. The big one was definitely older. He had the swagger as well as the looks.

"Hello," Dante said, stepping off the trail to stand next to Liz. "How's it going?"

"Excellent. Just taking a breather."

"I hear you. I feel we've climbed halfway to God."

The big one gave an appreciative snort, and took a swig from the two-liter soda bottle that served as his water container. "Is that where you're headed?"

Liz glanced at Dante to see if he thought this an odd remark. He smiled good-naturedly and said, "Well, maybe eventually, if I'm lucky. But today, just to . . . what's the place, Liz?"

"Sunrise Camp."

"Yes, Sunrise Camp," Dante said.

The man nodded. "You on a short trip, or doing the whole JMT enchilada?" He raised his eyebrows when he said "enchilada," and gave it a Spanish pronunciation.

Liz frowned at the possibility he meant it as a slight on Dante, but checked herself. He seemed friendly enough otherwise. "The entire JMT," she said. "At least that's the plan."

"That's a lot of quality time for a couple."

Liz didn't know how to respond.

Dante stepped in. "How about you?"

The brothers exchanged looks. The younger one said, "Depends on how we feel. Could be a long trip. Could be a short one."

Dante nodded as if this were the sort of free-wheeling adventure he wished he could join.

"Well," Liz said, anxious to leave these two behind, "have fun whatever you do."

"We always do," the younger brother said.

She started down the trail, with Dante behind her, and stopped at the creek's edge. On the opposite side, one path followed the stream uphill, while another led downstream for a while, before dissolving into the forest.

She turned to the men, and pointed at one path, then the other, with her trekking pole. "Do you happen to know which way it is?"

The older brother pointed upstream.

"Thanks."

Aware of the eyes on her, she gingerly crossed the creek, stepping on half-submerged rocks and using her poles for balance. The added weight of her backpack meant a small slip could result in a fall. When she arrived safely on the far bank, she waited for Dante to cross and turned left up the hill.

The trail followed the stream for a stretch, then cut steeply up the slope. Her pack felt heavier with each step. The footing became uneven, and she had to concentrate to avoid a misstep. She could hear Dante breathing hard behind her. Twenty minutes after they'd crossed the creek, she stopped, panting.

"Does this look right to you?"

His face was flushed with exertion. "You're asking me?"

"I don't know. The trail hasn't been this lousy."

"Maybe it's just this piece."

They struggled uphill on an ever-worsening trail for another fifteen minutes. And then the path disappeared.

"Damn it," Liz said, and jammed her pole in the dirt.

They retraced their steps to the junction. The brothers hadn't moved. They regarded Liz and Dante from their side of the creek.

She tried to keep the irritation out of her voice and pointed to the downstream trail. "It's this way."

"Really?" the older brother said. "I was sure it was the other way."

The younger one added, "Thanks for saving us the mistake."

"No problem," Dante said, waving.

They started off again. Before the trail veered to the left, Liz looked over her shoulder. The older brother stared in her direction. Given the distance, she couldn't be certain, but she thought she detected a smirk on his face.

Chapter Two

At six thirty, the sun hovered above the horizon, and they stopped for the day. The campsite overlooked Long Meadow, a vast expanse ringed with pines. The Echo Peaks and Matthes Crest stood guard in the distance. Tawny grasses in the meadow awaited the first precipitation since early May, and the tops of the peaks had lost their snow.

Dante groaned as he lowered his pack to the ground, then sat on a fallen log to take off his boots. Liz unpacked the tent and began clearing pinecones and other debris from the rectangle she'd chosen for their shelter.

"How are your tootsies?"

He crossed his ankle over his knee and examined the damage. His boots were new, as was the rest of his gear and clothing, but unlike everything else, he'd refused Liz's advice on which boots to buy. She agreed that his choice, Italian Zamberlans, were fantastic boots, but doubted he would have time to break them in and suggested he pick a lighter, more modern style he could wear off the shelf. He'd ordered the Zamberlans, and she had packed plenty of moleskin.

"Several, but not all, of my toes have sore spots." He pointed out the red areas and turned his foot over. "And this looks perhaps like a blister on my heel."

Liz unfurled the groundsheet with a snap. Blisters on Day One. Not a good start. "Tomorrow morning please mole-ify all of them."

"Okay, Mama." He sniffed his underarm. "I smell like a pig!"

"Well, you're in luck. I read there's a standpipe nearby because of the High Sierra Camp. We don't have to filter water, and if you carry it away from the pipe, you can wash, too. Luxurious, huh?"

"Yes. It's wonderful that, after today's efforts, I will be treated to a bath in a saucepan."

"A cold bath in a saucepan."

"Of course."

She clipped the tent ceiling to the arc of the central pole, then fitted the crosspiece through the grommets, forming the roof. "Ta-da!" She'd hoped Dante would clap, but he continued to worry his toes.

A hiker came around a stand of trees a dozen yards away. Though the light was failing, he wore sunglasses and had trouble finding his way. He wasn't anywhere near the trail.

"Hey, there!" She waved at him. "Are you lost?"

"Maybe." He took a step, caught his toe on a log and stumbled a few steps before righting himself. She guessed he was orienting by sound. "I'm looking for the High Sierra Camp."

"Oh, lucky you. I hear those camps are swank."

Probing delicately, he took baby steps toward them. "I hope so. I just learned about it today."

Dante looked up from his podiatric pity-party and addressed Liz. "Why aren't we staying there?"

"Because we're stoic." She noted Dante's pout. "Well, some of us are. Besides, you have to reserve months in advance."

The man stopped dead. "Are you shitting me?" He unclasped his hip belt and threw the straps off his shoulders as if they were the strangling arms of a rabid orangutan. The pack hit a boulder with a crunch of metal and glass.

Liz said, "Was that a camera?"

The man ignored her and she regarded him with concern. She couldn't figure out why he hadn't taken off his sunglasses, nor could she fathom why anyone who seemed so unhappy about roughing it would be backpacking alone. Dante, at least, had a reason for being here, even if he had no clue what he was getting himself into. She had tried to warn him, but when he began to take her warnings as evidence for her lack of feelings for him, she backed off. But this stranger was another story. Why would he put himself through this? Did he lose a bet?

The man kicked his pack several times, shouting, "I'm gonna kill him! I'm gonna kill him!" with each kick. Spent, he staggered in a small circle, tripped on a rock and came down hard on his hip. "Goddamn fucking rocks everywhere!"

Dante jumped up to help him but realized he was barefoot and sat again. He didn't do bare-foot. "Are you okay?"

The man had lost his sunglasses in the self-induced fray and was searching for them on his hands and knees.

"Are you visually impaired?" Liz asked, thinking the impairment was more likely mental.

For some reason, this question calmed him. He looked straight at her.

"Oh!" She pointed at him and couldn't help jumping up and down in excitement. "You're that guy!" She turned to catch Dante's eye so he could verify her I.D., but he was digging in his backpack. "Dante!"

He didn't look up. "What? I'm trying to find my camp shoes."

"It's that guy! The one in the movie!"

"Oh, here they are." He bent to strap on the shoes. "My feet are killing me. What movie?"

Liz continued to point at the man, so when Dante finally finished with his shoes, he'd know whom to look at. The man sat on a rock in the *Thinker* pose and rubbed his hip with his free hand. He seemed to be reminding himself to refrain from betting on a day never getting worse.

"The movie we saw last week. He played the dumb cop." She shrugged at the man in apology.

He raised his hand. No offense taken. "Matthew Brensen," he said. "Just to end the suspense."

"That's right!" she said, then caught herself. "Of course, you would know that."

"I would."

Dante walked over, introduced himself and Liz, and shook Matthew Brensen's hand. The actor was not a big star—he'd never win an Oscar—but was famous enough that his embarrassing moments had a better than even chance of ending up on *Entertainment Tonight*.

Brensen said, "Aren't you going to ask me what I'm doing out here?"

"Having a bad day?" Liz offered. The excitement of a celebrity sighting was wearing off. She was tired and wanted to eat dinner before it got any darker and colder.

He nodded sadly. "I let my fucking agent sign me up for a lead in a goddamn backpacking movie. Smart, right? But, okay, I go with it. Expand my scope and all that horseshit. Then the director says I need to find out what it's like."

29

The anger flared in his voice again. He spread his arms wide. "So here I fucking am. And you know what it's like? It fucking bites!"

Dante nodded sympathetically. Brensen pulled out his phone, and cursed when he couldn't get a signal. Over their heads the sky was chambray blue, fading to pale pink at the horizon. The setting sun cast an amber glow on the distant peaks. A handful of deer had gathered in the meadow, heads low.

"Tell you what," she said to Brensen. "Dante's about to have a cold bath in a saucepan. You're more than welcome to join him."

The next morning, as soon as she judged it light enough, Liz crept out of the tent, leaving Dante dead to the world. Their body heat had warmed the interior; leaving it was like walking into a freezer. She pulled her fleece hat from the pocket of her down jacket and slipped it on, tugging it over her ears.

She poured water from a Nalgene bottle into the pot—the only one—and lit the stove. The quarter-sized circle of blue flame hissed, and she smiled. Morning in the mountains. She climbed a nearby granite shelf to get a better view, her thighs complaining about yesterday's hike.

No questioning how Sunrise Camp got its name. The meadow stretched two miles in front of her, cast in near darkness, but the sun had found the

Cathedral Peaks, painting them a warm orange, a promise for the coming day. The air was completely still, her breath in her ears the only sound. It was morning distilled, the sun rising on a quiet world, a mute witness. To Liz, it was both the oldest miraculous event, and the newest. This one belonged to her, and she to it.

She swallowed hard and shivered. Hugging herself, she descended to the campsite. The water would be ready. Coffee beckoned.

While Dante slept on, she prepared for the day. She retrieved the bear cans from where they had stashed them last night. The cans were large bear-proof plastic cylinders in which the Park Service required they store all their food, toiletries and trash. Liz and Dante each carried one, which, with careful planning, could hold food for ten days. Although, as Dante pointed out, not the food you really wanted and not enough of the other kind either.

Numb with cold, her fingers fumbled with the catches on the lids, so she used a spoon handle to open the cans. She rehydrated milk for granola and set aside the food they'd eat during the day (energy bars, trail mix, wax-wrapped cheese and dense bread) so the bear cans could stay inside the packs. After she drank her fill of water, she went to the standpipe and refilled the bottles. Brensen's pack rested against a tree. Next to it lay a gigantic larvae—Brensen in his bag. Only the top of his hat showed. He'd been too pissed off to bother with his tent, a fine decision as long as it didn't rain.

She returned to their site, stuffed her sleeping bag into its sack and deflated her air mattress. As she worked, the line dividing dark from light marched across the meadow. She looked at her watch. Seven thirty. Time to wake Sleeping Beauty.

Dante had never been a morning person, and he certainly wasn't going to be a convert this morning. The sleeping bag was warm, he mumbled from inside, and his legs and shoulders felt as if he'd been pummeled by a prizefighter during the night.

"Wasn't me," she said, cheerfully. She reminded him that today was mostly downhill.

"As in 'it's downhill from here'?"

She bit her tongue to stop herself from reminding him he had asked to come, that it had been his idea. It was too early in the trip, and too early on a pristine morning to go down that road. Instead, she began disassembling the tent around him. He held out while she removed and folded the fly, but when she slid the pole out and the tent collapsed on him, Dante relented. Once he was up, the cold accelerated his preparations and within twenty minutes, they were on their way.

The trail took them past Brensen, firmly lodged in his cocoon. Liz commented it was a shame his face wasn't visible so they could take a photo and send it to the tabloids when they got to Tuolumne Meadows.

Dante twitched with excitement. "There's reception there?"

"So they say."

"*Bueno!*"

"And a store with lots of food."

"Really?"

"And beer."

"Beer!"

"And campsites with plasma screen TVs, Dolby sound and reclining chairs with cup holders."

His footsteps stopped. "Really?"

Liz turned, put her hands on his shoulders and kissed him. "No."

"But you weren't joking about the beer, right? Because there's nothing funny about that."

The prospect of evening refreshments buoyed Dante's mood for several hours, right up until the moment he was splashing water on his face and slipped into Cathedral Lake. He was soaked from the knees down. All he could do was change his socks and march on. The moisture would worsen his blisters, but at least the terrain over the remaining five miles to Tuolumne Meadows was relatively flat.

They knew they were close when they passed three dozen Korean tourists wearing sneakers and Vans instead of boots. Signs pointed them to the campground, an enormous maze of sites, most of which were occupied. And not simply occupied but fully inhabited. TVs glowed through the windows of RVs bigger than school buses. Generators hummed. People in tidy clothing watched them pass from screened-in picnic tables and lounge chairs. Liz felt like a refugee carrying all her worldly possessions through a city that had never known war.

She couldn't understand the attraction of parking a rolling house in a national park. For her, the section of the John Muir Trail from Yosemite Valley to Tuolumne Meadows was a gauntlet to run. Sure, the scenery was beautiful, but she resented having to suffer crowds to enjoy it. They would be turning south tomorrow, toward the wilder reaches of the trail. It could not happen soon enough.

In an ocean of RVs, the backpackers' campground had a throwback feel, but with the amenities of a picnic table, a fire ring, a bear locker and access to a store, running water and real toilets, it was barely camping. Dante was delighted. He dropped his pack at the first open site, changed his shoes, asked her what she wanted from the store and took off.

Liz did some reconnaissance to find a quieter site. Not far from the entrance she passed a yellow tent. No one was around. On the picnic table were two blue backpacks she recognized as belonging to the brothers they'd met yesterday. She headed in the opposite direction and selected a site with a measure of privacy. She tore a page from a small notebook, drew an arrow on it and returned to Dante's pack, where she wedged it under a strap. Returning to the site, she began to make camp.

A half hour later, Dante showed up with his arms loaded. He grinned and said, "Guess who I saw at the store?"

"Another celebrity?"

"No, those guys from yesterday. Remember?"

"How could I forget? They were pretty weird."

"I don't understand why you say that. Payton and Rodell were extremely friendly."

"You're kidding me, right? About the names?"

"No. Payton and Rodell Root. From Arcata, wherever that is."

"Northern California. Way, way north."

"Maybe it's a regional thing. Anyway, they didn't name themselves."

"I guess not."

"They met some guys having a bocce game later. They invited us."

"Later? When later?" She checked her watch. Nearly six already.

"Eight or so."

"Eight or so, I'm asleep. We have to leave early tomorrow. Aren't you tired?" Stupid question, really. If there was a social activity, he was game. Always.

"No! My feet hurt, but I'm good." He unpacked his haul: beer, cold cuts, bread, chocolate and ibuprofen. Dante's food pyramid.

"Dante, I'm serious about leaving early."

He frowned. "What's the rush? I love it here." He held up his phone. "I've got three bars!"

"You know what the rush is. We have to make it to Muir Trail Ranch, the halfway point, before they close for the season. Otherwise, we have no food for the last nine days. If we don't walk an average of fourteen miles a day, we won't make it. You know all this."

"Okay, but I also know this is supposed to be a vacation. And so far it doesn't feel that way."

"It is a vacation. A strenuous one."

"That's a . . . what do you call it? An oxy-mormon."

"That's a detergent popular in Utah. I believe you mean 'oxymoron.' "

"Yes, a moron. Because only a moron would design such a vacation!"

She leaned toward him and met his gaze. "Is this you giving this your best shot? Because I'm distinctly underwhelmed. I didn't come here to play bocce. I didn't come here to drink beer, although I'll be having one in a minute. And, to be completely frank with you, I didn't come here to be your cheerleader, your butler or your mother." She stood. "Do what you want. I'm leaving at seven thirty tomorrow." She grabbed a beer and walked away.

She went to bed alone. As exhausted as she was, she didn't fall asleep for a long time. Someone setting up camp in a neighboring site repeatedly shone their flashlights on her tent. Then they spent ages talking loudly on their phones. Several times she thought about getting up and confronting them, but the freezing temperature kept her inside. Besides, she'd had enough confrontation for one day.

Dante woke her when he unzipped the tent and wriggled into his sleeping bag. He didn't say anything, nor did she. She checked her watch—it was one fifteen—but she was past caring.

She awoke at dawn and crawled over Dante to get out. He was a champion sleeper. He fell asleep the second he closed his eyes and slept through earthquakes, parties, fireworks, thunderstorms and, most impressively, the frantic high-pitched barking of their neighbor's dog. Usually she thought it indicated he had a clear conscience. Today she thought it indicated he was lazy.

When she retrieved the cans from the bear locker and placed them on the table, she saw Dante had left out his socks—the relatively dry ones. They had absorbed the dew and were primed to maximize blister potential. She shook her head and gathered what she needed to make coffee. Not long afterward, Dante surprised her by emerging from the tent of his own volition. He was no beacon of joy, but at least she didn't have to collapse the tent on him.

They left the campground and picked up the trail at the bottom of a gentle slope, Liz in the lead and Dante trailing behind. At the bridge spanning the Lyell Fork of the Tuolumne River, an older couple was poring over a map and sharing an apple. They exchanged greetings but Liz didn't stop to chat. She was chilled and wanted to keep moving. Today they were finally going to leave the developed part of Yosemite, and she was eager.

"You don't have to walk so fast," Dante called after her.

She slowed a little. "I'm not walking fast. I'm just not hungover."

He caught up to her with a hobbling step. "I'm not hungover either. I'm disabled."

"Wet socks plus new boots equals unhappy feet. Isn't the moleskin helping?"

"I didn't have time to put it on. You were in such a hurry."

She whipped around and stared at him. "So it's my fault? Dante, how have you survived thirty-two years?"

"By driving when I need to go ten miles, and occasionally taking public transportation."

She picked up her pace. "If you have reception, try calling a cab."

Complaining, Liz believed, was a matter of opportunity and practice, and Dante had had plenty of both. As the youngest of four children, and the only boy, he was routinely indulged. Had he contained an ounce of malice, he would have become a despot. His sweet nature and abundant charm guaranteed that when he did grouse about the fundamental unfairness of life, he would be forgiven. Because he was an optimist, he did not complain routinely. That, and because he never had it that bad.

Liz was the only child of an egocentric mother and an absentee father, and had lacked an audience for her grievances. Her practical nature also made her disinclined to complain. A problem could either be fixed (usually by her) or it couldn't, and confusing the two was a waste of time. She instead directed her efforts at improving what she could—hence her job providing limbs for people who needed them—rather than railing at an obviously flawed universe. Find a problem that matters, fix it and shut the hell up about the rest. Growing up, she kept her own counsel, eschewing the gossip and social maneuvering that drove other girls' relationships, and had few friends because of it. She never intended to be awkward, or to hide. It was simply who she was and how she was raised.

Eventually, as her world widened, her habit of not expressing her hopes, disappointments and desires tripped her up. Because a lie or, more accurately, the absence of truth, was akin to grit in an oyster. Once it had been covered with a silky crystalline coating, again and again, it didn't feel the same. No one could see it—it's not as though someone could pry her open—and the currents of time kept moving past her. But Liz could feel pearls of the lies and subverted desires inside her, lodged in her soul. They presented a problem she didn't know how to fix.

Chapter Three

The trail up Lyell Canyon required little concentration. The base of the canyon was broad and flat, with golden meadows on either side of a winding river. The trail didn't do anything fancy, starting on the west side of the riverbank and continuing along for nine miles. After that, the map told her, the river narrowed to a rushing creek, and the trail climbed steeply to Donahue Pass. But for now, it was either easy going or monotonous, depending on how one looked at it. River on the left, forest on the right, and Potter Point and Amelia Earhart Peak dead ahead. The sky was clear, and the warming sun lifted the dew off the grass. A walk in the park.

Which was why Dante's silence worried her.

He was thinking hard about something, something serious enough to overwhelm his usual compulsion to talk. Normally she would welcome the quiet, content with the company of her own thoughts. But now her only thoughts were what Dante was contemplating as he took one step after another behind her. There was no point in asking him before he was ready, only a matter of how far up the canyon they would travel before he let her in.

It turned out to be six miles. She told him she was ready for a snack. She left the trail and set her pack down a few feet from the river's edge. He joined her and accepted the energy bar she offered. As she unwrapped hers, she scanned the water for trout. Within a few seconds, she spied a fish whose wriggling disrupted its camouflage against the mottled olive green riverbed. It darted under the shadow of rock and vanished.

"Liz," Dante said from behind her. "I think I made a mistake." She turned. His eyes were dark and a knot had formed between his eyebrows. "I shouldn't have come. I should have stayed home."

"The blisters are bad, huh?" she said, knowing blisters weren't the issue.

"Yes, but that's not it."

Her stomach twisted. All the frustration she had been swallowing over the last three days rose to the back of her throat, acrid. "It's hard! This hike is really hard. I tried to be realistic with you about it. I warned you." The chastising tone of her voice made her wince. She coiled the wrapper of the energy bar around her finger, unfurled it and coiled it again.

"You're not understanding me. I didn't come because I was sure I could do it, and I'm not thinking about leaving because I can't."

She bit her lower lip. It wasn't about the hike. Of course not. She just wanted it to be. "Why did you want to come then?"

He picked up her hand and held it between his. "Because I thought I would lose you if I didn't." His voice dropped. "I thought you knew that."

She did. She didn't.

She wasn't certain what she knew. She was angry with him, but was that fair? He'd acted out of desperation, fueled by fear and love. Why else would he have insisted on coming? It was so obvious she almost laughed at the audacity of her stubborn denial.

He squeezed her hand. "Say something. Please."

This was the moment in which she should explain everything. Valerie's voice spoke in her head, telling her not to be such a pussy and spit it out. Liz could tell him about the pregnancy and how confused and scared she had been, and how sharing the news with him (clearly the right thing to do in retrospect) had been impossible because she was certain he'd want to have the baby. He was Catholic and had a moral streak as wide as Lyell Canyon. She, on the other hand, maintained she had nothing against religion but was holding out for one that revered the periodic table. Unfortunately, as much as humor helped her cope with the mistakes she'd made, it appeared useless in preventing them. If only she could graft a simplifying moral structure into her brain using the technology she designed for artificial limbs.

Telling Dante she'd been pregnant would lead to confessing to the abortion. During her interior rehearsals, this was where she forgot her lines. That confession, however worded, would inevitably lead to owning up to her ambivalence about living with him. Except for fleeting moments when she forgot her own painful history and she was simply happy, she hadn't found level footing, the graceful certainty she'd done the right thing by moving in.

If she somehow managed to admit to the abortion (highly unlikely), and if Dante was still listening (inconceivable), she would have no choice but to explain why her actions had nothing to do with him. He would be relieved, and possibly encouraged, because it meant they'd have a chance after all—assuming he suffered an episode of amnesia regarding the abortion. But his relief would be misguided. And to explain why, she would have to voice something she had never told anyone, not even Valerie. When he heard that story, he would leave and never come back.

Which, from the look of things, might happen anyway.

She took her hand away on the pretense of pushing her bangs from her eyes.

"I wanted to do this hike alone. I wasn't leaving you."

He shook his head. "But you've been distant for a while. Like you're making plans without me."

"I was. I was planning this trip. And then you started having an issue with it."

"Only because it seemed so . . . so, I don't know, *necessary* to you."

"And your problem with that is what? I'm too independent?"

He frowned deeply. She could see the answer was "yes." She felt sorry for him, because her "independence" was, in part, a product of all the things he didn't know about her. She kept truths from him because he wouldn't love her otherwise, and she wanted his love. Her secrets were wrapped in a cloak of self-sufficiency she could both hide behind and hold up as a virtue. Independence was a flag American women waved proudly, and Liz knew Dante was drawn to this in her. His mother was a highly emotional woman who could do little more than breathe on her own, and his entire family had suffered because of it.

"Too independent? Of course not," he said.

"Look, Dante, I was actually fine with you coming along if you really wanted to. And if you

44

respected the way I wanted it to be." Not entirely true, but true enough to state with conviction.

He regarded her with skepticism. "I think you were testing me. And I failed."

"Now you're feeling sorry for yourself. Why couldn't you just have let me go? It could have been that simple."

"Simple for you, Liz. Not so simple for me. Not when I don't understand what's going on with us!" He took a couple of steps back, turned away from her and threw his hands in the air. "Shit!"

She pulled a bottle from the outside pocket of her pack, unscrewed the lid and drank. She watched as Dante opened his pack and began unloading it. She knew what was happening but said nothing. They'd pretty much covered it, at least what they were willing to say. Dante lifted out his bear can and placed it next to the pack. He leaned on it with one hand and dropped his chin to his chest.

"You were right about the boots. They destroyed my feet. I probably wouldn't be able to continue anyway."

"I'm sorry about your feet. And everything else." The truth, in its entirety.

"Let's go through all the gear. I don't want you to be missing anything you need."

They emptied the backpacks and bear cans and spread everything out on the grass. It reminded Liz, and probably Dante, of a similar array on their dining table the night before they left for the mountains.

She repacked her bear can with enough food to last until Red's Meadow, where she would pick up the first of two resupply buckets they had shipped. Red's was four days away. The second resupply would be waiting at Muir Trail Ranch, fifty miles farther south. The tent and cooking gear went on her pile as well, in addition to the rudimentary medical kit and the Ziploc bag containing an assortment of safety items: nylon cord, an extra tent stake, a flare, waterproof matches, zip ties, replacement shock cord for the tent pole, and a patch kit for the tent. Her pack would gain a few pounds; two can live almost as lightly as one.

She placed the water filter among his belongings. He gave her a questioning look.

"Trying to save a pound. I'm going to use the Aquamira." The purification tablets were backup. They killed everything they needed to, but not immediately. And if the source water contained sediment, it would stay cloudy.

"There aren't enough."

"I'll get more at Red's."

"I thought you preferred the filter."

She shrugged. Dante bent his head in apology. The choices she would have made at home in preparation for a solo trip were different from the ones she faced now. She'd have brought a smaller tent, for starters. The one she'd purchased when she thought she'd be alone was narrow and low to the ground, shaped like a chrysalis.

The process of divvying up their gear and supplies was what she imagined happened when cohabiting couples broke up: her stuff from before, his stuff from before and, the sticky part, the stuff they had bought together in the buoyant hope they'd never see this day. But instead of books, serving dishes and throw pillows, these were tools of survival. She picked up the compass —a dial set in a rectangle of clear, hard plastic— and closed her fingers over it. She squeezed and the sharp corners dug into her palm.

Dante contemplated his pile of clothing. "Why don't you take my gloves? They're warmer than yours." His eyes asked her to confirm they still shared a life. *Mis cosas son tus cosas.*

"They're too big. I'd fumble with everything." She handed him the car keys. "You might not catch the shuttle to the Valley in time."

He stared at the keys as if they were runes. "I'll figure something out."

Liz placed her fingers lightly on his forearm. "It's up to you about Muesli. Valerie's expecting to have him the whole time, so either way."

He exhaled loudly and stuffed the rest of his belongings into his pack. For now, the cat offering had been enough. He could tell himself that if he had the cat, she would probably follow. He was rushing to leave now. Ripping the Band-Aid off.

47

She methodically reloaded her pack, working with all the deliberation Dante no longer needed. She positioned each item with care, the heaviest things close to her center of gravity, the lighter things wherever they would fit. The business of getting it right soothed her. She paused to scan the skies. A few innocent puffs of cloud had appeared above Mount Lyell, cloaked in a glacier. She laid her waterproof jacket on top of the bear can, next to her snacks, where she could readily find it.

Dante hoisted his pack onto one shoulder, then leaned to the side and wriggled the other arm under the strap. He clicked the hip belt buckle and straightened his cap.

"You sure you don't want my phone?" This was tantamount to offering his leg.

She shook her head.

"I'm going to worry about you."

She could see he meant it. "Don't. It's only a walk." She stepped closer and kissed him. His lips were so warm and tasted of salt. Heat rushed through her body. She stepped back to stop from giving in to it.

Dante's expression had changed. A moment ago he had been ready to leave without a scene. Now he appeared frozen in place and crushed, and she regretted the kiss.

He said, "Was that our last kiss?"

"I thought you were leaving."

"I am. But before I go, I want to know."

"Why is it up to me to say?"

"Because you seem to be making all the choices."

"It's a hike, Dante."

They stood at arm's length, eyes locked. The river murmured beside them, the only sound.

"Liz," Dante said softly, his hands on her arms. "Was that our last kiss?"

She spun free. "How the hell should I know?" Turning away from him, she pulled tight the toggle on the main compartment of her pack, tucked in the strings and strapped the top section securely in place. She stuffed two Nalgene bottles into the side pockets and checked her pants' pockets for her map, pocketknife and lip balm. After she scanned the ground for anything she might have overlooked, she lifted the pack onto her shoulders, clipped the hip belt and slipped her hands through the straps of her trekking poles.

Liz cut diagonally across the meadow. As she rejoined the trail, she looked the way they had come. The trail was empty. She was, at last, alone.

Chapter Four

Leaving Lyell Canyon should have been harder than it was. She was loaded down—by her pack, by her guilt, by the heaviness in her heart. But when the river gave up its meandering and shrank to a creek, and the open meadows gave way to the forested slope, Liz felt strong. Her legs had been thick with soreness all morning, but now, in the middle of the afternoon, they were ready to climb again. Maybe she was gaining strength. Maybe her body had given up fighting the commands delivered by her brain. Maybe she was relieved Dante was no longer behind her, pulling her thoughts in his direction, derailing them. Maybe she was happier this way.

Despite the elevation gain, the temperature climbed into the eighties. She mopped sweat from her face with her sleeve and drank a liter and a half of water over the course of five miles. Remembering she could no longer simply filter and drink, she stopped to fill the empty bottle. The tablet would work its magic, and the water would be clean by the time she needed it. It would taste metallic and sour, but those were the breaks.

Switchbacks led her from one side of the mountain to the other and back again, winding through pines standing close, like soldiers amassed for battle. Finally, the trail straightened and the trees thinned. She emerged onto an open slope of low, smooth rock, punctuated by small clusters of trees. A few were snapped off at head height, perhaps by an avalanche. Others had been struck by lightning, charred trunks roughly broken, leaving black fingers pointing at the sky.

At nearly ten thousand feet, exposure was a fact of life.

And with it came views. She stopped and gazed across the valley through which she had walked. The canyon floor seemed impossibly far away, and so changed from a few hours before. The mountains had seemed larger when she (and, for a length of it, Dante) had traced their base. Now they were mere hills, the true mountains arising from behind, soon to overshadow the lower ridges as the sun fell. The river was no longer a gently flowing body of water, varied in color and course, but a uniform ribbonlike trace, as an idle child might make in a meadow that could have been sand.

Perspective, she thought, requires distance. And she continued up the trail, which, that day, only went higher.

She arrived at Donahue Lake at four o'clock. She checked the map and considered continuing on to the tiny unnamed lake above this one, but she was too tired and footsore. The emotional and physical exertion of the day had finally caught up to her. Besides, the small, scattered clouds from earlier had coalesced above the mountains. Too risky to climb nearer to them, especially because the higher lake might not afford a protected campsite.

A handful of hikers were already encamped at the lake, including the older couple she and Dante had seen near Tuolumne Meadows early that morning. Liz figured the couple must have passed unnoticed while she and Dante were arguing. She gave them a self-conscious wave as she skirted their site. They were talking and drinking, and lifted metal cups to her in salute. She heard them share a laugh as she proceeded to the east end of the lake. There she found a site with a solid windbreak, and a view of the lake and of the glacier on the north slope of Donahue Peak.

Crouching behind a large boulder, she changed into shorts, then hurried barefoot to the lake edge to wash before the sun lost its strength. The spot appeared to be private, but there might have been occupied sites she hadn't noticed, so she stripped down only to her sports bra. She stifled a scream as she stepped into the nearly frozen water and rubbed the dirt off her legs. She already had a sock tan even though she applied SPF 70 sunscreen several times a day, and her hands bore red patches from the pole straps. As she washed, her feet became numb—a wonderful sensation after a punishing day inside boots. She splashed water under her arms and onto her face and neck, no longer shocked by the cold, but invigorated. It amazed her she could feel so hot and exhausted and burdened one minute, and so refreshed the next. Carrying a backpack up a mountainside was similar to beating your head against a wall.

She was hammering a tent stake in place with a rock when she heard footsteps.

"Hey, Liz." It was the younger Root brother, Rodell. He wore a hunting jacket over a red wool shirt, and his knitted watch cap met his eyebrows. No Patagonia for him. He carried a dish out in front of him like a collection plate.

"Hi." She set the rock down and stood.

"I brought you some fish."

"Fish?"

"Yeah. We had all sorts of luck down in that creek. Too much for just us." He patted his stomach with his free hand.

She remembered Payton's misdirection and strange looks. Not the sort of people she wanted to be indebted to. But she saw no reason to be rude.

She smelled the trout as she came around the tent, and her mouth filled with saliva. In the dish lay two small orange-fleshed fish, already boned. What had she eaten today? Oatmeal, nuts, a granola bar.

"It smells amazing, but I've got plenty to eat."

"Dante told us you like trout."

Her antennae twitched. "You saw him today?"

"Yeah, down in the valley. He told us about his feet."

She waited for him to elaborate on the conversation.

"This is getting cold."

Her stomach growled and her hands reached out for the plate before she knew she had decided to take it. "Thanks a lot. Really."

"You got a fork?"

"Spork." She picked it up from where she'd left it next to her bowl and cup, showed it to him, and took a bite. "Oh, boy." The fish tasted of the river itself.

He grinned, showing teeth that hadn't seen braces. "Go on. Finish it. I need my plate for breakfast."

She took two more bites, then stopped in mid-chew and fixed her eyes on Rodell. "Did Dante ask you and your brother to look out for me?"

"Look out for you? No. Nothing like that. Can't see why he would, to tell the truth. Any fool can see you can take care of yourself."

She nodded and went back to her fish. Maybe Dante was right. Maybe these guys were all right after all. She quickly finished, and after she returned the plate and thanked him, he left.

The clouds, it turned out, gathered not for the purpose of producing rain, but for adding drama to the sunset. Liz had brushed her teeth and moved her bear can away from the campsite. Wearing all her warm clothing except her gloves, she sat on a fallen log and watched the world grow dark.

Whatever colors the landscape had lacked during the day—this time of year mostly gray granite, dark green pines and tan grasses—were painted across the mountains and sky in the twilight. Magenta clouds rippled across a lavender background, setting off the indigo peaks. The display was mirrored on the lake, twin lava lamps spilled above and below. The colors deepened with the encroaching darkness, as if an unseen hand were squeezing the last drop of beauty out of the day. She'd paid a high price to witness this, but didn't see how it could have been otherwise. Dante had turned back, hurt and confused, in surrender to her wishes. If the choices were indeed all hers, as he had claimed, she would bear the consequences.

The mountain slopes lost all texture, but the ridgeline lay firm against the heavens. Between the clouds, a star appeared. Like a hole punched in a postcard held to a light, it shone from another world, and another time, reminding her of why she had come. Here, at the edge of this lake, on the broad flank of this mountain range, under the boundless sky in the middle of nowhere, she was small and bare and completely inconsequential, as was her past. Water, rock, air—it cared nothing for her and would judge her not. On this journey, she would travel deep into the indifferent wilderness to discover what was possible for her, and what could not be undone.

A cloud winked out the star. Liz was limp with exhaustion. The cold moved inside her, blurring her edges. She shivered and rose.

While she could still find her way, she returned to the tent and crawled in. She stripped off her outer layer, folded her jacket into a pillow and lay down, zipping her bag closed. A faint breeze luffed the tent fly. Her toes tingled as they warmed. Soon, she slept.

At eight the next morning, she was finally ready to go. She'd been reluctant to leave the toasty confines of her sleeping bag that morning. Once she'd braved the cold, she'd taken an hour to make breakfast and break camp. She vowed to not be such a pansy about the cold in the future. Once she got moving, she generated her own heat quickly enough.

She hoisted her pack, which should have felt lighter than yesterday, but didn't. When preparing for the hike, she'd taken pains to pack lightly, and selected only the essentials for safety and comfort. She enjoyed the game, carefully considering each item, not only because she would have to carry it, but because the exercise of deciding what she needed mattered to her. Rain pants and fleece pants? (No, thermal leggings and rain pants would do.) Headlamp and flashlight? (Yes. They were backup systems, and if she had to work with her hands in the dark, the headlamp was indispensable.) She discovered her decisions were more about what she didn't take than what she did, and did not carry a phone, a GPS or an iPod. She wasn't wedded to electronics in her normal life, so unplugging wasn't a shock.

But she also brought no books, no folding chair, no pillow, no razor, no jewelry and no booze. And, as it turned out, no boyfriend.

She scanned the site to ensure she had packed everything. It looked exactly as she had found it. "Leave no trace," the wilderness permit insisted. Well, she'd abided by the rules. No one would know she'd been there.

Within an hour she was at the pass, the first on the John Muir Trail to afford three-hundred-sixty-degree views. She snapped a couple of photographs, drank some water and started down the other side. On the trail below Liz recognized the couple who had also camped at the lake, and admonished herself for failing to get a jump on these nearly geriatric hikers. She wondered whether Rodell and Payton were ahead of or behind her, not that she wanted to race anyone. Rather, because she was hiking alone, it was prudent to have a sense of where the closest human beings were. Ranger stations were few and far between, and at this time of year more likely than not unmanned.

She'd been excited about the day's hike—the first on her own—but the trail conspired against her. Now that she had left Yosemite National Park and entered the Ansel Adams Wilderness, she could plainly see which organization had more money for trail maintenance. The footing was rough, even dangerous in places, and absorbed so much of her attention that she could not enjoy the walk. In places, stone steps had been cut into the slope but were sized for mules, not people. She was forced to use her poles as crutches, bracing before each long step and lowering herself down. On other sections, the trail consisted of grapefruit-sized rocks with sharp edges, which shifted and ground against each other as she trod on them. She worried about twisting an ankle.

The poor trail persisted all morning. She stopped at midday above Thousand Island Lake to eat and give her feet a short break.

The trail might have been brutal, but the scenery did its best to compensate. The lake lay at the base of Banner Peak, the most glamorous mountain Liz had seen so far. Unlike the pale gray granite predominant in the Sierra, this mountain was dark as charcoal, dialing up the contrast on both the deep blue sky and the white of the snow traces along its ridge. The peak and the lake, sapphire blue and dotted with rocky islands, reminded her of those drawn in the final chapter of a storybook, the land in which the heroine finds the object of her quest.

You're not going to complete your quest sitting on your ass, she thought.

As she closed her backpack, a bearded man approached, heading the way she had come. He was about her age and moved with the steady gait of a seasoned hiker. They exchanged greetings, and he asked where she was going.

"Mount Whitney."

"Yeah? I'm doing the whole thing, too. In the other direction, obviously." Nearly everyone who attempted the JMT traveled southward, as Liz was, to avoid climbing the highest mountain in the continental U.S. on the first day.

"That's good. Because the trail's going to wear funny unless people walk it both ways."

He laughed. They chatted for a few minutes about trail conditions and campsites, then the man pointed over her shoulder. "Looks like there might be weather in our future."

She pivoted. Sizable cumulus clouds had gathered to the north, some with bruise-colored undersides. Overhead were just a few small clouds, but she reminded herself to be vigilant. She asked the man if he would attempt to go over Donahue Pass today.

"Not if those clouds mean business. I'm not in that much of a hurry."

As if to punctuate his meaning, a gust of wind pushed past them with a low whistle. The surface of the lake turned dull. Liz wished him a safe hike and, strapping on her pack, resumed her descent toward whatever patch of ground she'd call home tonight.

Liz had hiked and backpacked in the southern Sierra—near Mineral King and all around Kings

Canyon National Park—but never here in the north. She had been avoiding Yosemite and the area she was now traversing because of crowds, and because, when she'd lived in Santa Fe and Los Angeles, the southern hikes were closer. As she skirted the shore of Thousand Island Lake, ever more scenic with clouds casting dramatic shadows, she realized that places this gorgeous were crowded for a reason.

She had first planned to hike the JMT seven years ago, when she was married to Gabriel. They had done a few short backpacking trips together while they were dating, but nothing approaching this marathon. Gabriel postponed the trip several times for one reason or another. Two seasons went by before she realized it would never happen, and it had nothing to do with hiking. By then their marriage was unraveling, without discussion or argument. To this day, she didn't know whether Gabriel had seen the end for them coming. But this was clear: the day he knew for certain was also, and not by coincidence, the day he died.

Until late June, when she and Dante attended Gabriel's sister's wedding, Liz thought what had happened with Gabriel was behind her, like Tuolumne Meadows and Donahue Pass. She had believed, or at least hoped, that if she kept walking, the past would disappear beyond the horizon, and she could carve a new path, with

Dante. She had been wrong. She'd lost her bearings, and twisted in on herself, entangled and bound tight, unable to gauge the direction of the wind or the magnitude of the coming storm.

Chapter Five

The first raindrops fell as she arrived at Garnet Lake. A group of young Japanese girls huddled around their GPS unit, which was powered by a solar panel the size of a magazine attached to the top of a pack. Liz almost asked if they needed help, but decided against it. The trails were well marked. The only reason she consulted her map was to assess her progress and learn the names of peaks, rivers and passes.

The wind had picked up and, with the sun mostly occluded by the clouds, the temperature plummeted. She rounded the corner. The lake was streaked with whitecaps, and she ditched the vague idea she had to camp on the shore. Instead, she continued south, crossing the wooden bridge at the outlet and heading toward the next rise. Halfway up, rain began to fall steadily. She put on her waterproofs and drew the rain cover over her backpack.

It was a long three-mile slog to the nearest water source, Shadow Creek. She didn't mind the rain per se. She hadn't expected to spend eighteen days outside without some discomfort and inconvenience. Rain was only water. She could deal with rain.

What she couldn't deal with so casually was a thunderstorm. She'd been terrified of thunder and lightning since her father took her camping when she was nine. He came to Santa Fe, where she lived with her mother, two or three times a year. Her mother called it visitation, although Liz found out later they had no legal agreement. To Liz, her father's visits felt like kidnapping. He was a virtual stranger and took her away against her unvoiced will. They never went to his house in Virginia, where she knew he had a family—a complete one. He claimed he enjoyed camping with her so they could be alone. But even as a child, she knew better. Camping was what he could afford, at least for her. She imagined his other family never had to sleep in a tent. She imagined he took his real kids to Disney World, and stayed in a hotel with a pool.

But Liz had no choice in the matter—not at that age—so camping it was. The spring she was nine they went to Bandelier National Monument, a short drive from Santa Fe. As soon as they arrived, they set off on a hike. Either her father got lost, or he misjudged the distance, because when the clouds gathered and the air smelled of tin cans, they were nowhere near the car. They were, instead, on the exposed ridge of a canyon. The skies opened as thunder rumbled. Raindrops fell, attacking her bare skin like darts. The nape of her neck tickled. A loud crack made her jump, and rang in her ears. The first bolt of lightning struck close by. Fear gripped her insides. She wanted to run. She wanted to disappear.

Her father moved to pick her up. But she knew what every kid knew about lightning: you didn't want to be the tallest. Let him be the tallest. She threw herself on the ground, flat as she could, pressed her cheek into the gravel and shut her eyes tight. Her father tried to pull her upright, but her arms found a rock and she clung to it with all her strength and kicked at him, screaming. Thunder boomed in her ears and rolled through her chest. She saw her death: a bolt of lightning sliced through her like a giant sword. Terrified of the pain, and the empty unknown that would follow, she writhed against the dirt to burrow in.

Eventually, the storm relented and they found their way back to the car. Her father took her home the same evening, filthy and shaken. At the door, he said to her mother he had no idea why Liz was so scared of a little lightning.

In early summer, when she was first planning to hike the JMT, Dante asked her how the weather would be.

"Mostly clear, and cold at night. But it could rain, or even snow. Probably a thunderstorm or three."

"You do remember that you hide under the bed when there's a thunderstorm? Last time you shook so hard it rattled the frame."

"It's bad enough without you exaggerating. But I'm not about to spend my whole life burdened by an irrational fear."

"Why not? That's my plan."

"Do you even have an irrational fear?"

"Yes. Yes, I do. I'm afraid you'll never have sex with me again and I will die a sad, lonely and very frustrated old man."

They'd laughed, and made love on the couch. That was months ago.

By the time she arrived at Shadow Creek, the rain had become drizzle. She put down her pack and searched for a campsite. After following several rabbit trails off the main path, she found a small site with an established fire ring not far from the river. She suspected there were other campsites downstream—the terrain was leveling out—but after nearly fourteen miles, half of it in the rain, she was more than ready to quit. She wasn't going to quibble about where she pitched her tent.

The tent would have been up quickly except she drove a stake into a tree root, which gripped it tightly. She spent twenty minutes digging, pulling, twisting and cursing before she got it out. When the tent was erect and secure, she threw her pack inside and climbed in after it, leaving her boots, pack cover and rain suit in the vestibule. She blew up her air mattress and became light-headed. She'd not eaten nearly enough today. Tempted as she was not to bother with the stove and eat her next day's lunch instead, hot food sounded better. She set up the stove in the vestibule and ate an entire packet of instant mashed potatoes which, to her surprise, actually did taste like a loaded baked potato, as advertised. She washed it down with water and realized she'd forgotten to fill her second bottle. Back out into the rain.

By seven o'clock, she'd organized her gear and stashed the bear can outside the door. If a bear wanted to play with the can in the rain, he could come over here and get it. Other than what falling water had accomplished, she hadn't washed or bothered to brush her teeth. Her limbs were leaden. She wanted only to lie inside her sleeping bag, close her eyes and wake to a sunny morning.

In her dream, she stood alone aboard a tall ship on a high sea. Tattered sails whipped around her. The ship groaned and pitched, and the mast snapped in half with a deafening crack that startled her awake.

Her heart was racing as she sat up. It was pitch black. Rain pelted the fly and wind shouted through the trees. Her mouth went dry as she realized the breaking mast in her dream had been thunder. Her fingers searched along the inside surface of the tent until she found the mesh pocket and pulled out the flashlight.

A low boom sounded in the distance. She froze. A loud burst of thunder, like wood splintering against rock. She dropped the flashlight. As her hands scrambled to find it, the thunder growled twice more, louder each time, as if it were coming for her. She grasped the flashlight and turned it on. It didn't provide the comfort she'd hoped for. The shadows in the tent, combined with the undulating movement of the wind against the fly, brought only another dimension to her fear. She turned the flashlight off, but kept it in her hand.

Liz closed her eyes and pulled her hat over her ears to muffle the sound of the storm. She wriggled deeper into the sleeping bag as her mind struggled to rein in her emotion.

I'm not in the open.

I'm not the tallest thing around. (Thank you, trees.)

I'm not at the top of a pass holding a forty-foot metal stick in the air.

I don't have to go anywhere.

She realized it had been raining long and hard enough that water might be streaming under the tent. Her mattress was waterproof but the rest of her gear remained vulnerable. She cursed herself for not digging a trench around the tent to divert the flow. A couple of inches deep would have done it. She sat up again and shone the light across the tent floor. A two-foot section in the corner was dark with moisture. If it kept raining, the whole tent would be soaked.

Shit. Time to put on your big-girl panties.

Liz's hands trembled as she crouched in the tent opening and put on her rain suit and boots. The zipper on the fly jammed. She took a deep breath, backed the zipper up and tried again. Success. Not wanting to see more than she had to, she kept the flashlight focused on the ground. She circled the tent, stepping over the guy lines, and found where a rivulet flowed toward it. Using her bootheel, she scraped a shallow trench. The water flowed into it obediently.

She had almost completed the trench when a rolling boom made her stomach clench. She slammed her heel harder into the earth, determined to finish the job and seek refuge. An explosive crack startled her. Her foot skidded on the slick mud. She threw her arms out to regain her balance, and the flashlight sailed out of her hand, landing ten feet away, pointed uselessly at a boulder.

Liz moved to retrieve it. A flash of lightning lit the sky. The silhouettes of the trees and boulders appeared for an instant. Ten yards away, a shape, the head and torso of a man, was framed between tree trunks. She screamed. She darted for the flashlight, her boots slipping with each step. As she picked up the light, she fell onto one knee, pushed off the ground and wheeled around. She held the flashlight in both hands and shone the beam where the figure had been. It was gone. Her breath came in gasps as she jerked the light from place to place, searching. A peal of thunder rumbled up her legs and into her gut. She ducked into the vestibule of the tent, crouching like a rabbit under a bush, and turned off the light.

When she was once again in her bag, she told herself nothing would happen to her that night. She told herself the person she saw standing in a thunderstorm at two in the morning was probably a hiker camped nearby who'd gone out to pee, or to solve a problem with his tent as she had. This area wasn't particularly remote and would attract backpackers doing shorter trips, not just JMT through-hikers. (She pushed aside the competing thought that someone hiking for the weekend surely would have seen the forecast and changed their plans.) She made the argument that it could have been the older man hiking with his wife, since Liz's pace matched theirs, or even Brensen the actor. He had been behind her, but could have churned his anger into speed and caught up.

Liz told herself all these things, and many more, as she lay awake, shivering and hoping for dawn. But neither the logic nor the repetition of these lectures could alter her feeling that the man she had seen was Payton Root, and that whatever business he had outside in the middle of a thunderstorm had everything to do with her.

Chapter Six

As soon as she left the tent in the morning, she searched the vicinity for other hikers. She found no one, and began to question whether she had seen anything at all. In the dark, in the rain, while freaking out over the storm, it could have been anything. Or nothing. It's not as though she had seen the figure move. Now the storm had passed, the sun was out and, more to the point, she was unharmed. It wasn't much, but after a harrowing night, she'd take it.

While she drank her coffee, she studied the map and got more good news. Red's Meadow was a little over ten miles away, mostly downhill. A piece of cake. She'd arrive there a full day ahead of schedule. The thought of what awaited her at Red's cheered her. Not only would she be reunited with her bucket but, compared to camping, Red's was a Marriott. It had a store, a restaurant and showers.

She packed the tent wet and hit the trail.

A half mile along the older couple were storing gear in their backpacks. Liz called good morning to them, and they waved her over. Closer now, she judged they were in their fifties. Their names were Paul and Linda. "Like the McCartneys," Linda said proudly. They chatted with Liz about the storm ("We were hoping you were all right") and their previous long hikes (in Chile and the Pyrenees). Linda was talkative and perky. Paul, a Brit, was tall and slim and more reticent, with a self-deprecating sense of humor. Liz enjoyed them both. She left them to finish their packing.

"See you at Red's!" Linda called after her.

"If you beat us there, don't drink all the beer!" Paul added.

She arrived at two thirty, dropped her pack and entered the store to claim her bucket. The man behind the counter accepted her receipt with a heavy sigh and brought the bucket out from the store room. She paid him five dollars for a shower, two dollars for a towel and two more for a small bottle of shampoo. If Dante had been there, she'd have bought a razor for her legs, but he wasn't, so why bother? She carried everything outside, and returned for a Häagen-Daz chocolate-chocolate ice cream bar. *Carpe diem.*

Humping both her backpack and the twenty-five-pound bucket the half mile to the camp-ground was harder than the ten miles she'd covered that day. Last night had caught up to her. Too little sleep and too much adrenaline. Her shoulders ached and her feet felt as if they'd been run over by studded tires. She put her sodden clothing and gear in the sun to dry, then dragged herself along the footpath again to grab a shower and a burger.

She let the hot water pour over her for an ecologically incorrect amount of time, and had to agree that cleanliness was right up there with godliness.

The café, like the store, was decorated Western style with knotty pine paneling, deer and bear trophies mounted behind the counter and an ancient upright piano in the corner. There was a short counter with red stools and six tables covered with plastic red-checkered tablecloths. Brensen sat near the piano and waved her over. Tanner and thinner than when she'd last seen him, he was working his way through a six-pack of Sierra Nevada.

"Sit here if you want." He pulled out a chair. "You look surprised to see me."

"Well, the last time I saw you, you weren't exactly in the spirit of things."

"True, true."

The waitress delivered his burger. The smell of it made Liz realize she was starving. She ordered one.

Brensen opened a beer and handed it to her. "I got up that morning with my ass frozen to the ground. But there wasn't anyone around to complain to, so I started walking. Got to Tuolumne Meadows in time for the party and thought maybe this wouldn't be so bad after all. Of course that was before all the rain. Christ." He paused as if remembering something. "Where's Duncan?"

71

"Dante."

"Dante. Yeah." He glanced out the window. "Having a shower?"

She traced the pattern on the table with a finger. "His blisters were killing him. He went home."

Brensen put down his burger and studied her. "Maybe he wasn't exactly in the spirit of things."

She met his gaze. "Maybe. It's not everyone's idea of a good time."

"No kidding. I'm trying not to fight it. Hell, I haven't been this alone since . . . ever." He chuckled. "Now I know why my exes got sick of my company."

She didn't follow celebrity news, so she had no idea how many times he'd been divorced. He was in his forties, handsome, rich and, at least today, not a total jerk. So she guessed a few. "Are you married now?"

He shook his head. "I'm taking a break from making a mess of things."

"What a coincidence. So am I." She winced, embarrassed to have revealed herself. His candor had caught her off guard. Maybe this was how actors were: open about their inner worlds, and perceptive about those of others. Or maybe it was Brensen's beer talking.

The waitress brought her food. A hiker came over to their table and recited several roles Brensen had been in, as if he were delivering news. When he finally left, Brensen said, "For what it's worth, we're each the common denominator in our own lives. It always seems as if it's us."

And sometimes it really is. But she nodded in agreement to stop the discussion. She was too tired to talk about failed relationships. She concentrated on her burger, which she knew was mediocre but nevertheless tasted like heaven.

Later, at the campsite, Liz turned her attention to the bucket.

She sliced through the layers of packing tape Dante had applied around the rim, broke the seal on the lid and transferred the contents to the picnic table. Oatmeal, hard salami, cheese, energy bars, granola, muesli (which made her miss her cat), dry milk, a half dozen dinners, Starburst (her obsession), M&M's (Dante's), more sunscreen, toothpaste and biodegradable soap. Twice as much as she needed, much of it packaged in two-serving bags. It would take a while to sort it out.

The bottom layer of the bucket consisted of several bags of trail mix. Under them she spied something blue. She lifted the bags aside and pulled out an envelope with her name on it in Dante's slanted handwriting. She slit it open with her knife.

Mi carina,

We made it to Red's Meadow! Congratulations to you (and me)! I've never walked 56 miles. Well, perhaps over the course of my life, but never so quickly.

I wanted to tell you how much it means to me that you've let me accompany you on your trip. It is your trip, the same way it is your life. I want to share both with you. As you know, I'm not a big fan of adventure (except in films) but I hope to learn why you want to do this crazy trip.

We haven't been so close recently. I can't understand why, because I love you the same. Maybe by now we are better.

Happy trails to us!

Dante

P.S. I must be nearby, so kiss me and tell me you're glad I'm there.

Liz folded one leg underneath her and sat on the bench. She pictured Dante writing the note at the kitchen table in their condo, cautiously optimistic that his actions and determination would right their ship. His brow would have been furrowed in concentration and with worry, but he would not have doubted he was doing the right thing, both for him and for her. Confidence was one thing he'd never been short of.

They'd met at work. She'd been on her way to the mail room to retrieve a set of circuits she'd ordered when Dante had come flying around a corner. She'd had to jump aside to avoid a collision.

"Sorry!" He stopped and considered her. His forehead was beaded with sweat. "Any chance you're in IT?"

She shook her head. "R & D. What's wrong?"

"I've got a big presentation in five minutes and the projector's on the brink."

"You mean 'on the blink'? It's not talking to your laptop?"

"Yes! Can you fix it?"

She followed him to the conference room. A few dozen keystrokes later, the opening slide of his presentation appeared on the screen, with his name and title in the lower corner.

Liz stood. "There you are, Dante Espinoza."

"Fantastic!" He smiled broadly and stepped closer. His eyes were the darkest chocolate brown she'd ever seen. "I could kiss you!"

She shoved her hands in her pockets.

He backed up. "Oh, I shouldn't have said that. That's workplace harassment."

"It's fine. I mean, what you said is fine. I knew what you meant and it was okay. Maybe not that way, but I didn't take it that way." She felt blood rush to her cheeks. If only he would stop smiling at her.

"You have an unfair advantage."

"I do?"

"Yes. You know my name."

"Oh." She stared at him dumbly, her brain operating with an abacus instead of neurons. "I'm Liz."

"You saved my life, Liz. Thank you."

"It was simple."

He laughed, an easy sound. "Only for you." He gestured at the people filing into the room. "Time for my performance. I don't suppose you'd allow me to thank you more properly after work. Perhaps a drink?"

"Today?"

"Or a more convenient time. And only if it suits you."

She hadn't gone out with a man in three years. Not that this was a date. She'd done him a favor and he was being polite. Colleagues often had drinks after work with no romantic intentions.

"Today works."

"Great. Six at Freddie's?"

"Six at Freddie's."

"See you then. Wish me luck."

"Luck."

She slid out of the room, wiping her sweaty palms on her trousers. She hurried down the corridor, Dante's smile in her mind, forgetting entirely about the package waiting in the mail room.

Now tears stung her eyes as she read his note again. She set the paper down and watched a jay alighting from branch to branch. It squawked loudly, raised its black crest in excitement and flew out of sight. Dante would have known what sort of jay it was—and probably the Latin name, too. He had a thing for birds.

And he had a thing for her. She felt sorry for him. She regretted moving in with him and getting caught up in his version of her. To him, she was someone who could return his love whole-heartedly. She doubted she could. He assumed the force of his love would erase the tragedy of the death of her husband, her first love. That tragedy followed her like a hungry, mangy dog, but Dante believed he could free her from it, set her life on a different path, one leading to a happy ending. Kiss me! As if he were her frog prince. She wanted it to be true, but wishing didn't make it so.

She'd deluded herself into thinking she could escape her past by submerging it, and had kept one secret from Dante, then another, and another. If he knew the truth, if he knew what the real tragedy was, he wouldn't love her at all. He'd regret inviting her for a drink at Freddie's and everything that followed. But now they were caught, and it was her fault.

Liz stared at the letter and felt herself collapsing away from Dante, in shame and in fear. Her breath snagged in her chest and she rocked back and forth, biting her lip to keep from sobbing. He deserved someone better than her. At the very least, he deserved the truth.

If she came clean, she would break his heart,

and her own. She might endure that, but she was dead certain she could not bear to see his face when he found out his beloved widow had blood on her hands.

Chapter Seven

When she returned to the café the next morning, the last person she expected to see was Dante. But there he was, sitting at a picnic table, leaning on his elbows and fiddling with his phone. She scanned the area for his pack but didn't see it anywhere. He looked both bored and anxious. And of course he was there to see her.

Her first impulse was to avoid him. What would another confrontation accomplish, other than more pain? Nothing had changed since they'd parted three days before, despite his note and the feelings it had provoked. She was well rested, fully supplied and poised to continue her southward journey. All she needed to do before rejoining the trail was eat breakfast and turn in the bucket for recycling. Neither was imperative. She could duck behind the store to the footpath that led across the road to the JMT. He'd be left thinking he'd missed her and she'd be gone, hiking alone as she'd intended. That was, after all, why she was here.

She hesitated. Avoiding him was childish. She

approached the store, leaned her pack against a post and began transferring the extra food from the bucket into the trash.

"Liz."

She tossed a handful of energy bars into the can.

"Liz." He put his hand on her arm. "How are you? How was your hike?"

A bag of trail mix, the extra sunscreen, into the can. She held a packet of M&M's in her palm.

He moved in front of her and tilted his head to better see her face. She focused on the bucket. His voice was soft with concern. "Two nights ago, did you have a thunderstorm? I was worrying about you so much."

That night. Her heel digging into the mud. The driving rain. The waves of fear cascading through her body as the thunder rumbled. The world exploding in light, the silhouetted figure appearing between the trees.

A shiver slid down her spine. She chewed her lip to control her emotions and handed him the M&M's.

He smiled as if nothing had happened. "Let me buy you breakfast."

The café had just opened but was already half full. They took a small table next to the counter. As the waitress poured coffee, Paul and Linda came in and sat near the door. Linda caught her eye and waved cheerfully. When Linda's gaze fell on Dante, a bemused expression took over her face. Oh, the predictably topsy-turvy lives of young couples! Liz gave Linda a weak smile and picked up her menu.

They ordered. She asked Dante what he'd been doing since Lyell Canyon, which was not quite the same as asking why he was here.

"I took the shuttle from Tuolumne, then a taxi." Before she could ask why he didn't drive, he went on. "I've been thinking. And walking. Eating. Mostly thinking."

"You didn't go home?"

His face drooped. "I couldn't."

"So you've been hanging around? Like a trail groupie?" She meant it lightly, but it came out a little harsh.

"I was waiting for you."

The plates arrived, and they ate in silence except for Liz nervously tapping the tip of her knife on the table. Dante stole glances at her as if she might do something unexpected, such as run out the door or spontaneously combust. They'd almost finished eating when she noticed him watching the McCartneys. Paul whispered something in Linda's ear that made her laugh. She kissed him on the mouth and stole a strip of bacon off his plate. He pantomimed shock.

"I want to be like them," Dante said.

"Old?"

"Happy. Easily happy."

She almost made a sarcastic comment about

how the McCartneys probably had screaming matches twice a week or were actually married to other people, but was weary of her own cynicism. She gave honesty a shot. "Me, too. But I haven't got a clue how to get there."

"Neither do I."

"Let's interview them."

Dante shrugged as if to say there were worse ideas. "*Mi carina,* I want to tell you again how sorry I am I wasn't a very good hiking partner."

"It's okay. It's not for everyone. Notice the wilderness is mostly empty."

He chewed his toast and nodded. "I've been thinking about it for three days, and I get it now."

"Get what?"

"I get that you need to have this journey, and you don't want to cut corners or have to talk to me all the time, or take care of me. I should have been prepared to do the trip your way, the right way. And—I think this is important—you don't want to have to work on whatever's going on with us while you're doing it. You must have your reasons, and I hope you will share them with me eventually. But even if you never do, I should respect them."

"Thanks, Dante." She sipped her coffee and wondered what else to say. He didn't have to intercept her at Red's to deliver his message. It would've kept until she finished the hike. Still, he had come to find her, and his speech was touching, despite sounding rehearsed and stilted. She reached her hand across to his, and as she did, looked up and saw the Root brothers settling into the adjoining table. Startled, she yanked back her hand and knocked over her coffee.

"Shit!"

She jumped from her seat, but the damage was done. Her pant leg was soaked. Dante handed her his napkin. She blotted her leg, then stopped and told him she'd take care of it in the restroom. The waitress arrived and began mopping up the spill with a cloth.

"Sorry," Liz said, as she threaded her way through the tables. She pushed open the door, and looked over her shoulder. Half the café was staring at her. Dante's face betrayed concern and confusion. Probably he was wondering why she was so skittish. Payton Root caught her eye—he'd been waiting for it—and winked.

She jogged past the store to the bathrooms. She'd left her jacket behind and rubbed her arms as she ran. The single-stall room wasn't heated. The chipped sink (cold water only) stood under a crooked mirror with failed backing. It was border-line Third World, but at least there were paper towels. She wetted one and rubbed the stain.

Why did Payton Root rattle her? He hadn't done anything. She'd seen him only twice, maybe three times, if she counted the split second during the storm, which she couldn't honestly do, as it might have been anyone—or no one. During their first encounter on Day One of the hike, had he really acted strangely enough to justify her reaction? She tried to recall exactly what he'd said, and how he'd said it. Something about this hike being a lot of quality time for a couple, and a possible ethnic slur directed at Dante. But Dante hadn't picked up on it. Instead, the Roots were his fast friends. Unlike her, he had spent an entire evening with them in a drunken bocce tournament. And Dante was the people person. She was the geek and should defer to him in interpersonal gray areas.

She gave up on the coffee stain. What difference would it make when she was on the trail again? She tossed the paper towel into the overflowing trash, and leaned over the sink to examine her reflection. She organized her bangs and tucked the sticking-out wisps of her hair behind her ears. More pointless vanity. In a couple of days she could have a giant wart on her nose and wouldn't be the wiser.

She considered the hypothesis that Payton was attracted to her. She had a history of being the last to know when men were drawn to her, which undoubtedly accounted for how few men she had dated. They had to write their intentions in the sky in plain English if they wanted to get through. If Payton was interested in her, it would explain why he seemed a bit odd. He was sending signals she wasn't receiving. Hadn't he just winked at her? And the first day, when she and Dante had left the Root brothers at the stream, she'd turned to see Payton smirking. At the time she'd taken it as a sign of his satisfaction in sending them in the wrong direction, but now she considered the possibility he was checking out her ass.

It was a theory.

She went into the stall for a pee. Her thoughts turned from Payton to Dante. He was making a real effort, and she knew he believed every word he said. But she didn't get why he'd waited for three days to apologize again, then drive home. Unless he wanted reassurance. She didn't know how much she could honestly give him. He'd be waiting for her now, worrying about her reaction to his apology and her quick exit. Maybe he had more to say, like that their relationship wasn't working and he was bowing out. She wasn't the only one who could make decisions. Her throat closed, and she felt queasy. Well, if that was what was coming, she'd be spared having to break his heart in other ways.

When she came out of the bathroom, she found him sitting on a picnic table with his feet on the bench.

"I have something to show you." He jumped off the table, unzipped a large duffel bag he'd stowed on the other bench, and pulled out a pair of hiking boots. "These are amazing. So comfortable—and light!" He handed her one. "See?"

She turned it over. The tread was unusual—protruding nubs in a circular pattern. "Interesting tread. But why . . ."

"And look at these!" He showed her a plastic bag full of small bandages. "The man who sold me the boots said they're incredible." He pulled one out. "See? They're gel. They don't fall off either. And if they do . . ." His hand disappeared into the bag again. "I've got this!"

"Duct tape?"

"It's waterproof and slippery on the outside so it doesn't rub. And it won't come off until you rip it off. The man said all the hikers use it."

Liz put two and two together. "You're not thinking of coming with me again, are you?"

His face was shining with hope. "If you'll have me."

"Dante . . ."

"It'll be different." He took her hand. "I promise."

She looked away. It wasn't his promises that worried her, but her own. She'd vowed to try to put an end to the careening quality of her life, and was relying on the empty trail in front of her to straighten her path and align her actions with her intentions—or at least provide no impedance to whatever decisions she made, including whether she should stay with Dante, and whether she was capable of becoming anyone's wife, or mother.

This didn't require absolute solitude. She expected to meet other people on the trail—had looked forward to it, in fact—but only for a little company, and only on her terms. She wanted to walk through the mountains, her pack on her back, making the small daily decisions about when to stop, which dinner to prepare, where to pitch her tent. *Her* tent. To do all this in the silence of the wilderness, and sleep alone with only a thin sheet of nylon between her and the star-filled sky. It hadn't yet been the contemplative trip she'd planned, but neither had she given up. In fact, her hopes had been revived when Dante left in the first place.

Quashing that hope were the Root brothers, who were hiking at the same pace as she was. She wasn't privy to their plans, but whatever the distance, she expected to encounter them again, perhaps daily—or more. It wasn't logical to factor them into her decisions, but she also couldn't ignore the way she felt about them. She didn't think she could outpace them, and she couldn't afford to slow down and miss her resupply. Whoever they were and whatever they wanted (perhaps nothing), Payton and Rodell were almost certainly a lasting feature of this hike.

As were thunderstorms. She'd downplayed both their likelihood and their impact on her. Now that she'd had her first official storm-induced trauma, she'd stopped deluding herself.

Between strange men and terrifying storms, quitting was a viable option. She could leave with Dante, take the shuttle or a taxi to Yosemite and drive home. She pictured the long, quiet ride west. She saw herself unloading her pack, the piles of underused gear and uneaten food returned to the kitchen table.

She tasted the disappointment and tossed the idea aside. She wasn't ready to bail out. There wasn't reason to. She wasn't injured or sick or demoralized. Even Brensen hadn't yet quit.

Her eyes sought Dante's. His head was bowed, his eyes half closed, as if bracing for a blow. She studied the angle of his cheekbone and the curve of his ear. A wave of tenderness came over her. If she didn't let him rejoin her now, she would almost certainly lose him. She blinked back tears and breathed out slowly to steady herself.

However firm her plans and valid her reasons, on this particular morning she could not turn her back on him and walk away.

Dante let go of her hand, taking her silence as refusal. He sighed and said, "I got you something." He scrounged in the duffel and handed her a narrow paper bag. "Your favorite wine. I was surprised they had it in Mammoth. I even took it as a sign things would work out. Pathetic, isn't it? I planned for us to share it tonight because that's when I thought I'd meet you here."

He'd keep pouring out words until she stopped him.

"Tell you what. Let's transfer it to a Nalgene bottle. It'll go great with the beef stroganoff we're having on the trail tonight."

His mouth formed a small circle of surprise, and he pulled her into his arms. He smelled of cheap hotel soap. The weight of his body against hers was familiar and comforting. She wished she could purr.

He said, "I lit a candle for us at mass yesterday."

She whispered into his ear. "Don't tell God, but I threw away most of your food."

"I forgive you." He kissed her deeply.

"We'll go Dumpster diving." She pressed her hips against him. One kiss and he was hard. "But first we should celebrate."

He moved his hand to her rear end. "I stayed in a cabin here last night. I could show it to you."

Her entire body was turning liquid, pouring into her groin. She nuzzled his neck. "Please."

"If you insist."

She lay with her head on his shoulder, their legs entangled in the sheets. A trapezoid of light from the cabin's small window captured dust motes kept afloat by invisible forces. Dante planted a kiss on top of her head.

"We should get moving. I expect there are many miles on our agenda."

"Uh-huh," Liz murmured into his chest. She had more inertia than the mountains beyond the window. "Fourteen."

"Only fourteen?"

"That's my boy."

"*Vamos!*" He yanked the covers off and kissed her bare hip.

She sat up and glowered at him. "Cruel."

They quickly washed and dressed. She straightened the bed. They'd stashed their packs on the porch, but she asked, out of habit, "Got everything?"

They scanned the room and stepped outside. Leave no trace.

After their team bonding exercise, Liz and Dante reorganized their backpacks again. She had rescued some of what she'd thrown away, but they were short on snacks because Dante had eaten the ones he'd packed out. While he refilled his bear can, she went into the store to stock up.

She paid for her purchases and pushed open the door. Rodell and Payton had joined Dante. She said hello.

"We're glad to see you've got company again," Payton said.

What exactly had Dante said? She changed the subject. "So where are you headed today?" If she had some idea of their destination, she and Dante could stop short of it or leapfrog past them.

Rodell tipped his head behind and to the left. "South."

"Like we said before, we make it up as we go along," Payton said, clamping a hand on his brother's arm.

"It's part of the game," Rodell said.

Before Liz could decide whether she wanted to know what he meant, Brensen charged toward them from the back of the café, red-faced, his phone to his ear. Oblivious, he weaved through picnic tables, trash cans and hikers, berating whoever was unfortunate enough to be on the other end.

"I told you a million times not to negotiate with those assholes. You do work for me, don't you?" He came to a halt and scuffed his boots, sending up a cloud of dust. "What do you mean it's a partnership? I learn the roles, I make the movies, I earn the goddamn money, and you suck up your ten percent!" He plastered his hand against his forehead as if to prevent his skull from breaking open.

He ranted on, and Rodell and Payton exchanged looks. The older brother strode over to Brensen and poked his shoulder. Brensen spun to face Payton's chest, raised his head and noted the man's stern expression.

The actor said into the phone, "Hang on a minute." He snarled at Payton. "What do you want?"

"I want you to keep it down."

"Really?" He pulled himself a little taller. "I'm conducting business here."

"I don't give a shit what you're conducting. No one wants to listen to you. This is the wilderness."

Brensen snorted. "Not while I've got reception."

Payton stared him down, immobile.

The actor pointed at his phone. "Do you mind?"

The bigger man's voice was a low growl. "I just said I did, didn't I?"

Rodell approached them, cleared his throat and said, "Payton, he's a pissant. Not worth your trouble."

Payton stepped closer until his boots nearly touched Brensen's. Dante caught Liz's eye and frowned.

Brensen squirmed a couple of steps back, ran his eyes up and down Payton, nodding his head in recognition. "I knew there was something familiar about you."

Uncertainty flashed over Payton's face. And a trace of fear.

Brensen pointed his phone at him. "I think I played you. Yeah. Lead role in *Down and Dirty in Appalachia*."

In one step Payton was toe to toe with Brensen. The actor recoiled an inch, then scowled and held his ground. Payton set his jaw, stretched his arms along his sides, and spread his fingers wide.

"Now, Payton," his brother cautioned, "we're not shopping for trouble."

The café door slammed. Payton exhaled and nodded at Rodell, who grinned. The older brother addressed Brensen. "Lucky for you I'm in a sunny mood this morning, Hollywood, and eager to get on the trail." He thrust a finger at the phone clutched to Brensen's chest. "Better finish your call because once you're in the woods again there won't be anybody answering." He spun away, retrieved his pack from beneath a tree and swung it over his shoulder. Rodell did the same, with a grunt.

As they left, Payton tipped his cap to Liz and Dante. "See you lovebirds later."

Dante waved at them. A moment later they disappeared behind the store. "I don't think I've seen that movie. Have you, Liz?"

She didn't answer. She was watching Brensen as he paced in front of them, checking his phone display over and over.

"Hello? Can you hear me, damn it? Hello?"

Chapter Eight

Her pack lighter again, she led Dante up out of the valley from Red's Meadow Resort. The morning air harbored the night's chill, but the sun, climbing with them, promised warmth. The dusty trail traversed the slope through a sea of pines, although they bore little resemblance to the tall, majestic trees near Red's. This was a scene of devastation.

They stopped at the top of the slope.

"What happened here?" Dante asked.

"Maybe giants have been playing pick-up sticks."

The hillside extended a mile or so in front of them, dropped into a shallow valley and rose to an escarpment on the other side. Thousands of mature lodgepole pine and red fir, each seventy feet or more in height and as much a four feet wide, had been snapped in half or ripped out of the ground and tossed aside, root-balls dangling in the air.

Yesterday, when Liz had approached Red's, she'd seen acre sections of forest similarly destroyed. She'd guessed an avalanche was the culprit, although the terrain didn't seem steep enough, and the uprooted trees didn't point downhill, as she would have expected. She'd meant to ask someone at Red's about it, but forgot.

The source of the devastation baffled them. Liz pointed to a nearby tree that had been sawn in half. "They've had time to clear the trail, so Pine-ageddon probably happened a while ago."

Dante said, "Whatever it was, I'm glad I was somewhere else."

Liz imagined the noise the trees would have made as they snapped and fell crashing to the ground by the hundreds. It must have sounded like the end of the world. She shivered. "Let's get out of here."

They marched across the broken landscape, silenced by the overwhelming scale of the damage. After a half hour, they entered intact forest. She wondered how long it would take until a passing hiker wouldn't realize a boundary had been crossed.

Pine-ageddon was by far the most interesting thing they witnessed all day. The trail never left the forest. Where the pines were sparse and a view was possible, there was nothing to see. The surface of the trail was either fine dust or pine needles, both easy on the feet. Dante insisted on taking the rear position for most of the way, and blew his nose frequently because of the dust Liz inadvertently kicked up.

They had lunch at a verdant stream crossing. A few larkspur and asters hugged the banks, remnants of what would have been a riot of blooms earlier in the year.

"Those flowers remind me of the last people left at a party," she told Dante.

"I wish I'd seen the party in full swing."

"It's crazy pretty. Unfortunately, the mosquitoes crash it every year." She decided to hike the JMT in September partly because, from the snowmelt until the end of August, mosquitoes threatened to exsanguinate hikers. She liked flowers, but not that much.

He handed Liz a bag of trail mix. "When were you up here in the summer?"

"Here? Never here. But Gabriel and I went for a weeklong trip out of Mineral King. We had to eat in our tent because the mosquitoes swarmed into our mouths." She rarely spoke about Gabriel to Dante, or to anyone else, for that matter. The more she talked about him, the more the public version of their relationship stuck in her mind. As much as she avoided thinking about how their marriage really was, she also didn't want to forget.

"Sounds disgusting."

"They attacked Gabriel in particular. He'd get furious with them."

Dante said, delicately, "I didn't know he had a temper."

"He didn't. He just hated mosquitoes."

Dante brushed crumbs off the front of his pants. Liz suspected he wanted her to keep talking about Gabriel but was reticent to ask. It went beyond the understandable hesitation of knowing about his girlfriend when she had belonged to someone else. Maybe he was afraid of her dead husband. She hadn't met anyone who asked a follow-up ques-tion once they'd learned about Gabriel's death.

"Come on, *amigo*," she said as she stood. "We're behind schedule."

At Duck Lake, twelve miles from Red's Meadow, they agreed it was time to start searching for a campsite. In fact, it was past time; she was bushed and Dante had gone quiet, a sure sign of exhaustion. They dropped their packs and began hunting along the shore, their shirts clinging to their sweaty backs. She was puzzled as to why Duck Lake sounded familiar. After fifteen minutes of fruitless searching, she thought it might be among the prohibited camping areas listed on their wilderness permit. She dug the permit out of her pack. Sure enough, no camping at Duck Lake. Too tired to complain, they set off for the next water source: Purple Lake. Two miles more, uphill for the first half, then a sharp slide to the tiny lake. Liz hoped to God there were empty campsites.

When they came around a bend, the lake materialized before them. Its surface held a perfect reflection of the scree slope that poured from the granite peak towering over its southern end. Liz heard a commotion and turned to see Brensen, twenty feet away, brandishing a tent pole and chasing a chipmunk.

"Get out of my food, you fucking rat!"

She laughed and Brensen spun toward the sound, catching his boot on an exposed root. He stumbled headlong toward a tree. At the last

96

second, his hands flew up and smacked the trunk, breaking his fall. As they crossed the grass toward Brensen, Liz wondered if he did his own stunts.

"Fucking squirrels!" Brensen said, by way of greeting. "That bastard tore into my cashews."

"It was a chipmunk," she said. "And it's lovely to see you again, too."

"Chipmunk, squirrel, rat. Who cares?" He adjusted the waistband of his pants, smoothed his hair, and addressed Dante. "Hey, Duncan. Good to see you back in the game." He raised his eyebrows at Liz.

She returned the look, magnified to ridiculousness. She and Dante said, simultaneously, "It's Dante."

"Dante, yeah. I knew that. Losing my mind up here. What a goddamn boring hike today. If I didn't hate pine trees before, I do now."

"Hey, Liz," Dante said. "Do you think it was Mr. Brensen who killed all those trees right after Red's Meadow?"

Brensen smiled for the first time. "I wish. Funny enough, I can tell you what happened there. The Devil's Windstorm last November. After it went through here, it blew into L.A. Made a hell of a fucking mess."

"Wind did that?" Liz said.

"Up at Mammoth, near Red's, it blew a hundred eighty miles an hour. They said it was a fluke event. The jet stream, instead of staying north of thirty thousand feet, decided to touch down in the Sierras."

"That's insane," Dante said.

"If you ask me," Brensen said, picking up his tent pole, "this whole goddamn place is insane."

Brensen had snagged the only campsite on the shore of the lake, but there were others on the far side of the outlet stream. Liz deposited her pack at the first one.

"I hope you love it, because I'm whipped," she told Dante.

"It's paradise."

She set up the tent while he inflated the mattresses and fluffed the sleeping bags. He set beef stroganoff on the burner and she headed to the stream for water. Lake water was fine, but moving water was better.

She marveled as she had each evening at how much better she felt once she'd shed her pack, made camp, washed and changed into her (relatively) clean sleeping clothes. As she picked her way around boulders and over logs, her leg muscles felt sore, but comfortably so, as though content to walk farther with a normal burden. Her body impressed her. She typically asked it to work hard an hour a day during a run or at the gym. Now she had suddenly asked it for ten times the effort, and it had responded—not without com-plaint—but it had responded all the same. Countless neuromuscular junctions, firing away, thousands of times a minute, tens of thousands of coordinated impulses orchestrated by her brain, functioning smoothly behind the veil of her consciousness. If only her emotional self was a fraction as capable.

She knelt in the grass at the lip of the stream. Water burbled over mossy rocks. On the opposite bank, a robin probed the coarse turf as if it were a suburban lawn.

"You up here on vacation?" Liz asked it.

It cocked its head as if considering the question, bounced to a hillock and flew away.

She propped a bottle between her feet and began pumping. The jet of water hissed as it sprayed into the empty bottle. So long, Aquamira. Fresh water was on the way.

"You alone?"

Her hand slipped off the pump handle and hit the bottle, knocking it over. She righted it and swore under her breath.

She knew it was Payton before she looked up. He stood too close, casting a looming shadow. The sun was setting over his right shoulder, blinding her. She blocked the sun with her free hand. His mouth was half leer, half smile, but she couldn't make out his eyes under the bill of his cap.

She said, "You shouldn't sneak up on people."

"I wasn't sneaking. I didn't want to shout from over there"—indicating the way he'd come—"and ruin the quiet for everyone."

She wanted to stand, but he hadn't given her enough room. "Can you back off so I can put my arm down?"

He crouched. His knees were an inch away from hers. "Better?"

Her face flushed, and her pulse picked up. "What do you want, Payton? I'm busy here."

"I asked you if you were alone."

"I would be if you left." To busy her hands, she dropped the float in the current and resumed pumping.

"I can do that for you." He reached for the pump.

She blocked him with her elbow. "Back. The hell. Away."

He snorted and inched backward—a retreating spider. "Here?"

"Try Ohio." She gripped the pump tightly to calm her hands.

"Now, now. I'm just trying to talk to you." His tone was conciliatory. "I came here to ask you something."

The water hissed into the bottle. Ssshhh. Ssshhh.

He picked up a slender stick, holding it like a baton. "Rodell seems to think you're afraid of me. But I disagree. I think it's something else."

Her hand stopped in midstroke.

He waved the stick in front of her, as if teasing a kitten. "What do you think, Liz?"

She capped the bottle and scooped up the

equipment, holding it to her chest as she rose. Tubes dangling and dripping, she strode past him toward her campsite.

"Have a nice evening," he called after her. "And don't worry. No chance of a storm tonight."

Liz lay huddled in her sleeping bag facing Dante, who was on his back, eyes closed. She couldn't imagine how she would feel now if he weren't there beside her. She hadn't said anything to him about Payton. What could she say? Replayed in her head, no sentence or gesture was anything worse than awkward. Except it had been.

Until the incident at the stream, it had been a good day. Dante's appearance at Red's and his apology touched her. Even the boots he bought— not to mention the duct tape—meant something to her. And the sex didn't hurt his case either. As she'd hiked today, she had been grateful for the monotony of the scenery because it freed her mind to think about him. He was committed, he was reaching out to her, he was trying to give her what she wanted. Bending over backward, in fact. He wanted to be with her, to be close to her, to live with her and was willing to meet her at least halfway. She should think herself lucky.

And what had she done for him? Mostly protect him from herself, from her secrets, lies and misgivings born out of keeping the truth balled up and under wraps for too long. The half bottle of wine she'd had with dinner had loosened her. She wanted to be close to Dante, to let him in, just a little.

"Are you asleep?" she whispered.

"No. Just enjoying the sensation of not moving."

"I'm with you. That was a lot of territory to cover." She paused. "I was thinking of something today." She paused again. "When I was in college, I was walking to class and this guy in a wheelchair cut in front of me. I fell over a curb. My knee was bleeding badly. He saw what happened but just wheeled away. Didn't say sorry or anything. So, this older man, a professor probably, helps me up. I must've looked shocked because he says to me, 'Just because someone's in a wheelchair doesn't mean he isn't an asshole.' "

Dante rolled over to face her. "What are you saying?"

"It's the same when someone dies young. Everyone thinks of them as an angel flying up to heaven. The marriage the person had gets the same pass."

"Are we talking about Gabriel? And you?"

She nodded.

"But I thought you two were happy."

"You and I have never spoken about it."

"We haven't?"

"No."

"Maybe I heard it from someone else? Valerie?"

"Possibly. Like I said, it's what people think.

No one dares to ask, because it's taboo. Some-one's dead, suddenly dead, you don't ask those questions."

Dante looked as if he was about to dip his toe in a pool of piranha. "Were you happy?"

Liz exhaled. She'd half expected him to take this first tidbit in a different direction and speculate about what trouble might be hiding in their relationship. After all, she and Gabriel were old news, but the secrets she kept from Dante were right here, walking with them every step of the way.

"No, we weren't. Not for most of it." There. She'd said it. Now what? How long would the entire story take to unravel?

Dante propped himself up on an elbow. "And no one knew?"

"You'd be surprised. People see what they want to see."

"But you must have been happy when you first got married."

"I thought so. Optimistic, anyway."

"You weren't married very long, right?"

"Less than three years."

"So what changed?"

Liz almost said Gabriel had. It was an easy reach, especially since he was gone forever, and Dante had nothing to go on but her say-so. "I'm not sure."

He turned onto his back and examined the tent

ceiling. "Well, you guys were pretty young." He was marking the distance between her failed marriage and their relationship.

"I was twenty-one when we got married."

"That's young."

Age had to be the reason. No one to blame, just immaturity. She said, "Maybe I didn't know him as well as I thought I did."

A long pause. "How well do you suppose you know me?"

"Oh, Dante. That's such an impossible question for me. Getting closer to someone doesn't necessarily clarify anything. It's like staring at an electron micrograph. You're closer but nothing's any simpler."

"So much for optimism."

"I'm trying to figure it out. I really am."

"I know, *carina.*" He leaned over and kissed her lightly. "I'm so tired. Let's sleep."

She repositioned her makeshift pillow and settled into her bag, her limbs sinking into the ground. She conjured an image of Gabriel. His features were vague, but distinct enough that she winced with shame. Maybe she had never seen him for who he was, never understood what he wanted from their marriage. Maybe she never realized that she, the person who had had so little, was the one who wanted more.

Chapter Nine

Liz and Gabriel went to high school together in Santa Fe, but ran with different tribes, or, more accurately, he was a member of a variety of tribes while she had only a small circle of friends, mostly two. She might have been more than a bit player in high school except her sarcasm and wit were underappreciated. That and she didn't give a damn about being popular.

Gabriel Pemberton didn't have to give a damn about being popular. He just was. And he managed it without being a jerk most of the time. He was handsome in a clean-cut, East Coast prep school way, and disarmingly candid, and girls found their way to him. He befriended them all and dated only three. It could have been forty. Liz was not a prospect. She was more than pretty enough, but chose not to put herself forward. Boys, including Gabriel, assumed she was aloof, awkward or a lesbian, possibly all three. In truth, she didn't think much of men, and teenage boys did nothing to argue the opposing case. She went out a few times with a couple of boys from other schools (simpler all around), but thought she might wait until the selection improved, or she died, whichever came first.

They both ended up at UCLA, he on a track

scholarship (middle distances) and she because it was the best school that offered her a place. In the spring of their second year, they met outside a dorm party where he was helping a friend vomit into the bushes. She watched them from the steps, deciding if she would wait for Valerie, already a half hour late, or simply return to her aunt's house. By the time she'd thought it through, the vomiter was taking a nap on the lawn. Gabriel climbed up and sat beside her.

"You're Liz, right?"

"Guilty." She was surprised he remembered her. "And you're the fellow who needs no introduction."

He flashed his knock-the-girls-out smile. "You cut your hair. I like it."

She'd worn it chin length when everyone in high school had tresses streaming down their backs. Now it was cut in a pixie-style. "You like guinea pigs. What a coincidence. So do I."

For the next two hours their conversation flowed as freely as the beer they were missing upstairs. Turns out, sarcasm is an acquired taste. As for Liz, it was now permissible to fall for a guy like Gabriel. In a city of fifteen million, teeming with actors, would-be actors and surfer dudes, he really wasn't all that popular.

In the days that followed, their conversation continued between classes, over meals and, after two weeks, in bed. They talked as if no one had ever listened to them before. For Liz, this was more or less true, particularly where men were concerned. She had grown up without them. Her mother, Claire, was a sculptor with a small talent and a large trust fund. When Liz was eight, she asked her mother why she and her father were not married. "We're both much too selfish." Liz took it as the truth, at least about Claire. Her father did marry, but she had no idea how it turned out, because her mother waved aside her questions with a bored flick of her wrist. And Liz never dared to ask her father directly.

So she lived with her mother in solitude. Claire fed and clothed her, but played with her or read to her only sporadically. Some days she'd invite Liz into her studio and hand her sticky lumps of clay or pots of watercolor. More often she'd ignore her, not assiduously, but as if she'd forgotten she had a child. There were nannies from time to time, but Claire couldn't adhere to any sort of schedule, and they soon left for steadier work. When Liz was a teenager, she asked her mother why she'd bothered to have a child. Claire wasn't offended by the question.

"Every woman should have one. I thought it would be interesting."

Apparently not.

From an early age, Liz learned to keep her own company. When she tired of her books and toys, she began to disassemble household objects using a screwdriver and various kitchen implements. She began with simple things—a picture frame, a stapler, her desk chair—but soon graduated to toasters, radios and door locks. Claire was amused and told her daughter that if she couldn't put whatever it was back together, she'd buy a replacement. Liz electrocuted herself only once, when she reversed the wiring on a night-light. It hurt enough to ensure she would not make the mistake twice.

Wiring was easier than making friends, but Liz's humor and lack of malice guaranteed she always had one close friend, which was plenty. When she was old enough to compare her family to others, the contrast evoked more curiosity than self-pity. Fathers were the strangest element, present in her friends' lives at sports games, dinner tables and movie nights, followed closely by doting mothers. She knew about boys from school. They were like her, but louder.

In junior high, the simple understanding of people and relationships she had assembled crumbled under the burden of puberty (hers and everyone else's). Claire moved them from Seattle to Santa Fe in the middle of seventh grade. "For my art," she explained, and Liz could not voice her anxiety over losing her tiny social toehold. As a newcomer to the school and her own body, she turned to sitcoms for information about families. Her favorite was *Home Improvement*, because she also learned about carpentry and power tools. She survived high school and braced herself for college.

She needn't have worried. Even before she began dating Gabriel, she had Valerie's friendship and enviable accommodations in her aunt's house in Beverly Hills, a half mile from campus. Claire's sister, Georgette, was a professional socialite whose ridiculously large mansion was filled regularly with celebrities, politicians and the merely rich. The glitterati didn't attract Liz (she failed to recognize the names of most of the people her aunt went on about), but she did appreciate her lodgings. Her aunt installed her in the au pair suite, for which Georgette had no use, as she had no children and, during Liz's tenure, no husband. The suite was as large as her Santa Fe home but, more important, completely private, with a view of the lush gardens. She'd seen the dorms. The cramped quarters she could live with. All those noisy, sloppy kids she could not.

Georgette was indifferent to Liz's activities and made few social demands on her, asking her only from time to time "to say hello to some people." For these occasions, she'd provide Liz with an expensive outfit and trot her out for show. "This is my niece, Elizabeth. She studies medical engineering next door. Isn't she lovely?" Liz wasn't thrilled with being treated as an accessory, but it seemed a small price to pay for what she received in return.

Gabriel listened to Liz's story as he would a documentary about an aboriginal people in a remote and hostile country. His history couldn't have been more at odds with hers, balanced and normal in every way. Liz had long known his father was a Presbyterian minister who, together with his tall, handsome wife, had raised five children, none of whom, she suspected, had ever been left alone with a screwdriver and a toaster. The Pembertons were well respected. It was what gave Gabriel, the middle child, his easy confidence.

From their courtship conversations, Liz pieced together a more complete tableau of the family. The youngest son, Daniel, had Down's syndrome, but even this seemed more of a blessing than an affliction; God had given them Daniel because they were that good. The Pembertons perpetrated all manner of charity among areas of Santa Fe Liz had no contact with: Rotary Club, Meals on Wheels, Boys and Girls Clubs, soup kitchens, hospice groups and Native American reservations. The most her mother had ever done was donate art supplies to the schools when she ran out of space at home.

Gabriel could readily have become a sanctimonious bore, but didn't. He was serious about his goals (he wanted to be a computer jock), but was typically lighthearted (although never goofy). Liz warmed to the idea that there was something to all this God talk—the Pembertons' version of it anyway—and sensed she'd missed an important part of her development. She had gills while other people were breathing with lungs There was, however, no point in dwelling on it, as it was too late to grow up differently.

She waited for Gabriel to voice a complaint about having wanted to play video games instead of working at a food bank, or having to suffer personalized sermons from Pastor Pemberton, but he never did. This made her worry he was too good for her by far, and she might represent a spiritual and emotional charity case to him. When they'd been dating three months, she got up the nerve to ask him what he saw in her.

"What do you mean? You're amazing."

"I am? I thought I was cynical, aloof and unusually twitchy."

He laughed. "You are. Twitchy, I mean. And, yeah, you can be pretty cynical, but who could blame you, the way your parents were. Are. I don't think you mean it."

"I don't?"

"No. I think you want what everyone wants."

"And what's that, pray tell?"

"A normal life."

So she shouldn't have been surprised when, the day after they returned to Santa Fe at the end of the semester, Gabriel invited her to meet his family. Liz had been concerned Pastor Thomas Pemberton and his wife, Eleanor, would be less than thrilled about their son's choice of a Godless geek for a girlfriend, but if it was true, they hid it well. She was asked to join them for dinners, walks, charity events and, of course, at church. The pastor's sermons weren't as sermony as Liz expected. Some were posed as friendly suggestions, which an individual could take or leave. Others were parables, delivered in a way to make the ending seem more of a question than an answer. She asked Gabriel's father how much time he spent creating a sermon.

"Usually twice as long as I need to."

The internal yapping of her cynical self was soon drowned out by the Pembertons' collective genuine good nature. They weren't the least bit stodgy, mixing the work of church and family with laughter, self-deprecation and a good deal of wine. The eldest daughter was married, and brought her two toddlers to see her parents a couple of times a week. Everyone took turns watching the children, including Liz. As she shepherded them away from myriad dangers lurking in the Pembertons' childproofed home, she realized it was pure chance she had survived her mother's lackadaisical parenting.

When Liz wasn't working at Radio Shack, she was with Gabriel, and usually his family, too. Her mother dropped comments about never seeing her, and said one day she had missed Liz while she was in California. Liz answered with a shrug, and doubted it was true.

"It was so quiet without you," Claire said.

"Maybe you should get a cat, Claire." She had been on a first-name basis with both her parents since high school.

"Or a dog?"

"No. A cat." Dogs expect too much.

Gabriel asked Liz to marry him on the anniversary of the first time they met, on the steps of the same dorm. She said they were too young, but what she meant was he couldn't possibly love her as much as he appeared to. Six months later, he asked her again, and she refused him in the same way, for the same reason. Finally, on their second anniversary, Gabriel led her to the steps once more. His eyes pleaded with her. His love was palpable.

Gabriel was the first man to love Liz, to truly love her. So she said yes.

Her father, Russ Kroft, showed up at the wedding to give her away. Every time Liz thought of that phrase, "give me away," she wanted to laugh, or puke. Gabriel and his earnest family had quashed most of her cynicism, but she had a secret stash of it for her parents. She'd have been content to walk down the aisle alone, but Eleanor Pemberton couldn't bear the thought.

"Whatever he is or is not, he is your father. You don't want to regret this opportunity to help him become a better man." Gabriel's mother could utter this with a straight face and mean it. There wasn't a hope in hell that Russ wanted help from Liz—and she doubted he was keen on self-improvement—but she couldn't tell Eleanor that.

The last time she'd spoken to Russ was more than two years ago. He had called to say he would be in Santa Fe in a few days' time and hoped to see her. She had informed him she had been at UCLA for nearly two years.

"You don't say," he said. "What are you studying?"

"Biomedical engineering."

He let out a low whistle. "You don't say. Good jobs in that field?"

"A few."

"Well, good luck with that."

"Thanks."

A long pause. "I guess that means I won't see you next week."

"I guess not." And it's way too much trouble to get to Los Angeles.

"That's too bad. It's been a while. What? A year?"

"Two."

Another whistle. "You don't say. Santa Fe would have been convenient."

114

"I'd move the university for you if I could, but it's awfully big."

He guffawed. "That's a good one' Okay, I got to go. You take care."

" 'Bye."

The conversation about the wedding hadn't been much better.

"Hey, Russ."

"How's my girl?"

She bristled at the expression. "Fine. I called to say I'm getting married."

"You don't say. Who's the lucky guy?"

"Gabriel Pemberton."

"Sounds fancy."

"He's somewhat fancy. The wedding's three months away, on June twenty-fifth." She steeled herself. "I don't suppose you could make it."

"In Santa Fe?"

"Yes."

"June twenty-fifth?"

She could hear him riffling through a date planner.

"By golly, it's your lucky day!"

Please tell me you have a colonoscopy scheduled.

Russ said, "I'm in Colorado Springs the twenty-third. That's close, right?"

"Spitting distance."

"Count me in, then. How old are you now, anyway? Nineteen?"

"Twenty-one."

"Well, old enough anyway."

"Claire said she'd take care of your tux."

"She's a fine gal, your mother."

"Yeah, you guys are the best."

When Russ showed up for the wedding, Liz saw he had gained a few pounds since she and Claire had last seen him and wriggled uncomfortably in his tux. Liz concentrated on Gabriel as they inched down the aisle, ignoring Russ's stately nods at the guests, all strangers to him. When Russ handed her off to Gabriel, her groom winked at her and the second chapter—the better chapter —of her life began.

After the ceremony, they rode in a limo to the hotel reception, where she weathered the obligatory father-daughter dance. He wasn't a bad waltzer. As the song wound down, he reached into his pocket and slipped a folded hundred-dollar bill into her hand.

"For you and Gabe. Get yourselves a little something."

"Um, thanks," she said. "But I don't have any-where to put this."

"Oh, you've got lots of places. Aren't you wearing a garter? Or just put it . . ." He tucked two fingers down the top of his vest, then pointed at her chest, wrapped in white satin. "You know."

"Wow, Russ. You must go to some fun weddings."

"You bet I do. See you later." He searched out Claire and finagled a dance. The sight of Russ and Claire slow-dancing was surreal, as if the people in the photos that came with a picture frame had shown up in her life.

When all the formalities were over, Gabriel followed Liz up to their suite so she could change out of her gown. He poured her a glass of champagne and undid, one by one, the thirty-two covered buttons on her spine. The bodice of the dress fell forward.

"Thank God," she said. "Now I can eat."

He cupped his hands over her breasts and nibbled her neck. "Me, too."

She leaned against him and moved his hands into an embrace. "Hey, husband."

"Hey, wife."

"We should get back into the fray before they start spreading rumors about us."

"Yeah, and you should get some food." He released her. She stepped out of the dress and he took her glass while she changed. "I wanted to ask you something. Quinn and Pablo and some of the other guys are playing Ultimate in the morning. They want me to come."

"Tomorrow morning?"

"Yeah."

"As in the morning after our wedding?"

He finished off her drink and shrugged. "I

know. But most of them are leaving right after the breakfast."

"You'll see them there." She tucked her blouse into her skirt. "They're all invited."

"Yeah, but a little Frisbee with the guys . . ."

Liz slipped her feet into her flats and stood.

"You look nice," he said. "So, are we cool about tomorrow?"

She wished he hadn't asked. How could she tell him not to see his friends? But she wasn't about to start her married life yanking a leash. "Sure. Now lead the way to the buffet."

Chapter Ten

Liz and Dante stopped for a drink at Virginia Lake, a sapphire expanse with a broad, open eastern shore and rimmed on the far end by the Cascade Range. Horsetail clouds filled the sky like waves upon an ocean. The formation usually meant good weather, but Liz kept an eye on the clouds all the same.

They reached Tully Hole, an enormous meadow dotted with chest-high corn lilies. Fish Creek snaked through the amber grasses. The heat rose with them as they climbed steeply out of the valley, the creek babbling alongside. Over their heads, the horsetails fled and flat-bottomed cumulus clouds moved in. They arrived at Squaw

Lake in the early afternoon and set down their packs.

A jaylike bird, gray as granite with crisp, black wings, emitted a harsh squawk from atop a stunted pine.

Liz asked Dante, "Who's the loudmouth?"

"*Nucifraga columbiana.*"

Her mind searched through the Latin roots. "Nut fragmenter from the land of Columbus?"

"Yes! Clark's nutcracker. It buries nuts from pinecones in the fall, then digs them up even before the snow melts in the spring."

"You do know how weird it is that you know everything about birds and yet you yourself are rarely found in nature."

He shrugged. "Blame my uncle. Every summer I spent a month with him in Monterrey. The coolest room in the house was the library, and the only interesting books—to a kid—were his bird guides. He had dozens."

"And you memorized them all?"

"They are fascinating creatures. At least on paper."

While she filtered water, Dante examined the map. "Squaw Lake, Warrior Lake, Chief Lake, Papoose Lake, Lake of the Lone Indian. How charming to have a theme. Oh, here's another one."

"Teepee Lake?"

"No."

"Native American Lake?"

"I think this was pre-P.C."

"Casino Lake?"

"No. It's Brave Lake."

"I was about to guess that." She pointed at the darkening sky. "We need to make tracks. Those clouds mean business."

"Silver Pass is only another mile and a half. Then again, it's a doozy. Almost eleven thousand feet."

"Hi-ho, Silver."

Liz set a blistering pace to the pass. Her arms worked like pistons, pushing down and behind on her trekking poles to take a portion of the strain off her legs. She'd been hiking nearly a week now, and was stronger and lighter than she had been at the start. She had adapted somewhat to the altitude, although when climbing rapidly up a steep grade, she would have paid good money for more oxygen.

Dante, she could tell, was suffering. He hadn't put in the miles she had. But he was doing his best not to fall behind and wasn't complaining about his feet or anything else. She hoped he could keep it up until they got over the pass, and down the other side, because with the possibility of a thunderstorm brewing, she couldn't imagine waiting up.

They left the tree line behind and pushed onward. In a short while, they passed an overweight man resting against a boulder taking photographs—the first person they'd seen all day. They exchanged greetings but didn't pause to talk. Liz considered warning him that, if he was going to go over the pass, he should hurry, but figured anyone could see what those clouds meant.

She reached the top first and strode across the small flat area to see what lay on the other side.

"Shit." She had hoped for a protected area— with lots of trees—closer to this side of the Silver Divide, an east-west ridge. Instead, what she saw was a barren plain stretching for miles. In the center was the trail, a line drawn down the middle of a page.

Dante appeared next to her.

"Congrats, *amigo*," she said. "Your first real pass."

He swept his hand in an arc. "It's fantastic."

And it was. She had been so preoccupied with the weather she hadn't taken in the view. The long, sloping escarpment, dotted with stands of whitebark pine and tiny lakes, gave way to row upon row of granite crests. Above them, the clouds, paler in the distance and also stacked in rows, cast bands of sunlight and deep shadow onto the mountains, highlighting the relief.

Liz felt small, and fortunate.

A raindrop landed on her arm.

"Time to boogie."

They scrambled down the switchbacks on the steep south face of the Divide, gravel crunching underfoot as they descended. At every turn, Liz glanced at the darkening sky. She wished the switchbacks would end so she could put distance between herself and what the clouds foretold. She needed to go *away,* not just down. She dared not go faster, though, and risk a fall. A long fall.

At last they arrived at the open slope tilting downhill toward the forest. Silver Pass Lake lay on their right, but even from the trail they could see there was nowhere to camp. Not during a storm. Liz looked over her shoulder at the pass where inky clouds had formed a solid shroud. Midafternoon and it was as dim as dusk. She picked up her pace.

Dante called out from behind. "It's okay, Liz!"

A crack of thunder rang across the plain. She cried out. A wave of panic flowed through her and sloshed in her stomach. She concentrated on the trail in front of her and fought the urge to throw herself on the ground and cover her head with her arms as she had in Bandelier when she was small.

Dante was at her heels. "Don't worry. We'll be fine."

She was not fine. Several oversize raindrops fell. Above the pass, the thunder rolled and boomed. Her heart beat in her throat. She was compelled now not to prostrate herself, but to flee. She would have broken into a run, but her pack was too heavy. Instead, she strode as if she was cross-country skiing, poles flying out behind her.

A gust of wind carried the smell of ozone past her.

The rain fell harder and the wind picked up. Her thighs and shirtfront were soaked. She tucked her chin as rain needled her face, eyes glued on the trail. From the pass, the plateau had appeared immense. Here, with the storm chasing her like a runaway train, it was endless. Her breath was loud in her ears as she fought to ignore the burning in her legs. She hoped Dante had not fallen behind but she dared not turn to face the storm clouds.

Rain continued to fall in sheets, but the thunder grew no closer. They descended out of the plain, and the widely spaced clumps of whitebark pine gave way to heftier lodgepole pine. No longer a bull's-eye for lightning, Liz slowed down. After a short while, the trail wound across a boulder-strewn hill and dropped to run alongside a small stream.

She shouted over the wind. "What about somewhere here?"

"Looks good."

The rain turned to hail. The pellets stung her bare arms and bounced off the ground like jumping beans. She ducked off the trail, into the woods bordering the stream. Dante followed. They picked their way among rocks and fallen trees. A hundred yards along was a campsite. Liz threw off her pack, the hail pecking at her exposed back, and found her rain jacket. She put it on, and zipped it up. The hail stopped. In the distance, a low growl of thunder.

Dante listened, rain jacket in hand. Another grumble, farther away. The storm was leaving, at least for now. He cupped his hands to his mouth and shouted at the sky. "Is that it? Is that all you've got?"

Liz dropped her head back and yelled, "So long, sucker!"

Dante grinned at her, his eyes sparkling with excitement. Drops of rain, or sweat, dripped from the bill of his cap. He stepped closer and brushed the hail from the brim of her hat. "Hail Lizzy, full of grace."

She laughed, relief flowing through her like a storm-fed river.

"It crossed my mind," he said, "that if we could arrange for more thunderstorms, we could be done with the whole thing in three days."

"Right. But I doubt my heart could take it."

They set up camp, marveling at what a superb site they'd stumbled upon. Nestled in the trees, they had a view of the clearing through which the trail wound. The stream was nearby and there were two large logs for drying clothes and sitting. For hors d'oeuvres, Dante cut them each a chunk of hard salami and a piece of cheese.

He pointed at several birds hopping among stones at the edge of the clearing. "Look! It's a flock of gray-crowned rosy-finches."

"Really? Should we be excited?"

"This is their typical habitat, but I've never seen one before."

"Well, you keep an eye on them. You know what gray-crowned rosy-finches are like. I'm going to the river to wash off the day."

While drying her feet on the riverbank, she heard voices. She rinsed out her underwear (she wore her clean ones; these were for tomorrow), collected her things and returned to camp. Dante was near the clearing with the Root brothers, who, judging by their sodden clothing, had been caught in the same storm. To her dismay, Rodell and Payton headed into the woods, and began to search for a place to camp. She prayed there wasn't a flat rectangle of ground for miles.

Either she hadn't prayed hard enough or had addressed the wrong gods, because within five minutes, Payton lowered his pack and Rodell followed suit. They weren't forty feet away. She thought about suggesting to them, in the friendliest manner possible, that perhaps in these millions of square miles of wilderness there might be another ten-by-ten-foot spot for them tonight. But she couldn't see doing it. There was no rule, other than common courtesy, about camping in someone else's bubble. As long as it was a legitimate campsite (no vegetation, previously used, not on top of a water source), they had the right to camp wherever they pleased. And, when it came right down to it, even if it weren't a legitimate site, she'd hesitate to say anything. She wasn't a vigilante preservationist. Especially not when it came to a standoff with the Root brothers.

Thank God Dante was here.

She organized her pack and sneaked glances at the neighbors. In contrast to her and Dante, who divided their chores, the Roots worked in tandem. Rodell held one end of the ground cloth and Payton the other, lowering it to the ground like a prayer mat. Instead of a tent, they had a tarpaulin anchored at the corners with trekking poles. Rodell telescoped the poles for the head end so the tarp slanted toward their feet. They chatted in low voices as they worked, and laughed several times. When the shelter was finished and they'd filled it with mattresses and bags, Payton laid a hand on Rodell's shoulder and gave it a squeeze. They were kind to each other; Liz had to give them that. And Rodell looked up to Payton, his big brother. It was written in every gesture.

She wished, not for the first time, for a sibling. The closest thing she had had growing up was Brioche, her marmalade cat. One of her story-books featured a cat named Muffin, so Liz asked her mother for names of fancy muffins. She rejected Danish, Cupcake and Bearclaw, seriously considered Fritter, and finally settled on Brioche. Brioche was compliant enough and tolerated dress-up, patiently listened to stories and never tired of games of chase. Still, Liz would have preferred her own species. A half sibling would have sufficed. They could have shared holidays and vacations and a parent, whom they could have fought over and complained about. Her girl-friends were the next best thing to a sister, and she was grateful for them. They all had siblings, and often two dedicated parents, in addition to her friend-ship. An embarrassment of riches.

Rodell caught her watching them, and waved. She returned the wave and joined Dante, who was struggling to extract the stove from its pyramidal container.

"Allow me," she said, extending her hand.

She squeezed the sides of the container and pulled the stove out with two fingers. It consisted of a central hub, the size of a caramel, that screwed onto a fuel can, forming its base. Three pointed prongs, each the length of a finger, were attached to the hub. To fit in the fist-sized container, the prongs swiveled and folded to lie flush along the hub. She twisted and lifted each prong in turn.

"You look as if you're in love with that thing," Dante said.

"I am. Look how they cut holes along each prong to make it lighter." She screwed the hub onto the fuel can, and placed her hand across the open prongs. "The pot balances perfectly on these little points. The jet is an inch in diameter but boils water in a few minutes. And this is cool. This rectangular hoop is the gas control. So simple. So beautiful."

"So hungry. Let's eat."

By six o'clock they had finished their chili and washed the dishes. Liz was brushing her teeth (away from the camp because the toothpaste might attract bears) when the Root brothers crunched through the undergrowth separating the campsites and approached Dante. They stood talking a moment. Before she could rinse and spit, Dante pointed to a log and the men made themselves comfortable. Liz sighed and picked her way through the forest toward them, wondering how rude it would be to crawl straight into the tent.

Payton, his long legs stretched in front, followed her movements as she lowered herself next to Dante. "Heck of a storm today, huh?"

"Were you at the pass when it hit?"

"Were we ever! Dante said you had hail, too."

"For a couple minutes. It was a drive-by."

Payton let go a short laugh. "Go on," he said to his brother. "Tell them what you did up there."

Rodell shuffled his feet, considering. "Oh, all right. But so long as everyone knows it was a dare."

This'll be worth staying up for, Liz thought.

"So, we're at the very top, right? And the sky

was dark as midnight and the clouds hung low and heavy. Like the end of the world was coming. What do you call it? The eclipse?"

"Apocalypse," Liz said.

"Yeah, that. A big one. Anyway, I'm standing there, waiting for the thunder." He got up, assumed a wide stance and turned his face to the sky. "My knees are shaking like crazy and Payton is laughing his butt off."

Payton smiled. "I wish you could've seen yourself."

"Then the thunder goes 'Boom!' Right there! I swore a bomb went off inside my head. So I throw my arm up like this," he thrust his arm above his head, "and stick my hiking pole way up in the air!"

"Holy crap!" Liz said.

Payton's eyes locked on hers. "Your own personal nightmare, I take it?"

How the hell would you know? She held his gaze, refusing his challenge. "Sounds like a bid for a Darwin Award."

Rodell either didn't understand or refused to take offense. "Got away with it."

Dante said, "That's quite a story. Who dared you? Your brother?"

"Yeah." He shot a glance at Payton, who closed his eyes and nodded once, slowly. "We do a lot of dares. It's a game."

"Like Truth or Dare?" Liz said.

Payton said, "Just like that. We've been doing it since we were little."

"I'll bet your parents were thrilled."

"Wasn't any of their business. It was only between us."

Rodell said, "Daddy didn't approve."

Payton narrowed his eyes at his brother. "Like I said, it wasn't anyone else's business. Thing is, we ran out of truths a long time ago."

"In 2001, wasn't it?"

"It was. Late October. No secrets left."

"Not a one."

"So now all we've got are dares."

The failing light dimmed another notch. The trees froze in the hush. Liz reached for Dante's hand, warm against her suddenly cold skin.

Dante spoke in a cautious tone. "Sounds exciting. Or dangerous. Or both."

"That about covers it," Payton said.

"Sometimes it's funny, too," Rodell said, and fell into a fit of laughter, snorting like a pig. He bent over, holding his stomach, and snorted again and again. "Isn't it funny sometimes, Payton?" Another snorting fit. After a few more bouts, he gathered himself and wiped his mouth with his hand. "Remember the time you and that girl— Brenda, wasn't it? Remember? She didn't—"

"Yeah, yeah," Payton interrupted, unsmiling. "Sure I remember. But no one wants to hear about that. Not right now." He stood and reached a hand out to Dante. It was as thick and broad as a slab of meat. They shook.

"Stay dry," he said, and nodded in the direction of his campsite. "We're right there if you need anything."

As soon as the Root brothers left, they climbed into their sleeping bags. It was pitch black inside the tent. Liz lay with her eyes closed, listening. The footfall of someone approaching would have been deafening in the still night, but she listened all the same.

"Dante?"

"Um-hmm?"

"You don't think those guys are weird?"

"Unusual, yes. But not necessarily weird."

"Volunteering to be a human lightning rod isn't weird?"

"It's not different from swallowing goldfish or tipping cows or whatever else Americans do in college."

"Except the Roots aren't wasted when they're doing it."

"True." He pulled an arm out of his sleeping bag and wrapped it around her. "These bags are very unromantic."

"Sadly, yes. In about two minutes you'll have an armsicle."

"Maybe Rodell was exaggerating. No one saw him do it."

"Good point."

And that was the problem with the Root brothers. No one ever saw anything.

She awoke and waited for the sun to scale the eastern ridge and provide at least the hope of warmth. The metallic clink of cups and dishes from the other campsite told her the brothers were up. Dante stirred. She kissed him and left the tent. Payton and Rodell were folding their tarp in the minuet of housewives folding a sheet. Fold, step together, touch hands. Fold, step together, touch hands. The good news was they would be well on their way before she and Dante were ready. Odds were the Roots would make camp first, and they could leapfrog past them. Not that it mattered much. In two days they would all converge at the same place: Muir Trail Ranch. Everyone landed there to retrieve supply buckets and enjoy showers, food and Internet access. The last approximation of civilization for the remaining one hundred and ten miles.

She lured Dante out of the tent with a cup of coffee, and began breaking camp. He helped put away the bags and mattresses. She was removing the fly when Payton called out. "See you guys on the trail." He adjusted his cap and raised a hand in salute.

"Have a good walk," Dante said.

" 'Bye," Liz said, sweetly. *Go to hell. I double dare you.*

Chapter Eleven

Over the first four miles, they descended from their camp at ten thousand feet to below eight thousand feet to reach Quail Meadows.

Liz said, "Sounds like a suburban development."

Dante nodded. "And I suppose, because I can actually breathe here, we're about to go up."

She'd reviewed the map and knew what they were in for. Two thousand feet of climbing over two miles. A whopping one hundred eight-five stories.

The switchbacks began, zigzagging from one side of the slope to the other like a garland on a Christmas tree. She counted each time they made a left-hand turn. At the fifteenth switchback, Dante asked for water. She pulled the bottle from his pack and handed it to him.

"You first," he panted. "Air, then water."

She drank and passed it to him.

He gulped down half the bottle. "I was wondering if a story wouldn't make this easier."

"Only if I tell it. You'll pass out."

"Exactly what I was thinking."

"Any ideas?"

"As a matter of fact, yes. If you wouldn't mind,

you could tell me the story of what happened with you and Gabriel."

She opened her mouth to refuse, or deflect, but remembered she had started this conversation the night after Red's Meadow. "I'm not sure I know how."

"Start with the first time you cried."

"I don't cry very often."

"I know, *carina*. I know."

It was easier than she thought. With the empty trail in front of her, she could have been talking to herself.

"Gabriel got a job right out of college as a systems analyst in Albuquerque, which was how we ended up there. I think I told you that, right?"

"Right."

"It worked out fine for me because the University of New Mexico was putting together a program in biomed engineering. I did graduate work and earned some money as a teaching assistant.

"It felt like we were playing house. Gabriel would leave for work in the morning and come home by dinnertime. I had more free time, so I did most of the housework and cooking. I guess that's why it felt like playing house. It was all so grown-up, but even though I knew how to do all the tasks, it felt like someone else was doing them. But I figured all newlyweds go through that—at least they did on TV."

Dante said, "The idea of TV explaining life scares me."

"It's what I had." She rounded the corner of a switchback without pausing. "Anyway, on weekends we'd see a movie or go for a hike. On Sundays he went to church—I sometimes went, too—then Gabriel spent ages reading *The New York Times*. It was a habit he started in college. He said he never had time to read most of it when he was in school, but now he did. I thought it was a little odd—to read the book reviews but never the books, to read about sports but never watch a game—but so what? While he read, I talked on the phone with Valerie, or went for a long run.

"Every other weekend we'd drive to Santa Fe to see his family, and sometimes Claire. Claire was odd. She'd greet us at the door as if she'd forgotten we existed, and wasn't thrilled to be reminded. Then she'd recover a little, show us her latest work, and maybe even convince us to go to a gallery to see her friends' stuff. Claire was Claire."

"I don't think mothers like her exist in Mexico," Dante said. "I mean, when I met her, if I hadn't known she was your mother I never would have guessed. Except your mouths are exactly the same."

"They are?"

"Precisely."

Liz ran her fingers over her lips and tasted dirt and sunscreen. She adjusted her hat and resumed her normal pace. "Anyway, back to Gabriel's family. They seemed different to me than when we had visited from L.A. Or maybe they'd always been that way, only now I noticed because I was married."

"Different how?"

"For instance, Gabriel's parents never touched each other. They must have had sex a minimum of five times, right? And I don't mean pawing each other. I mean no pecks on the cheek, not a hand on an elbow. *Nada.* They were as kind to each other as ever, but physically they treated each other like lepers.

"The other thing was they mostly talked about other people, or causes. When they asked Gabriel or me about our jobs or whatever, they were ticking a box. We were married; we had promising futures, so we weren't interesting. I wasn't insulted by it, but over time it struck me as strange."

"It does seem odd not to be interested in your son's life. But usually there is a reason."

She continued around the next switchback and paused to face him. "Are you thinking about your father?" Dante's father had endorsed his son's pursuit of both an undergraduate and master's degree in the States because he believed Dante would return to take up the mantle of his hugely profitable business supplying weapons components to the Mexican and U.S. militaries. When Señor Espinoza realized his son had no intention of returning home, he was furious. Only his wife's emotional breakdown averted a complete dissolution of their relationship.

Dante's tone was somber. "Yes, of course, but I can dwell on failing my father another time. Right now I want to hear about Gabriel."

"You sure?"

He nodded and she led them upward again.

"Back to the Pembertons. They always drank—pretty sure I mentioned that—but the longer I knew them, the more they seemed to drink. It could have been because we were there mostly on weekends, when most people do their serious drinking. But I wondered about that, too. And all of it started me thinking about the normal life Gabriel said everyone wanted. I wanted. It got me wondering about what it meant."

"To be normal?"

"Yes. I thought it was the same thing as being happy."

"It would be nice if that were true." They traversed two more switchbacks. Finally, Dante said, "You haven't finished the story."

Liz took a deep breath. "After about six months at his job, Gabriel started playing around with video games in the evening. Not just playing them—he'd been into that in college—but designing them. It seemed hugely frustrating for him, because he didn't have a clue how to proceed. I don't understand much about computing, but systems analysts and programmers are different species. I suggested he take some courses, but he said he didn't have the time or the money. Which made no sense because he spent a lot of time working at it at home. Hours. He'd stay up late and have trouble getting up in the morning for work.

"This didn't happen all at once. It was insidious. I'd wake up in the middle of the night, alone, and find him asleep on the couch, or in his chair at the computer. Everything'd be a mess. Paper, DVDs, beer bottles, food everywhere."

"Didn't you talk about it?"

"Of course. He'd agree he should limit his hours and sleep in our bed. I even got him an alarm clock so if he drifted off he could wake up and come to bed. He'd do it for a while, then forget.

"I hated that I was verging on being a nag about it. But two years into our marriage, I pretty much only saw him at dinner. Sure, once in a while we'd go out, to see friends or whatever, and he'd be the way he used to be—not so distracted. I'd think we were back on track. He'd even say how great it was to be together and tell me how much I meant to him. But it never lasted. He'd go inside himself again, exactly as before. It dawned on me that his parents were completely focused outward and Gabriel was completely focused inward.

I couldn't get through to him." Her chest constricted. She hadn't thought about the details of what had happened in her marriage in so long. Her anxiety and fear were fresh, like a cut reopened while slicing a lemon. She fought it by pushing harder up the hill for several steps and the pain eased.

"I woke up one night, the fourth night in a row Gabriel wasn't there. I knew he was in the next room. I started crying." She paused, then forced the words out. "I was alone again."

Liz stopped. She knew without turning around that Dante's face would be full of pity. She didn't want to see it. She didn't deserve it. Tears stung behind her eyes, not only because her own story made her sad, but also because soon, too soon, she would disappoint Dante. She would break his heart. And when she did, he'd remember this moment and regret his pity. He'd wish he had never met her.

"Liz." The trail wasn't wide enough for both of them. Unless she stepped aside, he had to stay behind her.

"It's okay, Dante. Really."

He moved closer until only her backpack was between them. "It's not okay. It's sad. Extremely sad."

She ground the tip of her pole into the gravel, and fought the choking sensation in her throat. "It was a long time ago."

"How can someone love another person enough to marry them, then ignore them?"

Liz bit her lip and blinked back tears. "I wish I knew. Maybe it was me."

He sighed and placed a hand on her shoulder. "Let's get to the top and have lunch. I'm starving."

Dante had met Gabriel's family when they traveled to Santa Fe in June for the wedding of Gabriel's youngest sister, Etta. Liz would've preferred to avoid being inundated with reminders of her dead husband but could hardly refuse, as both Gabriel's mother and Etta had included personal notes with the invitation, urging her to attend and welcoming her to bring "a special friend" if she wished. She and Dante had laughed about it, and Liz referred to him as My Special Friend for a while. As they would be in Santa Fe, Dante assumed he would finally meet Liz's mother. Liz wasn't concerned about her mother's appraisal of Dante. If Claire could be counted on for nothing else, it was indifference.

The wedding was large and tasteful, and the Pembertons, whose numbers seemed to have increased exponentially, were warm to both her and Dante. But Liz was distressed. With her boyfriend and her dead husband's family in the same venue, her secrets seemed to rise to the surface and become nearly visible. It was irrational, but real enough. She drank too much at the reception and afterward Dante half carried her to the hotel room, where she attacked the mini-bar. He'd had a fine time socializing and dancing, and was tipsy himself. After three, maybe four, miniature Ketel Ones, Liz shucked her dress and pulled Dante into bed, forgetting—or was it not caring?—she'd left her diaphragm at home. The next morning, she was hungover and emotionally whipped. While she waited for Dante to return from Starbucks, she latched onto the idea of an escape: three weeks alone in the wilderness.

Over the next few weeks, the idea of hiking the John Muir Trail, and the subsequent planning and research, restored her relative calm. She studied weather patterns, emergency provisions and the logistics of resupply. She read backpacking blogs and books about the trail. She discovered the right equipment, the best food, the optimal pace.

And the unintended pregnancy.

Chapter Twelve

The day after the hailstorm, the Root brothers made camp first, as Liz had secretly hoped. She spied them setting up their tarp fifty yards off the trail at the edge of a broad meadow and pointed them out to Dante with her pole. Giddy with relief, she put her finger to her lips and tiptoed down the trail in an exaggerated fashion, lifting her knees high like a cartoon burglar. Dante squeezed his lips together to stop from laughing out loud, and followed her into the woods where the trail wound toward Bear Creek.

The bank of the river was lined with clusters of slender quaking aspen with silver-green bark and pale, shimmering leaves mimicking the movement of the water. Away from the river, red fir and lodgepole pine stood next to mountain hemlock, a graceful tree with a nodding top, resembling the peak of a wizard's hat.

Liz and Dante emerged from the forest onto an exposed rocky slope. There, and upon the wind-swept ridges above, were giant Sierra junipers, the largest sixty feet tall with trunks five feet wide. They were colossal beasts, with thick branches straining out of their trunks and covered in shaggy reddish brown bark. Liz noticed a cinnamon scent as she approached one towering over the trail. She stopped to pet it and leaned closer to inhale more deeply its rich scent.

"It reminds me of Chewbacca," she told Dante. "If we had the space and a couple hundred years, I'd want to grow one of these."

They chose a campsite next to Bear Creek, halfway between the creek and the trail, where a row of pines gave way to a granite shelf extending to the water. The creek was a dozen feet wide, cascading down the narrow ravine in a series of steps, with deep pools in between. The sun had fallen low in the sky, and the rocks surrounding the campsite struggled to hold on to the heat of the day.

As they made camp, ate dinner and cleaned up, they talked about what they'd seen that day and what tomorrow's hike might bring. Liz sensed Dante was waiting for an opportunity to turn the conversation to Gabriel again; there were pauses into which he might drive that wedge. She squeezed the gaps shut with easier words, and he went along with it.

Later, they sat side by side on an anvil-shaped boulder, facing the river and the setting sun. He took her hand, and she kissed him to stop him from talking. She pulled back and saw in his eyes the pity she had known had been lurking there all day. As before, she neither wanted it nor felt she deserved it.

At the edge of her vision, something moved. She turned to see a doe on the opposite bank, staring at them, tail twitching. Trailing a distance behind were two fawns with faded spots on their tawny coats.

She nudged Dante and slowly lifted her hand to point at the deer. The doe glanced over her shoulder at her fawns. One ran toward her, and the other gave chase. Every few steps, one would skip, kicking out its front foot like a dressage horse. She thought if they weren't deer, they'd be giggling.

Dante whispered, "The definition of a child: one who runs for no reason."

The fawns had caught up to their mother, who bent to nibble among the grasses. They copied her, but soon raised their heads and skipped away again.

Liz and Dante watched until the deer became vague shadows.

"Animal Planet programming is over for the evening," she said, getting up. "Bedtime."

He stood and encircled her in his arms. "I love you."

"I love you, too."

From then until she fell asleep in the dark rectangle of the tent, Dante beside her, she forgot about Gabriel, and the many things that made her doubt she could love at all. And in the middle of the night, as the nearly full moon made the river run silver, she dreamt she was a deer, and the dewdrops upon her slender hooves were diamonds.

All the next day they hiked through a wonderland. Lakes with crenellated shores and jetties of smooth, gray rock jutting into indigo pools, their surfaces a perfect reflective plane, broken intermittently by a ring left behind by a feeding trout. Stunted, ancient pines with white bark and dark green branches seemed arranged to balance the varied expanses of stone: honed sheets the size of playing fields, undulating granite waves, chunks of rock of every size. The mountains were everywhere today, appearing around corners, hiding behind one another, standing over the lakes as if they owned them. And above it all was the sky, painted the deepest blue. Liz and Dante tried different words for it, but nothing did it justice. They settled for That Color.

She finally felt they were not on a hike now, but in it. Her feet understood the trail without studying it, each footfall landing in a sensible place without conscious attention. She could tell from the rhythm of Dante's steps the same was true for him. When she climbed a steep pitch, the work in her legs was a feeling of strength, not pain. When she drank water she had taken from a stream, she realized it was the only drink she ever needed. Until now, her pack had been a very large albatross worn on the back instead of the front. Now she had made friends with it. Dante called his "my sleeping child," which touched her and made her profoundly sad.

It was a shame they would arrive at Muir Ranch tonight, having just found their stride.

Then again, a hot shower sounded like nirvana.

From Selden Pass the trail dropped three thousand feet into the valley holding Muir Ranch. A third of the way down the switchbacks began, wending in long arcs across a nearly treeless slope of manzanita bushes. After two switchbacks, Dante asked her to stop.

"See those people down there? Is that Payton?"

She could make out three figures on the far side of the slope, perhaps two switchbacks lower. Judging by size alone, Payton was among them. "I think so. And Rodell's sitting down?" The third person faced the other way. All they could see was a backpack.

"I guess we're about to find out."

In five minutes they were close enough to hear raised voices, and Liz had identified the third person as Brensen. If he was in one of his moods, it had all the makings of a sticky situation.

Payton noticed them first. Frowning, he lifted his hand in greeting. His brother's right leg was propped on a boulder, and his mouth was twisted in a grimace. Brensen stepped off the trail on the uphill side so Liz and Dante could join them.

"Hey," he said. "How are you guys?"

"We're great," Dante said. He pointed at Rodell's leg. "You okay?"

Payton said, "He took a hard fall. Wrenched his knee."

Liz said, "That's too bad. I've got an ACE bandage if you need it."

Rodell pulled up his pant leg to expose a neatly wrapped bandage. "Thanks, but we've got that covered."

"Problem is," Payton said, "he can't carry his pack down the mountain. And this fellow here"—

he jutted his finger at Brensen—"isn't inclined to help us out."

"I have to ask," Liz said. "Did this have something to do with a dare?"

Payton gave his brother an I-told-you-to-keep-your-trap-shut look. Rodell shrugged and rubbed his knee. "Like he said, I fell."

Brensen shifted his pack. "And like I said, I don't see how that's my problem."

"Liz," Payton said, "you're an experienced backpacker. Perhaps you could inform Hollywood here of the unwritten code of the wilderness."

"You mean, you should dig a six-inch hole before you poop?" The older Root brother was correct about the code, but she was not going to take his side without making him work for it. If only he were the injured one. She'd kick his good leg as she marched past him on her way to a hot shower and a real meal.

Payton nodded, as if taking her measure.

Dante, allergic to conflict, turned to Brensen. "I think what he means is that out here, where there are few resources, we are obliged to help our fellow hikers in need."

"Yeah, I've already heard the lecture. But it doesn't change the fact that there's no way in hell I'm going to carry anything more down this fucking mountain than I have to. I'm older than all of you. I've got my knees to think about."

"Your mistake," Payton spat, "is forgetting it

could've been you instead of Rodell here. Anyone can fall."

The obvious truth of the statement didn't make it any less chilling.

"If it had been me, I wouldn't be sitting here. I'd have ditched my goddamn pack, hopped or crawled or whatever to Muir Ranch and called my fucking agent to get me the hell out of here!"

Dante perked up. "There are phones at Muir Ranch? What about Internet?"

Payton was determined to have the final word. "Listen, Hollywood. Liz and Dante might give us a hand and they might not. But remember, from now on you won't be a couple hours' walk from getting bailed out by your agent." He pointed his meat slab of a hand south. "Down that way is nine days' worth of nowhere. What're you going to do if you get into a mess?"

Brensen flicked his hand impatiently. "I'm tired of standing here. You all enjoy the rest of your day." He trotted past Rodell and headed down the trail, Payton's eyes drilling into his back.

Liz was relieved it wasn't her. "Rodell, how heavy is your pack?"

"Forty-five pounds give or take."

She wouldn't have been surprised at that figure immediately after a resupply, but today everyone's packs should've been at their lightest. "You've gotta be kidding. What you got in there?"

"Stuff."

Dante said, "We can take some of it, can't we, Liz?"

"Sure. It's only a few miles." The code was the code.

Payton reached inside his brother's pack and pulled out the gear he wanted them to carry: the stove, the tent, a couple of fuel canisters, a half-empty bear can.

"Just don't give me any of his dirty socks," Liz said.

She fit everything inside her pack, except the tent, which she strapped to the outside, and the bear can, which Dante put under the top flap of his pack. He lashed his sleeping bag to the bottom.

Payton was stuffing gear back into Rodell's pack when a shirt fell to the ground. He scooped it up with lightning speed, but not before Liz glimpsed what appeared to be the etched handle of a pistol. Payton twisted casually to see if she or Dante had noticed, but Liz had already turned away to hoist her pack.

A gun wasn't illegal in the wilderness, except in the National Parks and unless you actually hunted with it. But, Liz wondered, if you didn't intend to shoot things, why would you bring it?

Chapter Thirteen

At the ranch, three women on horseback herded two dozen horses into a corral. Liz and Dante were forced to wait for the procession to pass. Liz wasn't much of a judge of horseflesh, but these made a good impression: shiny coats, flowing manes and tails, not a swayback in sight. Dante pointed out his favorite, a spirited palomino.

"What is it with men and blondes?" she said.

A woman in a battered safari hat returned to close the gate. They told her about Rodell and asked if someone could help him get off the trail. She nodded and said she'd take care of it.

"How far is the hospital?" Liz asked.

"Oakhurst's the best bet. But he'd be lucky to get that far tonight, unless he's really a mess. If he wants to leave here tonight, we'll ride him out to the road. That's four miles. He might get a lift from someone out of Jackass campground to the ranger station. That's another seven miles. They'd know what to do with him."

"Not a very convenient place to get hurt."

She nodded. "And this is the civilized part."

The resupply shed was adjacent to the corral. Inside the windowless room, a hunched woman peered at a computer screen and jiggled a mouse. When she stood, she came to just above Liz's waist. She was in her eighties and wore a plaid shirt with pearl buttons. Her polyester slacks stopped a few inches shy of her orthopedic shoes, revealing dingy white socks. Liz wondered how a person so small could have pants too short. The woman took her name, disappeared behind a rack of shelves, and reemerged, tipped to one side to counterbalance the bucket's weight.

Dante moved toward her. "Here, let me help you."

She waved him off. "I do this all summer, son."

They left Rodell's gear beside the shed, as they had arranged, and went to a nearby building to check in. Behind the counter in the cramped room, a young woman with hair like the tail of a chestnut mare was braiding a halter rope.

"Electricity's out. We'll run your card later."

Dante said, "Have you got wireless?"

"We do but we don't give out the code. The bandwidth is teensy." She pointed behind them to a laptop perched on a wooden crate. "Ten bucks for fifteen minutes, when it's working."

His shoulders fell.

Liz said, "It's better than nothing. You can try later."

The woman loaded them into a golf cart and began the tour. The ranch had a couple dozen buildings, most made of log. Half were cabins for rent. The rest were special purpose: a store, a kitchen, a lounge, a bathhouse and accommodations for the staff. Liz and Dante had reserved a tented cabin—a wooden platform with canvas walls and roof. These were clustered at the back of the property facing a large stand of aspen embroidering a bend in the river.

"Yours is the Tenthouse," the woman said. "My favorite."

The Tenthouse was perched eight feet off the ground and sported a deck at the front as large as the cabin.

They thanked the woman and climbed wooden steps to the deck. Dante pulled aside the curtain door and ushered Liz inside. There was a full bed and a twin, covered in matching quilts, a set of shelves and a bare lightbulb with a pull string near the bigger bed.

"So luxurious!" she said, running her hand along the stained and faded quilt. "I'd give it the full five pinecones."

"We'll need to put our sleeping bags on top tonight. There's no heat."

"But there are *sheets*. And dinner."

"Is there beer?"

"Sadly, no. But a washing machine."

"What do we wear while we wash everything?"

"Our birthday suits?"

He smiled. "I assume there's no dryer, so we'll need something to wear to dinner."

"Our rain gear, then. Kind of kinky, don't you think? Naked under Gortex?"

"You're a pervert."

"Not at the moment, but perhaps later. After you've had a shower." She pinched her nose and lifted her pinky.

"I understood love is blind."

"Perhaps. But my nose works fine."

The washer—a museum piece—sat on a patch of dirt outside a small building. A white-haired man, tanned only on his face and forearms, and naked except for underpants, was leaving as she arrived. He told her the wringer attached to the top of the washer was broken and pointed to the elaborate instructions written on the wall above the machine. Liz set down her laundry and began filling the tub with a hose. Once the load was going, she sat on the steps, content to watch the horses in the corral and absorb the warmth of the sun.

After a time, Linda approached with an armload of clothing and dumped it on the table next to machine. "Look at that thing! No wonder they don't charge to use it."

"And the wringer doesn't work, according to the guy who was here before. Too bad you missed him. He was about seventy and wearing nothing but his tighty-whities." Linda made a face. "So, you have to wring everything out."

"Well, cold-water agitation is better than nothing. Will you show me how to use it?"

Liz rose and indicated the faucet shutoff. "You

can't reach it from the washer, so you need to kink the hose. And the mud's slippery, so be careful." She turned on the agitator. "When you're finished, you stick this drain hose in there"—indicating a drain in the ground—"and flip this lever on the bottom. To rinse you do the same thing. Just remember to close the lever for the drain."

"Might as well use the rocks down by the river."

"Just about. I'm on my last rinse." She shut off the hose, flipped on the agitator and joined the older woman on the steps.

The McCartneys, she discovered, lived only an hour from her and Dante, in a small town in the East Bay. Paul was a research physician in pharmaceuticals (the sister field to Liz's) and Linda designed gardens. They talked about the hike—the sections they enjoyed the most, the condition of the trail and how much they were looking forward to a feast at dinner.

Liz turned the topic to celebrity gossip. "You've seen Matthew Brensen on the trail, right?"

"Are you sure it's him? I thought it was, but Paul said no. It seemed so unlikely."

"He's training for a part."

"He doesn't look very happy in his work."

Liz laughed.

Linda said, "What about those others? The huge guy and his brother, maybe?"

"Oh, them. You haven't talked to them?"

"We've been steering clear. They give me the creeps."

At last, confirmation. "Me, too. Was it something they did, or just a feeling?"

"A feeling, mostly. But last night we camped near them. Couldn't find anywhere else and we were wiped out."

"We saw where they were. Off the trail a ways, right on Bear Creek."

"Yeah, there. They made a big fire, which was fine because it's low enough. We don't make fires because we're too old and go straight to bed." She chuckled. "Anyway, we could smell them cooking something. Smelled like meat."

"Meat? Do you think they brought it from Red's?"

"That's what Paul said at first, but Red's was four days earlier. So I got out my binoculars—Paul gave me these fantastic ones for backpacking—and spied on them." She shrugged, excusing herself. "They were roasting an animal."

"An animal? What kind of an animal?"

"Bigger than a squirrel and smaller than a deer. We figured it was a marmot."

"A marmot? That is so gross."

"And illegal."

"Maybe not. Marmots are rodents and this is national forest, not a national park."

"But it's still gross."

"Extremely."

"We didn't think they'd shot it, though. Someone would hear a gun go off, don't you think?"

"Maybe." Liz related the story of Rodell's injury and the pistol she thought she saw in his pack.

"I guess the good news is we've seen the last of them."

"And no more marmot kebabs."

Liz enjoyed getting to know Linda, but by the time she finished the laundry she was starving. She followed Dante into the low-ceilinged dining room, and the aroma of barbecued ribs nearly knocked her over. Her eyes went to the buffet, crammed with platters of corn, potatoes, bread, beans and three different salads. Her stomach jumped for joy. She and Dante had carried as much food as the bear cans would hold, but not enough to compensate for the calories they'd burned. She estimated she'd lost at least five pounds. And tonight she'd do her best to put it all back on.

Her plate loaded for the first round, she scanned the long tables for a spot for two and noticed Brensen. To her chagrin, he waved them over. Maybe the food would make him less irascible. Dante stepped over the bench and sat beside Brensen, and Liz took a seat across from them.

Brensen introduced the couple next to him: his agent, Woody, a middle-aged man with an artfully unshaven face, and an almond-eyed blonde named Katarina. She had an Eastern European look and was not quite young enough to be Woody's daughter. Both were dressed in premium outdoor wear that had never seen weather, much less mud.

"They're here to check up on me," Brensen said, slathering butter on a chunk of bread. "Make sure I'm not cheating."

Woody dragged the butter dish away. "Or eating."

Dante said, "He's not allowed to eat?"

"They're shooting the movie backward. When he gets to Whitney, we need him skinny and tan, and—"

"—and fucking fed up," Brensen added, his mouth full.

"—and then he can start eating again."

Liz said, "I wouldn't worry about it. The John Muir Trail is a mobile fat farm." She turned her attention to her plate. The food was delicious and she wanted to make sure she got seconds before they cleared the buffet.

"Just riding in here was enough for me," Woody said. "I could've eaten the horse."

"That's terrible, Woody," Katarina said, in a teasing tone.

Brensen addressed Dante and Liz. "I was just telling them about Payton and Eli."

"Rodell," she said. "Payton and Eli are quarterbacks."

"Rodell?" said Woody. "Seriously? I couldn't make that up."

Brensen snorted. "Yeah, right? The Dubious Brothers. Did they get off the hill?"

"We think so," Dante said. "We haven't seen them since we got here." He changed the subject, probably not wanting to remind Brensen he'd behaved badly toward Rodell. "So, Woody, what's the news from the real world?"

"Well, the last couple days there's been a shit-storm surrounding General Petraeus. Resigned from directing the CIA for bonking his biographer."

"He led the surge in Iraq, right?" Dante said.

"Gives new meaning to the word 'embedded,' " Liz quipped.

Everyone laughed, except Dante. "I suppose they are both married."

Woody said, "Uh-huh. With kids I think. And get this. The title of the biography is *All In*."

Liz nearly spat out her water. "That's too much. I guess he's regretting not keeping his boots on the ground."

Woody nodded. "And it's not only the two of them. There's a whole network of army bigwigs and rich socialites who've been partying in Tampa and stealing kisses. Or whatever."

Dante shook his head. "It's disgusting."

"Way of the world, my friend," Brensen said.

"Well, it shouldn't be. Petraeus took an oath.

I'm talking about the one to his wife. And I'm guessing he's a Christian, so in front of God, too."

Liz kept her eyes on her plate, but detected the others exchanging glances.

Dante went on. "What? Is it wrong to expect someone, especially a leader, to show some moral strength?"

"You can expect all you want," Woody said, "but choirboys are outnumbered by ordinary louts five to one."

"Ten to one," Brensen said.

"I already counted you twice, Brensen."

"I think Dante is a romantic," Katarina said.

"Maybe I am, but that's not the point. After all, people choose to get married. No one forces them to. Then they behave immorally and everyone shrugs. It's the same as athletes taking performance-enhancing drugs."

Liz said, "Although if everyone takes them, the playing field is level."

"And if everyone bonks everyone else," Brensen said, "then everyone's a cheat and it doesn't matter."

"We're almost there," Woody said, "because I'm pretty sure it doesn't matter who the general screws. Except to the networks. They're having a field day."

"I believe his wife would disagree with you," Dante said. "And so would God."

"You speak for God?" Katarina asked, as if it were fine with her if he did.

"No, but Petraeus will be asking for forgiveness. I can't speak for his wife, but I wouldn't be surprised if God was getting extremely tired of people standing in his house and taking vows they don't have the will to keep."

The group was silent for an awkward moment before conversation turned to lighter subjects. Liz and Dante had their second helpings, and excused themselves to go back to their cabin.

They'd forgotten to bring a flashlight to dinner, and the moon had yet to rise, so when they stepped beyond the light emanating from the kitchen windows, darkness encircled them. Liz placed her feet deliberately and tried to remember if there were any ruts or large stones in the dirt road winding through the ranch. In the corral to their left, a horse nickered and snorted, then another joined in. She was about to ask Dante whether he thought the horses could see them, when he spoke.

"You might have stood up for me in that discussion."

"You seemed to be making your point just fine on your own."

"Maybe, but aside from jokes, you were pretty quiet on the subject."

She did not want to get into this now. Or ever. "Look, Dante. You're absolutely right. People should take their vows seriously."

"So why couldn't you have said that?"

"Because everyone believes it already. The problem is that what people should do and what they actually do don't line up very well. The road to hell . . ." She stopped short. "We go right here, don't we?"

"I think so. Isn't the light over there the bathroom?" They walked on in silence for a few moments. "I think couples should try harder not to act in ways that will destroy their relationship. And having sex with other people is bound to do exactly that."

She was tempted to remind him he had never been married. Had, in fact, never lived with a woman before her. She wanted to point out that people did stupid things, rash things—even calculated, deliberate, horrible things—to the ones they've promised to love until death. But he knew all that. Everyone did. He was willing to risk sanctimoniousness to drive home the point that lovers should remain true. Who was she to argue?

"You're right. You're absolutely right."

He slowed. "Liz, shouldn't the cabin be here already?"

Indeed it should have. She could make out where the trees met the sky and, faintly, a low building on her right, but she had no clue where the Tenthouse might be.

"Let's go back to the last place we recognized."

Dante tripped on something and swore. They retraced their route with halting steps, then went straight where they previously had veered to the right, away from what they thought was the bathroom light. The outline of a tented cabin appeared. Up ahead was the Tenthouse, crouched in the shadow of a wall of trees.

"Naughty of you, Tenthouse, hiding from us." Liz found the railing and ascended the stairs to the deck. She pushed aside the curtain and picked her way to the opposite wall where the light hung.

Dante moved close behind her. "We need to remember to not go anywhere without a flashlight."

She knocked her hand into the pull string and tugged it. The naked bulb blinded her. She blinked several times and noticed one of their sleeping bags had fallen to the floor. She picked it up, tossed it on the bed, and bent to arrange it. The bag on the far side was bunched. Reaching across, she pulled the other bag toward the foot of the bed.

A loud rattle, the sound of dried beans shaken in a cardboard box.

She yanked her hand away, clutching the bag. A snake. Its body, thick as a child's arm, lay coiled upon the quilt. Instantly, it whipped its head high, and retracted its neck, tongue flicking at the air, ready to strike. Its tail shook above the coils like an aspen leaf, emitting a constant rattle.

She gasped and jumped back, colliding with Dante and knocking him down in the doorway.

Her heart pounded in her throat. Only three feet away, the snake tracked her with its head, swaying and moving toward her, tongue darting.

She screamed, the sound ringing in her ears.

Dante scrambled to his hands and knees and crawled out to the deck. Liz stood frozen to the spot, legs dead, eyes fixed on the snake's head as it weaved from side to side.

Dante grabbed her arm. The snake lunged, missing her narrowly, and struck the air beside her. Dante pulled her backward. Her trance broken, she stumbled outside. Dante ran down the steps with Liz on his heels. He stopped at the bottom, but she flew past him into the darkness, and thought she heard, over the noise of her pounding feet and panting breath, a laugh that was not a laugh, coming from the woods close behind her.

Chapter Fourteen

She was trembling when they returned to the dining room, empty except for Paul, Linda and a trio of young men. Liz told them what had happened. Dante ducked into the kitchen to find someone who knew how to deal with snakes.

Linda patted the bench beside her. Liz sat. "Thank God you're all right. You want some water or tea?"

She shook her head.

"Aren't you in the elevated cabin?" Paul said.

"Not elevated enough, apparently."

"I can't imagine a snake going up there."

"Neither can I. And Dante was lying on the bed right before we came to dinner, so it couldn't have been there then."

"It might have been under the bed or somewhere you couldn't see it," Linda said.

Liz shivered at the thought. "True."

Dante and a man they'd seen earlier with the horses came in from the kitchen. The man's face was stern. "You sure it was a rattlesnake?" His tone suggested a lot of folks came through who couldn't tell a snake from a fence lizard.

"Yes. I got a really good look."

Dante said, "It rattled. Like in those John Wayne films."

The man peered at him sideways. "Okay, I'll go have a look-see."

Liz said, "I don't think I could sleep in there. Any way you could grab our packs and let us have another cabin?"

"Sure," he said. "If I don't find it and kill it, I wouldn't be sleeping in there myself."

He came back fifteen minutes later and said he'd come up empty. Liz and Dante followed him to another cabin—one with a real door. The bed was piled high with their gear and damp clothing.

"Sorry for the mess," the man said. "Didn't know what else to do with it."

They thanked him and he left. With few words, they organized their belongings, hanging clothes wherever they could, and went to bed. They lay awake a long time. Eventually, Dante's breathing slowed and he drifted off to sleep. Liz's thoughts turned away from her near-death experience with the snake to the topic that had occupied most of the evening: infidelity. And that was how she came to think about radishes.

Dante had taken Liz to meet his family a year after they'd started dating. He'd never said so, but the meeting was a hurdle in their relationship, whether for both of them or just her, she wasn't certain. He'd proposed the trip soon after their first discussion about moving in together, a discussion prompted by Liz receiving notice that her rented apartment was going up for sale.

"Let's visit them for Christmas," he said.

"This year?"

"Yes."

"That's in nine days."

"Yes! Spontaneous!" He opened his laptop. "I'll book the flights."

His parents lived in Mexico City but were spending the holidays in the city of Oaxaca, known for its clean air, mild climate and spectacular radish festival each year before Christmas. During their flight south, Dante briefed Liz on his mother's festival fetish. The majority of her travels centered on a festival, either within Mexico or farther afield: festivals of art, music, film and dance, celebrations of Day of the Dead and the feasts of saints, wine and harvest festivals—Felicia Espinoza loved them all. Her husband, Carlos, joined her if he could, but was often called away on business, at times suspiciously close to an upcoming festival. Carlos would then arrange for the company of one of their daughters or friends. Felicia was too high-strung and naive to travel on her own, given to wailing if a train were delayed, leaving her hand-bag in a hotel lobby or behaving inappropriately when strange men spoke with her, as they readily did, drawn by her expressive face and girlish laugh.

"You're lucky," Dante said, finishing off his in-flight tequila. "This one's only radishes. The summer I was eight she dragged us to Zacatecas for La Morisma. Thousands of people reenacting medieval battles between Christians and Moors in old Spain, including firing cannons. It was so loud I let go of my mother's hand to cover my ears and got lost. I wandered into the battle scene and nearly got my head chopped off by a broadsword."

"I can see why you'd prefer radishes."

A taxi deposited them in front of the Camino Real Oaxaca, a sixteenth-century nunnery converted into a luxury hotel. The bellman led them under broad archways and along Saltillo-tiled corridors lined with frescoes, and paused across from a courtyard with a tiered fountain. The shrubs were alive with birds. He unlocked a dark oak door, placed their bags inside and informed them Señor and Señora Espinoza were currently at the pool. They could, when they were ready, join them there.

"I never expected the nuns to have it so good," Liz said, exploring the room. It was decorated in colonial design with brilliant white stucco walls and beamed ceilings. An intricately painted wooden cat crouched on the dresser. Liz recognized the style as local, knowledge she'd presumably picked up from her mother, although she couldn't say when.

"We treat our sisters very well," Dante said.

The pool was crowded, but they easily spotted Dante's family. They were arrayed in a loose group of twenty or more, lounging on chairs, or standing at the pool's edge supervising their children.

"Dante!" someone cried, and every head turned to face them. Half were versions of Dante himself. Liz smiled and gave a self-conscious wave.

On the plane, he had schooled her about his sisters, brothers-in-law, nieces and nephews, but when the battalion of Espinozas and their spin-offs mobbed her, she forgot nearly every name she'd learned. Worse, she was blindsided by several unexpected aunts and uncles. Everyone talked at once in rapid-fire Spanish. She offered her cheek to them all.

Dante's mother threw herself at her only son, clutching at his back and sobbing as if he had returned unexpectedly from war.

"Mama," he said, taking her hands firmly in his and looking her in the eye. "*Todo está bien.*" All is well. He introduced Liz, and Señora Espinoza rallied, swiping the tears from her cheeks. "Call me Felicia," she said in English. "Please."

"*Gracias*, Felicia."

Felicia put her fingertips under Liz's chin and drew the attention of her husband, several yards away. "*Mira, Carlos! Que bonita!*" Heat rushed to Liz's cheeks. Señor Espinoza nodded at his wife and smiled at Liz, tight-lipped. Dante caught his father's eye and offered a nod, and a tentative smile, in greeting. Señor Espinoza turned aside. Dante had warned Liz that his father's reception would be cool and implored her not to take it personally. He had chosen to live in the States of his own accord, long before they'd met, so she was blameless. She understood the situation, and thought she was prepared for it, but she was not. The anguish in Dante's mother's embrace pained her, as did the sting of his father's scorn. At that moment she would have welcomed Claire's tepid disinterest. She reached for Dante's hand and held it.

The radish festival formally started in two days' time, December twenty-third, but the next day Dante's mother hustled everyone to the main plaza, the Zócalo, for a preview. Liz couldn't imagine it any more festive than it appeared. The Zócalo was bursting with people: busking musicians, vendors selling candy, balloons and hats, and onlookers sitting on benches in the shade of gigantic Indian laurel trees. The base of each tree was encircled with dozens of poinsettias, and lights had been strung between the lamp-posts. Booths of radish carvings lined the plaza perimeter and faced sidewalk cafés where people sat drinking and laughing.

Dante's father's attitude had softened overnight —at least toward Liz. He escorted her around the displays, explaining in fluent English the festival was the brainchild of two Spanish friars who wanted to create a marketing buzz for local produce. They instituted a competition for radish carving, and the indigenous people took to it with a passion. The radishes, some the size of watermelons, were carved in elaborate displays, many with religious themes. Liz admired radish cathedrals, radish nativity scenes (with tiny radish baby Jesuses), and a four-foot-high Our Lady of Solitude radish with an elaborately rendered crown and robe. The vegetable artists also exhibited vignettes of daily life: radish mariachi bands, radish markets and, her favorite, a radish agave farm and tequila distillery complete with radish people falling down drunk. If all the festivals were this bizarre, she could see why Felicia was hooked on them.

Carlos Espinoza explained the significance of the less obvious carvings, then excused himself to take a call. When he finished, he searched out his wife, who was photographing a carver spraying radishes with water, and guided her to a nearby bench. Liz watched the conference with concern. Dante's mother gesticulated wildly and threw herself against her husband. Her back heaved with sobs. Señor Espinoza waited a few moments until his wife had recovered somewhat, then returned to the group to pluck Emilia, the eldest, from the company of her sisters for another conference.

Dante appeared beside Liz. "What's going on?" she asked.

"I don't know. But it looks serious."

The Espinozas appeared to be berating their daughter, who hung her head. Carlos looked as though he was struggling to control his temper. Felicia clutched his arm and scowled at her daughter, who would not meet their dark glares.

"Emilia!" Señor Espinoza said sharply, attracting the attention of everyone around them. His daughter lifted her head, and he pointed in the direction of the hotel. Without a word to the rest of her family, Emilia gathered her two children and left.

Hours later, Dante returned from a visit to his parents' hotel room and told Liz the call had been from Emilia's husband, Rico, who was to join them in Oaxaca tomorrow. He had taken Dante's place in the Espinoza's company three years prior, preserving the legacy, after a fashion. Today he'd stopped at home after a business trip and discovered Emilia had left her phone behind. On it were several text messages providing him with incontrovertible evidence of the affair he'd long suspected his wife of having.

Dante slid onto the bed next to Liz. "She's gone home."

"Wow. Just like that?"

"Yes. And we won't be seeing her—or speaking with her—again."

"Ever?"

"Ever."

"But you don't know the story. It might be complicated."

"In our family, loyalty is never complicated." He hesitated, as if weighing whether to say more. He sighed and leaned back on the pillows. "And the matter of the company came up. Again."

Liz had been thinking of Emilia, Rico and their children. The business implications hadn't dawned on her. "If your family excommunicates Emilia, does it change Rico's position in the company?"

Dante shook his head. "My father didn't share

the details of their arrangement with me, but my mother begged me to move back. Literally. She was on her knees."

"That's awful." He looked crushed. Liz's mouth went dry at the possibility he had given in and would leave the States—and her. "What did you say?"

"I didn't have to say anything. My father answered for me. He helped my mother off the floor and said, 'Rico is my son.' "

Now Liz lay in bed at Muir Ranch with a sleeping Dante and realized he had not mentioned talking to Emilia in the ten months since the radish festival. Not long ago he'd said his youngest sister, Rosalinda, was spending time with Emilia in secret. Their parents had found out and given Rosalinda a stern warning, accompanied by the threat of a substantial hit on her inheritance. Liz could not fathom having three siblings, much less losing one by decree. What had been the price of a sister?

Liz stared into the darkness. Strictly speaking, she wasn't Dante's family, but she doubted that would change how he'd view her indiscretion. If Emilia and General Petraeus were damned, so was she.

Chapter Fifteen

Mike Wilson wasn't handsome or charming. He wasn't effusive or affectionate, or a particularly good listener. He wasn't wealthy or ambitious (not to a fault, anyway), and he hadn't planned on having an affair any more than she had. He didn't send Liz love notes or buy her sexy underwear. He didn't even buy her lunch. He didn't talk trash about his wife or assume Gabriel was a monster. And when they finally got around to it, he wasn't even good in bed.

Liz had taken the job at Extensor Labs while finishing her master's degree. Of the company's two hundred or so employees, Mike Wilson was the only black man, although that wasn't why she noticed him. She, Mike and two other men, Trenton Wu and an assistant known as Baxter, shared bench space. When she joined the group, they were developing biosensors that detected muscle activity and sent the information to a mechanical device, such as a prosthetic limb. The group reported to Stacy Stratticon, a ruthlessly driven scientist-turned-manager determined to advance in the company. Liz's group, with the exception of Baxter, called her Strap-it-on behind her back. She'd hired Liz because her thesis research suggested a promising new direction, and because, as a rookie, she came cheap.

Liz's relationship with Mike developed in the same insidious, incremental way that her marriage to Gabriel drifted away from her expectations. At the time, she did not see the two as related, because her husband had lost interest in her (if that is what happened) long before she felt anything more than friendship for Mike. In retrospect, however, it might have been muddier. The scenes she could play in her mind, but the feelings were harder to recall, submerged as they were under a sea of shame and guilt, then sunk to the bottom like a wreck after Gabriel died.

Trenton and Baxter ate lunch at their computers. Trenton played video games and Baxter caught up on Facebook and Twitter. Liz was glad Mike enjoyed eating outside because she had too much time alone at home. They talked about nothing of consequence: sports (Mike was into professional tennis and NASCAR), nonpolitical news, science and a little office politics. She knew he was married with no kids and he knew the same about her, but it was irrelevant because they were only having lunch. Occasionally, people from other lab groups would join them. Few women worked at Extensor, and Liz never clicked with any of them.

Before long, lunches with Mike became the social focus of her day. When she went home, she'd have twenty minutes at dinner with Gabriel

—much of it spent discussing household business —then would be on her own until bedtime. Mike wasn't exciting, and she wasn't attracted to him, but she came to depend on him to verify an essential truth: she was a human being someone could talk to comfortably.

She hadn't given up on her marriage, and continued to try to get through to Gabriel. She suggested outings, even midweek, but he turned most of them down, citing the need to make progress with what he had come to call "his real job"—the video game work. When she finally asked him point blank if he was dissatisfied with her, he said he couldn't understand why she would ask. Of course he wasn't. One night, a year or so after she'd begun working at Extensor, she had too much to drink and cried her eyes out in front of Gabriel, pleading with him to love her the way he used to, "to see her."

He handed her a Kleenex and squeezed her shoulder. "You wanted a normal life, Liz, right? Well, this is it."

In the morning as he left for work, he said she was drinking too much and might think about seeing her doctor about it. She called in sick and spent the day rereading the first Harry Potter.

What she was not able to foresee was that only so many lunches could be shared by two people unhappy in their marriages before one of them let their guard down. Neither Liz nor Mike knew their guard was up until he let his down. It could have as easily been her. She was telling him about a hike she had taken in the Sandias the day before while Gabriel was reading the paper (although she left out that part).

Mike put down his turkey sandwich—the lunch he had every day—and regarded her seriously. "You know, I'd have enjoyed hiking there with you."

She didn't have to answer. His guard had dropped a little, so hers did, too. She was picturing them hiking together and he could tell that she was because he smiled a little, and so did she. Their guard dropped another notch. Nothing had happened, and nothing would for a long time— not even a hike. But if Liz had to put her finger on it, she'd say that was the moment she began her affair with Mike.

If that was the beginning, it lasted fifteen months. They had sex twice. Once to get over the inevitable and once because they were sad. The sex wasn't great but it didn't matter. What did matter was how Liz came to feel when she was with him—not like a lover or mistress or soul mate, but a whole person. She was acceptable, and visible.

Gabriel had, in the beginning, made her feel special, and adored. She'd been suspicious of those feelings because they were novel and unexpected. But she went along with it and was swept up in his conviction. Too good to be true turned out to be exactly that.

Her relationship with Mike wasn't too good to be anything. She couldn't even speculate whether it was ultimately better than the normal life Gabriel was selling. How could she know while they were both married to other people?

Mike said once maybe people came into your life just to show you the way through.

"Like a guiding spirit?" she said.

"Yeah, exactly. Only flesh and blood."

"Of course. So it hurts."

The night Liz told Gabriel about Mike the air conditioner was running full blast but the house was still baking hot. The air temperature had been building all week, a slow fire feeding on the heat stored in the cement and stucco and asphalt of Albuquerque from one night to the next.

Liz made taco salads for dinner, and they each had a beer. The air was stale inside the house, so they went out to the tiny patio at the rear and sat side by side in plastic chairs facing a stucco wall. They could see the tips of the Sandias beyond their neighbor's roof.

She hadn't planned to say anything that night in particular. Her bare legs were glued to the seat, and she stared at nothing in the colorless sky. The weight of the hot air reminded her of the lead apron at the dentist's office.

Gabriel asked if she wanted to go to Santa Fe

for the weekend. The interval between visits to their families had increased with the distance between them.

A cricket rubbed a leg against its back, scraping out a dry chirp.

"I had an affair." She hadn't realized the affair had ended until she heard herself use the past tense. She turned to him, her movements dragging, laden with dread.

He'd been about to take a swig from his beer. His hand paused for a beat in midair, then he tipped his head back and drank. He swept his thumb across his lips, his gaze straight ahead. "That's not funny, Liz."

"I wasn't joking. I'm sorry."

He twisted toward her. "You had an affair."

"Yes."

"I don't believe it." His tone was neutral but his face, in sharp relief from the patio light, betrayed uncertainty.

She waited, unsure of what he would do and whether to say more, wishing she'd thought it through. Wishing she hadn't said anything.

His eyes locked on hers. She wanted to look away, but could not. Her throat cinched shut.

He said, "You're serious, aren't you?"

She couldn't speak. His face became blurry. She managed a nod and wiped the tears from her eyes.

He leaned toward her, his eyes dark. "Who is it?"

"It doesn't matter. It's over."

"Why should I believe you?"

"Because it's true. It's over."

He shook his head. "I can't believe you'd do this to me."

"I'm sorry."

"Sorry? That's it?"

She picked at the label on her beer, dredging inside herself for the words for feelings she did not understand.

"Why, Liz? Why the hell did you do it?"

"I'm really sorry, Gabriel."

He bent over his legs with his head in his hands. A few moments passed. He was breathing loudly through his nose, his shoulders rising and dropping with each breath. "You promised," he said to the ground, his voice thick.

Her mind flashed to their wedding day. She remembered how happy and relieved she had felt when Russ handed her to Gabriel, but the feeling was trapped inside a glass box, like a keepsake or a relic. As she stared at the nape of her husband's neck, she thought of coming out of the bedroom late at night and finding him hunched over his computer. She thought of how she'd come to resent Sundays and *The New York Times*. She thought of all the times he had promised to come to bed, to talk to her, to spend time with her. "So did you."

He sat up and glared at her. His jaw muscles scooted back and forth under his skin like trapped fish. "What the hell is that supposed to mean?"

"I trusted you."

"*You* trusted *me?* What did I do? Huh, Liz? What fucking crime did I commit?" He jumped out of his seat, strode to the wall, fists clenched at his sides. He spun around. "I can't believe you're making this my fault. What's wrong with you?"

Gabriel's anger and hurt came off him in sheets, smothering her. She shrank in her chair, her flash of righteousness gone. She was suddenly unsure she had tried hard enough to bring her husband back to her. Had she done anything? Had her marriage been terrible enough to justify this? A sinkhole opened in her chest. She gripped the edge of the chair in desperation. She was falling.

Gabriel stormed past her.

She stood. "Gabriel—"

He stopped at the back door and turned to her, his eyes red, his jaw set. "Save it, Liz." He yanked the door open, slamming it against the side of the house. She heard him pick up his car keys from the hall table and leave. She never saw him again.

Chapter Sixteen

Liz and Dante left Muir Ranch the following morning, facing the rising sun across Shooting Star Meadow. The grasses were burdened with dew. Liz, tired from a poor night's sleep, walked in silence. Dante trailed several steps behind her and offered small talk when they stopped to drink or have a snack. Their packs were at their heaviest, both bear cans filled to the brim with food for nine days. It was cruel, she mused, this fact should coincide with the climb ahead of them today, one of the toughest of the entire trip— a total of three thousand feet of elevation gain over twelve miles. The summation sounded gradual but the topo map indicated otherwise. The climb occurred predominantly in two sections, where the contour lines were compressed as if pinched shut. A long, hard day.

She had read online that some hikers avoid this scenario and instead resupplied after Muir Ranch. It wasn't straightforward. The southern half of the JMT was remote, tucked in the crease of massive mountain ranges on either side. With no easy way in or out, the mountains here were castle walls, ready to lay siege. To resupply, a hiker would leave the JMT and climb over, say, Kearsarge Pass, and hope to hitch a ride into Independence. After a night in a hotel, they'd pick up their bucket from the post office, return to the trailhead, and hike back to the JMT. Two days lost, if all went according to plan, and no closer to Mount Whitney. Most hikers, Liz included, could afford neither the extra vacation time, nor the hassle. They filled their bear cans at Muir Ranch and hoped for the strength to carry them up and up and up.

The trail followed one river, then another, reminding her of a dancer changing partners: a level waltz along the South Fork of the San Joaquin, a quickstep across Piute Creek, then a swing marathon all the way up Evolution Creek, the river pulling the trail into a closed hold in a switchback, and sending it away with a twirl, into the pines, again and again. Water raged down the steep canyon, poured over granite ledges and boulders as white paint, and landed in a froth in the pools below. Liz wiped the sweat from her eyes every few minutes and imagined standing under the falling water, an unending supply of ice-cold relief.

In the middle of the first climb, she stepped off the trail for a water break. "When we stop for lunch, we should soak our feet."

Dante nodded, too breathless to speak.

A half hour later they reached Evolution Meadow, where the creek, now flat and broad, intersected the trail. They changed into their camp sandals and tied their boots to their packs.

She dipped a foot in. "It's freezing!"

"Be careful what you wish."

The rapidly flowing water came midway up her shin, and the rocks beneath were slick. Each time she placed a foot on the river bottom she tensed, knowing a slight slip could make her lose her balance completely, toppling her and her pack into the water. Halfway across her feet went numb, and she couldn't be sure of her footing. The slower she went, the less sensation she had in her feet. She looked around to see how Dante was faring and found him already on the far bank, lacing up his boots. She continued in mincing steps and joined him a few minutes later, amazed she hadn't fallen in.

"Finally," he said. "An alpine activity I'm good at."

"You're good at many alpine activities."

"Like what?"

"Not freaking out at storms."

"That doesn't count."

"Remembering to apply sunscreen."

"I'll put it on my resume."

Liz thought for a moment. "How about lunch?"

"Oh, yes. I'm an expert at lunch. Perhaps even an opinion leader."

After they ate, they entered Evolution Valley. The creek had become a wide ribbon lying across an immense golden field. At the far end rose the Hermit, a bare lump of rock two thousand feet above the valley floor. The river bent south, and they pursued it, toward the towering peaks of the Evolution Range and true wilderness.

They rose above the timberline and picked their way along a sloping boulder field. Liz could feel the lake approaching. To her left, the western side of Mount Darwin canted downward and disappeared behind the wall of rubble they'd climbed. To her right, the backside of the Hermit did the same. In the middle would be the lake, and this arduous day would be over. The chill from the river had long since left her feet. She was exhausted; her legs trembled with each step. Only pride stopped her from breaking into tears.

Above the tree line, a lake is either seen not at all, or all at once. For the past four hours, everything Liz had seen was gray: gray trail, gray rock, gray slopes, gray mountains. The monotony made the minutes drag, and it was hard to feel as though they were making progress. Every small rise should have been the final one, but wasn't.

She concentrated on her footing as she climbed a broad slanting ledge. The trail leveled out and she raised her head. Everywhere was blue, blue, blue.

Now that she had arrived, she regretted having considered the lake as merely a spot on the map. This had happened before. She would arrive at the day's destination, so relieved not to have to walk a step farther that she forgot why she'd hiked there in the first place. Today, at the sight of Evolution Lake, gratitude, wonder and relief surged through her. The energy she thought had been completely expended, returned. It made no sense for a view to have the power to completely alter how she felt, but it did. The sparkling sapphire water spread out before her, and she laughed.

"Wow!"

Dante came up beside her, grinning. "Wow, indeed."

A wind blew from the south, crinkling the surface of the lake. They searched for a sheltered spot, and soon found one, tucked into a knoll two hundred feet from the water. A flat area, barely large enough for their tent, was surrounded on three sides by boulders taller than a person. Someone had built a knee-high stone wall on the open end. Liz took it as a sign Evolution Lake could prove to be a windy place. She scolded herself for forgetting to get a weather forecast from the ranger in the valley. At the moment, there was only the usual high-altitude end-of-the-day breeze, but that meant absolutely nothing.

Dante had unpacked and was setting up the kitchen. Liz positioned the groundsheet and erected the tent, crouching against the boulders that crowded the site. She searched the stuff sack for the bag of tent stakes, which she always rolled together with the fly. It wasn't there. She emptied her backpack and pulled her sleeping bag out of its sack.

"Dante, have you seen the stakes?"

"For the tent?"

"No, the New York sirloins. Seriously, I can't find them."

"You always put them in the tent bag."

"I know. After I count them. Twice."

They went through everything they had, which took less than five minutes.

He said, "What do we do?"

She regarded the tent, as if it might contribute a solution. "We've got one stake in the emergency bag, and I should be able to use rocks to hold down the corners."

"What about the extra string?"

"The emergency cord? I'll use it if I have to, but I don't want to cut it up otherwise."

Dante stared at her as if he suddenly realized his survival might very well depend on the length of a piece of nylon. "Sounds good to me."

"I wonder what happened to them."

He handed her a piece of salami. "Eat this. It'll take your mind off it."

A voice came from nearby. "Hello!"

Paul and Linda waved and climbed up to them. Linda said, "We're neighbors," and pointed to a stand of pines circling an enormous boulder. "On the other side of Bertha."

"She names things," Paul explained.

Dante cut them each a piece of salami, and they traded stories about the day's hike.

Liz said, "You been here long?"

Paul lifted a shoulder. "A couple of hours."

Liz was amazed fifty-somethings could set that kind of pace. "Hey, I hate to ask, but do you have extra stakes? All of ours went missing."

"That's weird," Linda said. "We came over to

see what your fuel situation was. We've got about a half a can, but the extra is gone."

Paul put a hand on Linda's arm. "Not that we're asking for fuel. We can manage. But sometimes people burn off their extra canister near the end."

Dante said, "We'll conserve ours."

Linda added, "And if we're below ten thousand feet, where there's plenty of wood, we can all use fire instead."

"That's why I wasn't too worried." Paul said. "Oh, I can help you a little with the stake situation. Hold on." He trotted off toward his campsite.

"He's got a lot of energy," Dante said.

"He does," Linda said. "Like a little boy."

A few moments later, Paul returned brandishing three tent stakes as if proposing they draw straws. Two were aluminum, the other red and slimmer. "Will this help?" He pulled out the red stake. "I found it on the trail today. Pretty expensive litter."

Liz took it from him, her mind spinning in ten directions.

Dante said, "That's exactly like ours. But I guess they're probably common."

"No," she said slowly, twisting the stake in her fingers. "These are fairly unusual. See how the cross section would be a Y-shape? They're called Groundhogs, because they hold extremely well, plus they have a favorable strength-to-weight ratio."

187

"Engineer?" Linda asked.

Liz nodded, transfixed by the stake.

"What's a groundhog?" Dante asked.

"A flatland marmot," Linda said.

Liz glanced at Linda, who she could tell was also thinking about the Roots. "Paul, where did you find it?"

"Near the Piute Creek bridge. In the middle of the trail. It struck me as an odd place. At a campsite, sure." He handed her the other stakes.

"Thanks a lot. It's getting blowier by the minute."

The McCartneys said good night, and Liz secured the fly and the guy lines.

As soon as the lake fell into shadow, the temperature dropped like a stone. Liz and Dante made dinner and stood huddled near the pines, their backs to the wind, and ate hurriedly. They scurried to the lake edge to rinse the dishes. The wind flew through the gap between the peaks, over a rocky archipelago, then swept across the water in gusts that pulled tears from their eyes. Liz, anxious to find relief from the cold, scrambled too quickly up the steep bank and tripped. Her knee hit stony ground, and dishes clattered down the hill behind her.

"I'm okay!" she shouted to Dante before he could ask. She rubbed her knee and bent it a few times. Nothing more than a bruise.

Fearing the strengthening wind, they stowed the

cooking gear in their packs instead of leaving it out as they usually did, and took refuge in the tent before the sun had abandoned the summit of Mount Darwin. They stripped off their rain pants and jackets, and wriggled into their sleeping bags, facing each other.

She dropped her head onto her folded jacket. "I am so damn tired."

"Me, too. How's your knee?"

"It'll be fine, and serves as a reminder. Haste makes pain."

He leaned over and kissed her cheek. "Sleep now. You had a bad night last night."

"Yeah. The good news is it's too cold up here for snakes."

"Good night, *carina*."

"Good night, *amigo. Te amo*."

"*Te amo*."

She closed her eyes, her lids falling shut like trapdoors. Gradually, her body heat warmed the cocoon, and her hands and feet melted. Her legs sank through the mattress and tent floor and into the ground. If twenty rattlesnakes appeared in the tent, her mind would run screaming, but her body would stay right where it was. She drifted off.

The howl of the wind woke her. The moon had risen, casting a low light through the yellow fabric of the tent. Above her head the tent bulged inward, throbbing with the pulse of the wind. She placed her hand against it and pushed, but the wind's strength was greater. Outside, branches scraped against one another, creaking. The gust eased, and the tent returned nearly to its normal shape. For a minute or more, the wind relented, blowing now, she guessed, as hard as it had when they'd been outside.

It was only a respite. From across the lake, she heard the wind gathering, whipping down the slopes and hurtling itself across the lake, closer and closer, louder and louder, then hitting the tent like a fist. The bulge above her head returned, pulsating. She rose to her elbow to see if Dante was awake, but his face was in shadow.

The tent would hold. She'd assumed the wind would not shift direction and had positioned the tent to face the force along its strongest side. She'd staked it as best she could. But she doubted she could sleep. Maybe during a steady wind, but not with intermittent gusts buffeting them.

Dante rolled over. "Not exactly a lullaby, is it?"

She tested the force of the wind again with her hand. "You should feel this. I wouldn't be surprised if it was blowing fifty, sixty miles an hour out there."

"We okay in here?"

"I think so. It's a strong little tent."

They listened to the wind howling across the lake. The gust slammed into them, lifting the edge of the tent floor near their heads two inches off the ground.

"Whoa," she said.

"I wonder how Brensen's doing in this. He's not very experienced."

"True. He can't pitch a tent to save his life. Probably he's outside swearing at the wind."

"You should try to sleep." He checked his watch. Its face glowed turquoise. "It's only ten."

She did, but to no avail. During lulls between gusts she heard Dante's soft snoring, which served to feed her growing frustration. Her body begged for sleep, but she could not supply it. Her mind was tuned to the wind, pointlessly tossing shreds of thoughts into her consciousness, spinning them around and around, then blowing them away again, into an unknowable space. She didn't want to think, if this could be called thinking. She wanted oblivion. The wind wouldn't let her have it.

For hours and hours, she lay not simply sleepless, but tormented by her sleeplessness. The more she strove to clear her mind, the more debris the gusts blew in. The tent was secure, holding them safe in their beds, but inside Liz was chaos. Snakes, Dante, missing stakes, Mike, Payton Root, Gabriel, wrenched knees, General Petraeus. Thunder. Lightning. Radishes.

Without sleep, she would go mad.

Facing away from Dante, she pulled her knees up to her chest and chewed her lip to stop from wailing along with the wind. She rocked herself in time to the pulsing bulge above her head. The pressure pushed against her heart.

A hand on her shoulder. "What's wrong?" He turned her over. She squeezed her eyes shut, afraid that in the moonlight she might see his pity for her. In a moment, he would want it back.

"I cheated on Gabriel! I cheated on him!"

He pulled his hand away. She opened her eyes. His lips were pursed with concern, but she couldn't see his eyes. He twisted away. "Oh, Liz." It came out like the last air in a balloon. "Did he know?"

She pictured her husband's face on that sweltering night, his disbelief morphing into pain and anger. "Yes—"

"But his family doesn't know? You're still friends with them."

"No one knows! No one!"

The wind bore down once again, as if to drown her out. She had the impulse to leave the tent to meet it, shout at it, run at it. Dare it to snatch her off this earth and take her away into darkness.

He was talking to the ceiling. "I don't see how you could do this. I know you were unhappy. I understand that now. But this?"

She sat up and threw her hands in the air. "I knew you'd react this way, because nothing's worse than cheating, right? In your little morality play, loyalty is everything! You don't get it!"

"What am I supposed to get? That you had your reasons? That he drove you to it?"

"No!" She stuck her fists against her temples. "I told him! I told him and he got up and he got in his car. He got in his car and he crashed it! I told him and then he died!"

She tucked her head to her knees and sobbed. The spasms, like the gasping wind, threatened to crush her. Dante put his arms around her. He held her until the spasms eased. She lifted her head to wipe her face and he zipped himself wordlessly into his bag. She lay down, and waited for the wind to scream across the lake and throw itself at the tent, at her, but it had steadied now, and howled in a single octave, not three. Shivering, she closed her eyes and pulled the bag over her face. She focused on the throbbing pain at her temples. In time, she slept. Her tears dried as frost.

Chapter Seventeen

The police came to the door the way they do in movies. A man and a woman, he with his hands crossed in front, she with her thumbs in her belt loops, both with serious, guarded expressions, as if showing sadness before delivering bad news was unprofessional. Information first, condolences after. You never know how people will react.

And, as in a movie, Liz knew why they were there as soon as she opened the door. Police don't stand on your doorstep, unhurried and grim, on the same hot August night your husband stormed out, for more than one reason.

"Is this the residence of Gabriel Pemberton?"

"Yes. I'm his wife." She almost asked them what had happened—even though she knew—but went along with the script. They were in charge. They had Gabriel. Somewhere, he was lying on— what?—a stretcher, a gurney. There would be blood. His clothes would be torn. She tried to remember what he had been wearing, but couldn't. Maybe his arm, or his leg was the wrong shape, or detached. Maybe he was still in the car, pinned by the steering wheel, or upside down, hanging from the seat belt like a parachutist. No, they would have taken care of that first, before they came here.

Heat radiated off the concrete landing. She felt it go through her, and put a hand on the doorjamb to steady herself.

The officers glanced at each other. "Do you mind if we come in?"

She turned and lowered herself into the nearest chair. She never sat in that chair. From this new vantage the house appeared unfamiliar. The officers sat on the couch—her usual spot.

They told her what had happened. He'd lost control of the car on Central Boulevard. He might have been speeding. They weren't sure. They would know more tomorrow. He hit a retaining wall, flipped. They said he was "already gone" when the paramedics arrived on the scene and hadn't suffered. They offered their condolences.

The woman said, "Can I get you something? A glass of water?"

She shook her head, eyes on the jute rug at her feet, following the pattern of the weave. Over, under, over, under.

The man said, "We need to ask you a couple of questions, if that's all right."

She nodded once.

"When was your husband last here?"

"About an hour ago."

"Had he been drinking?"

"We each had a beer at dinner. The last two." She felt a drop of water on her bare leg. She put a hand to her face. It was wet.

The man said, "We can do this later."

She looked up. "What else do you have to ask?"

"Was your husband depressed?"

"No."

"Then he went out because . . ." He leaned forward, narrowing the distance between them, making it easier for her to toss the answer.

"We ran out of beer."

The officers stayed while she made a phone call. She called Valerie, and kept it short.

"Okay," the woman officer said. "Someone's on the way?"

"Yes." But she neglected to say Valerie lived in Paris.

Valerie wasn't just the first person Liz wanted to tell about Gabriel; she was the only person. She did call the Pembertons that night, because there was no escaping it. She had killed their son. Her hands shook so much it took three tries to get the number right. Pastor Thomas Pemberton answered. She told him the bare bones of the story because that was all she could manage. A man used to dealing with death, he took the news calmly, or calmly enough, even asking Liz to confirm someone would be looking after her. Yes, of course. He said they would speak the next day, to make arrangements. At first she misunderstood what he meant. She thought it bizarre he would suggest arranging flowers when his son had just died, then the word locked into its context. Arrangements for the transition to the next world. For the pastor it was heaven; for Liz it was tomorrow, and all the days afterward, absent of Gabriel because of her.

She hung up and imagined the ripple of shock and sorrow as it passed from the pastor to his wife, to their other children (four now, only four), and to other relatives and friends, outward through their many branches of kinship, love and support, connections they tended with care. The community of people the Pembertons had nourished would now nourish them. They would all say, in their messages, that losing a child was the greatest loss of all, and wish them strength. Liz was the domino that fell, knocking Gabriel flat on his back, and starting the wave that set the Pembertons and their world in tragic motion.

She did not call her mother.

Valerie was ignorant of Mike. She barely knew anything about the problems between Liz and Gabriel. Or, more accurately, the problem Liz had with Gabriel, because he never acknowledged anything was wrong.

Valerie was her best friend. She knew her better than anyone else, but that didn't mean she knew Liz well. They met in college, not long before Liz met Gabriel, so Valerie knew only the Liz who was loved by Gabriel. She hadn't met the marginalized high school Liz or the Liz who played alone on her bedroom floor, tinkering with the guts of some machine. Liz in love with Gabriel was so much more acceptable than any previous versions—or that's how it seemed to Liz—so she filed her other selves away, and referred to them infrequently. She did so out of habit, not concerted effort. Liz believed she would always have Gabriel as he was during their courtship, so her life before him was irrelevant to Valerie, and to herself.

When Gabriel began pulling away, Liz talked to Valerie about it. Her friend laughed and said not to worry. He loved her madly, anyone could see it, she said. It was probably nothing more than the inevitable mellowing even the most romantic relationship experiences. Normal life. Had she used that phrase? Now Liz wasn't certain.

More than a year ago, Valerie moved to Paris to study at an art institute, and there never seemed to be a right time to talk since she'd left. Liz was reluctant to complain about Gabriel across such a distance, and the differences in their schedules discouraged her further. Morning in Albuquerque was dinnertime in Paris, when Valerie was either out, tired or on the wrong side of a bottle of wine. If Liz called during her evening, her friend would be groggy with sleep or impatient to start her day. It was too difficult, so she kept her own counsel more and more.

Valerie, and the rest of the world, never learned about Mike. For so long, there was nothing to say. She imagined the conversation.

"I eat lunch with a guy at work."

"Are you attracted to him?"

"No."

"Does he flirt with you?"

"No."

"Then why do I care about it?"

By the time she realized there was a reason for Valerie to care, she was too ashamed to tell, and too worried she might lose her best friend.

Liz hadn't planned to keep secrets from Valerie and she hadn't planned to lie to the police. The story about the beer came out of her mouth unbidden. She might have been subconsciously covering herself, so everyone would believe she was the tragic widow, instead of the cheating woman who'd shocked her husband and let him run out the door angry. Let him kill himself. Of course she was relieved she wouldn't have to get into it with everyone, to explain how Gabriel had ignored her, and how it made her feel. To explain Mike. How could she do that anyway? Her understanding of her marriage, her choices, her goals—everything—had collapsed. She didn't have anyone she could trust to help her figure it out—her go-to resource had always been herself—so she had buried the truth and let everyone think what they would.

And the lie, as it happened, worked out better for Gabriel. When she confessed to the affair, and used the past tense, she removed Mike from inside their marriage, where he never should have been. She hadn't meant to put him there, but he was there nevertheless. And because Mike was now out, he had to stay out, and she would stay out of his marriage as well. That couldn't transpire if the police—and perhaps Mike's wife and Valerie and the Pembertons—all knew about her affair. He would be everywhere in Gabriel's life, in the memories people carried of him. Gabriel hadn't deserved that.

After she called Gabriel's parents, she returned

to the chair she never sat in. The reality of her situation began to sink in. Gabriel was gone, and this part of her life was over. The longer she sat, the more she realized the lie was irrelevant. She hadn't gotten away with a thing.

Chapter Eighteen

She woke at dawn to silence. Her head ached, and her mouth felt lined with parchment. The confines of the tent threatened to smother her—she couldn't face Dante in there—so she grabbed her jacket and pants and crept outside.

The cold air was sharp in her nose. She walked up a small rise and faced east. The landscape stood immobile. She could not detect the slightest sign anything had happened during the night. The mountains remained stolid and mute above the lake, a sheet of midnight blue glass. The stunted trees held their resolute needles.

She returned to the camp, unpacked the cookware and stove, and set the water to boil. Dante squirmed out of the tent and regarded her as she spooned coffee mix into the cups.

"You been up long?"

"A few minutes."

She filled the cups with water, stirred, and handed Dante his. "What are we going to do?"

"What do you mean?"

"I thought you'd be going back."

He stared out at the lake. His cheekbones were red where they'd caught yesterday's sun. The short beard he'd grown since Red's Meadow— which she had thought sexy—now made him appear to be transforming into someone she might not know. Her throat closed and the skin on her palms tightened. She sipped her coffee to stop from crying. She didn't want him to go. She wanted him to want her. He didn't need to forgive her (her transgression wasn't his to forgive), or understand. Wanting her was enough. It had to be.

"No, Liz, I'm not going back. I promised I would do this hike with you, and that's what I'm going to do."

Because he, at least, knew the meaning of a promise.

They ate their breakfast without speaking. Liz carried the dishes to the lake, scooped water into the bowls and mugs, rubbed them clean with her fingers and walked away from the edge to toss out the water. She wiped the dishes dry, stacked them on the ground and stuffed her hands into her pockets to warm them. The tips of the peaks on the western shore, a pair of isosceles triangles, burned orange. The lake surface captured them, every detail of shadowed and sunlit stone painted upon the water, the far shore an uncertain demarcation.

She watched until her fingers regained feeling,

then gathered the dishes and climbed to the campsite. Dante was bent over his pack, his back to her.

"How far are we going today?" he said without looking up.

"Le Conte Canyon would be great. So, thirteen miles?" She began storing the dishes and cookware in her pack.

"Okay." He clicked the straps shut. "I'm almost ready, so maybe I'll see you at the pass, or later."

Her hands stilled. She should've expected he might not want to walk with her this morning, but the break in their routine unsettled her. He didn't seem angry, though, and probably only wanted time to himself. Her mind was so foggy she doubted she could manage a conversation anyway. "Sounds good," she said.

She heard feet on gravel and lifted her head to see the McCartneys crossing the gulley between their camps. Liz wondered if they'd heard her screaming last night and felt her cheeks flush. The couple smiled and waved as they approached.

Paul said, "Good morning. We wanted to make sure you didn't get blown away."

"No, we're still here," Dante said, his tone tinged with regret.

Paul and Linda exchanged concerned looks. Liz changed the subject. "Thanks again for the stakes. I'm not sure the tent would've held up without them." She scanned the piles of gear in front of her and peered inside her empty pack. "I didn't give you guys a fuel canister last night, did I?"

"No," Linda said. "You said you'd conserve, which was nice of you."

"That's what I thought. But I was so tired, I thought maybe I forgot." She began rummaging through Dante's pack.

"Is something wrong?" Linda asked.

"Yeah. Our extra fuel has spontaneously combusted, too."

They all looked at one another.

"What the hell is going on?" Paul asked.

Linda said, "Someone could have gone through our packs at Muir Ranch. Everyone has dinner at the same time, and our cabin was next to yours. Nothing's locked."

Dante shook his head. "Stealing a camera, or a nice knife, I could see. But fuel? Even at the ranch they were only charging eight dollars a can."

Linda said, "Eight bucks is eight bucks. Some people depend on other hikers' leftover food instead of resupplying. They end up with a free vacation if they steal fuel."

"I guess," Liz said, although she doubted the theory.

Paul said, "If we hike into Le Conte Canyon tonight—and that's our plan—we'll be low enough to make a fire."

Dante said, "Another primitive skill to add to my resume."

"That's the thing about primitive skills," Liz said. "You never know when you might need them."

The McCartneys returned to their camp. Dante swung his pack onto his back and adjusted his cap. "See you later."

"Have a nice walk."

He nodded as if this was exactly what he had in mind. "You, too."

She watched him go. He cut diagonally across the hill to meet the trail at the shore and turned south. After a few hundred yards he followed the trail away from the water, and began ascending a ledge at the base of Mount Darwin. Dante was tiny now, an ant moving slowly and steadily, significant in its being and in its purpose, and insignificant otherwise. If she took her eyes off him, she might not find him again.

He reached the top of the ledge and stopped. He might have turned to admire the view, or to see where she was, but it was impossible to tell. In a moment she would lose sight of him in any case, so she made her final preparations and set off. She had become chilled and walked rapidly, relieved to be on her way.

She left Evolution Lake behind and passed a series of lakes, each the same deep blue. Wanda Lake was the largest, lying in a basin a mile below Muir Pass and nearly divided in two by a peninsula. The trail came within an arm's length of the shore. As she skirted it, the surface danced, bejeweled by the early-morning sun.

She stopped to rest midway along the final climb to the pass and looked down upon Wanda Lake, a pool of indigo ink. In this treeless expanse was only ink, stone and sky. The granite basin held the pool within its rugged curves. Beyond the lake, the western slopes of the jagged peaks plummeted into an unseen valley where she guessed another measure of ink had spilled.

The vista reminded her of her first weekend in Santa Fe, when her mother had taken her to lunch at Coyote Café, and to the Georgia O'Keeffe Museum. She'd been dragged through countless museums during her twelve years—some a dozen times or more—and had never been inspired. Museums and galleries and studios were her mother's world. Claire was an authority, so Liz felt her mother automatically experienced more in the face of art than she herself ever would. Depending on her mood, Claire might offer commentary but she was usually lost in private reflection or engrossed in sketching in the notebook she always had with her. Liz was relieved when an audio guide was available to assuage her boredom, although she did admire line drawings, especially preliminary sketches, and the museum buildings themselves.

At the O'Keeffe museum she had left her mother's side and proceeded, as if called, to a canvas in the far corner the size of a large window. She stood a step away and peered through an ivory hole into an impossibly blue sky, where a faint moon hung. Her gaze slid to the bottom corner of the painting and a second ivory hole revealing again an ellipse of sky. She realized the ivory was bone and had the sensation of lifting out of her shoes. Her eyes were drawn through the hole in the bone. She felt if she were to lean forward, she would feel the bone's dry smooth-ness on her forehead. She was in the painting, and the moon was more real than she.

Liz returned to the museum most days after school. Each visit she would choose another painting, or let it choose her. Her hands dipped inside the cool velvet tunnel of a calla lily, and she lay at the foot of the round red hills and stroked their sides, which were sanded like the tongue of a cat. With her fingers she explored the openings in a coyote skull—weaving in and out of the nostrils and eyes—a skull she was certain had never belonged to a living animal, but had always been bare and exposed. In a painting entitled *Above the Clouds I* she stepped from one white puff to the next, the sky below as deep as the ocean.

She said nothing to her mother.

After several months, she could summon the paintings in her mind, and she returned to the museum only for new exhibitions. She kept a stack of postcards of her favorites in a drawer next to her bed, and entered an image before going to sleep, exploring and touching all the surfaces and their simple, beautiful meaning.

When she packed for UCLA, the postcards remained in her bedside table. They were emblematic of the odd, isolated childhood she trusted she could now leave behind. In any case, they lived inside her should she need them. And she managed without the skulls and mesas and morning glories until the night Gabriel died and she found herself sitting in the chair she never sat in, searching for O'Keeffes on her laptop. They got her through that first night.

Now she stared at the peaks surrounding her. It was utterly quiet, as quiet as her childhood bedroom before she fell asleep. These mountains were a far cry from Georgia O'Keeffe's mesas and canyons, and yet the feeling they evoked in her was the same. The simplicity of the scene, combined with the enormity of its scale, evoked a sensual reverence in her. And curiosity. If she dipped the tip of her finger in the ink, could she write upon the sky?

This was why she had come. Not to think, or learn, or seek absolution. She had come to enter into a world of pure perception, to explore this canvas of gray and blue. It was a place beyond reckoning, beyond sin. If she could exist there, she could bear the weight of existence completely inside herself. This, she believed, was necessary for love. She feared the answer would be no, but, at the moment, the question was still alive.

During her marriage to Gabriel, she'd lost hold of the strength she'd taken for granted as a child, when she had calmly reached into her toolbox, aiming to take the world apart and discover how it worked. Courage lay within easy reach of a child who knew nothing of how easily under-standing can unravel, leaving a set of rules that apply to nothing, and an empty heart.

Last night she'd delivered a truth to Dante, blown out of her by a windstorm. Today the trail was in front of her, and behind. Dante was there, following the same line, keeping his word. The high country, so simple, so beautiful, was indif-ferent to them both.

Chapter Nineteen

Dante was waiting for her at Muir Hut, a stone shelter built by the Sierra Club in 1930. He smiled for the first time that day.

"Welcome to Muir Pass. I finally beat you to the top of something."

She lowered her pack, pulled off her hat and wiped her forehead with her sleeve. "Lack of oxygen seems to suit you."

"I slept more than you did."

"Your conscience is clearer."

He took a step toward her. "I have things I'm sorry about. Everyone does."

She wondered what he meant. Probably something innocuous. "Thanks, but let's not have a sinning contest."

He put a hand on her arm, and looked as if he had something to say, but changed his mind.

"What?"

He picked his water bottle off the ground. "Here. Drink. You lost a gallon in tears last night." She accepted the bottle. "Oh, I forgot to tell you." He reached into his shirt pocket. "Look what was sitting in front of the hut."

A red tent stake.

They took a break from the long descent from the pass to eat lunch. Dante retrieved the tortillas, cream cheese and smoked salmon from his pack. Liz filtered two liters of water, and took a seat next to him on the grass.

"Someone's messing with us, Dante."

"Who would do that?"

"The Roots come to mind."

"You think they're behind everything. Rodell was injured, remember. They aren't even hiking anymore."

"So it seems."

"Why would they fake an injury?"

"I have no clue. It doesn't even work as a dare. 'I dare you to fake a wrenched knee so we can get those two to hump your stuff downhill'?"

"You're right. That makes no sense."

"Unless they were after Brensen."

"Why would they be after Brensen? You sound like a conspiracy terrorist."

"Theorist."

"What?"

"Conspiracy theorist. Not terrorist."

"Who cares, Liz!"

He was exasperated with her. She couldn't blame him, not after last night. She had half expected to be relieved having unburdened herself of a secret she'd held for years, but she wasn't. She felt tenuous. And she couldn't get the Roots out of her mind. "I'm just thinking aloud. Did you see Brensen at Evolution Lake?"

He shook his head.

"Me neither." She took a bite of tortilla. "I kind of miss his bitching."

Late that afternoon at Le Conte Canyon, they chose the largest of three campsites arrayed between the trail and the stream, the Middle Fork of the Kings River. The site was closer to the trail than she would have preferred, but they'd logged thirteen miles since Evolution Lake and it would do. A newly built rangers' station was visible a hundred yards away, nestled among the pines on the other side of the narrow stream.

She erected the tent, crawled inside and fell asleep instantly. She awoke to low evening light.

Tempted as she was to put her head down again and sleep until morning, hunger drove her outside. Dante wasn't around, but he had set up the kitchen. She opened a bear can and grabbed a handful of trail mix. Other than the night at Muir Ranch, she hadn't been full since they'd left Yosemite Valley ten days earlier. She'd gotten used to being somewhat hungry much of the time. But every once in a while, like now, if it wasn't for the obligation of rationing, she'd have eaten her way through the contents of both bear cans. And then crawled into the tent for another nap. Eight hours a day of hard exercise had turned her into a lean animal—a large cat that walked across its expansive territory and, after feeding, slept for days. At least that was her fantasy.

She scouted the area for dry wood to burn. On her way back to camp with a small armload of kindling, she spied Dante with two men on the bridge spanning the creek south of the camping area. He shook hands with them and left. When he noticed Liz, he raised a fuel can in the air.

"You can return that wood to its native habitat. This is almost full."

"Where'd you get it?"

"On the map I noticed there's another trail not far from here, coming out of Bishop. I figured there'd be people doing short trips, so I asked everyone who came by and scored on the third group."

"They just gave it to you?"

"They only had one night left, so I traded our nearly empty canister. I offered them five dollars, but they wouldn't take it."

She smiled. "I never thought of salesmanship as a wilderness skill before."

"Wherever people are, there's a deal to be made."

She admired his ease with people and his trust in the practice of give and take. He assembled transactions the way she assembled objects. His skill was more delicate than hers, as no deal was ever made without emotion: loyalty to a product, or a person; love for an idea; jealousy in not getting everything; and pride. Pride was always at the table. Dante respected all these feelings when he made a sale, and recognized them in himself. It made him an invincible negotiator. She had no clue how he made it seem effortless.

They needed to conserve fuel on behalf of Paul and Linda, and had collected the wood, so they built a fire anyway. She demonstrated how to arrange the kindling upon the ashes within the stone circle and handed him the lighter. "Torch it." Once the kindling caught, they angled larger pieces of wood against it.

"Wait a second," he said, taking a branch from her hand. He examined the Y-shaped piece. "We have a spare bungee cord, don't we?"

"Yeah, but—"

"But nothing. You're about to see some real wilderness shit now."

Within ten minutes he had fashioned a sling-shot. He scoured the campsite and creek bed for ammunition and rejoined her at the fire. Selecting a golf ball–sized rock, he pointed at the roll of toilet paper he'd placed on a log fifteen feet away.

"I am no doubt—how do you say?—rusty."

He cupped the rock in the sling made from a bandanna, raised it to eye level, squinted like an archer and released the rock. It hit the toilet roll with a soft thud.

"You nailed it!" she said. "Where did you learn to do that?"

"From the same uncle who was crazy for birds. He photographed them at the feeder. My job was to scare the squirrels away."

"Did you kill them?" She couldn't imagine Dante killing anything.

He shrugged. "A few. I tried not to. Most of them ran away as soon as they saw me."

They entertained themselves for a while setting up more difficult shots. Dante hit nearly every-thing.

"The fire's hot," he said, carefully adding another log. "We should eat."

She boiled water and rehydrated the lentil soup. They ate quickly. Dante moved to pick up the dishes, but sat again when Liz spoke into the fire.

"I never understood why Gabriel changed the

way he did. He was so in love with me, so into me, and then he—" Her hand mimicked the flames disappearing into air. "I don't get it."

"Neither do I." He hesitated. "Something was going on with him."

"Clearly."

"Did you ever think he might have been depressed?"

"Only long after it was too late. My go-to response—especially back then—was it's me, not the other guy."

"It must have been so terrible to not understand what was happening."

"Yeah, but Dante, if you're me, it almost always feels that way. And everyone called us the perfect couple. I loved Gabriel, but as for the rest, I had to take their word for it. Relationships were this big intricate mystery. Are."

He poked the embers, and a flame awoke and licked a charred log. "I can see why you think that, because you spent too much time alone when you were small. And you never saw your parents together, being a couple. Living together, being happy, being angry, being bored."

"Even an evil stepparent would have been more informative."

"Exactly. You're the same as someone who learns to ski when they're already an adult. It's hard to be natural at it. You've got no snow sense."

"Well, that's very encouraging."

He put his hand on the nape of her neck. She turned to him. "But we are not skiing. We are loving, and it's not as difficult."

"It's not? Remember I'm a shitty skier, too."

"I think it's actually very simple. I don't know what happened between you and Gabriel. Maybe you were too young—both of you. But don't blame it on love. There's nothing wrong with love."

It was dusk when they returned from filtering water at the stream. Linda and Paul were coming down the trail and eyeing the campsite next door. They spotted Liz and Dante.

Linda approached. "Are you going to think we're stalking you if we camp here?"

Liz laughed. "Better you than anyone else."

"Brensen's right behind us."

Liz pointed out the third site near the bridge. "It's tight, but it'll give him something to complain about."

The McCartneys lowered their packs with a shared groan. They both looked as if they could use a stiff drink.

Dante said, "Our fire is still pretty hot if you want to use it."

Paul glanced at Linda, who nodded consent. "Fantastic. I'll put up the tent, darling, if you want to get dinner started."

Liz observed the McCartneys unloading their

packs in the near darkness. She couldn't recall when they'd ever hiked this late into the evening. Whenever she saw them late in the day, they were already kicking back, clean and organized. Linda approached with a pot, two bowls and two sporks.

"Pull up a log," Liz said.

Linda nestled the pot in the embers. "I dislike cooking over fires. Makes such a mess of Harold." She noted their quizzical looks. "Harold's the pot."

Dante told her about the fuel.

"That was resourceful of you. Thanks." She peered over Liz's head at the trail. "I want to tell you about Brensen before he shows up. Last night, in all that wind, one of his guy lines got loose. The fly was flapping wildly, so he went outside to secure it. He forgot about a huge branch hanging over the tent and smacked his head on it."

"Ouch," Liz said. "How bad was it?"

"That's the thing. He says it was nothing, but he's got a lump on his forehead you wouldn't believe." She lifted the lid off the pot and stirred. "Not only that, but he's acting strangely."

"Brensen's normal is already strange."

"I know what you mean, but we think he might have a concussion. He seemed a little unsteady on his feet and twice he couldn't find where he was on the map."

"Sounds like me," Dante said.

Liz smiled at him indulgently.

Linda sighed. "We followed him all day because we were afraid he'd fall, or get lost."

"So what happened?"

"Paul got fed up. I can't blame him. Brensen wouldn't admit there was anything wrong. He kept yelling at us to stop babysitting him. Said we were ruining his preparation for his role." Her eyebrows flashed upward in disbelief. She peered into the pot again. "Harold has completed his work. Paul! In two minutes I'm eating yours!"

They ate dinner, cleaned up and headed off to bed. Liz and Dante were in their sleeping bags, drifting off, when a light swept across their tent. Someone swore under his breath. Light beams broke the darkness several more times, accompanied by the rustle of nylon and the clatter of gear falling to the ground.

Liz could hear Paul whispering nearby in his tent, but she couldn't make out the words.

"No, I got it!" Brensen said. "I can take care of my own tent!"

Paul hissed, "I'm not offering to help out of charity, you pompous idiot. I just want your lights off so we can sleep."

"So there's a curfew out here?"

"Sadly, no, but perhaps wilderness permits should require mental health screening. Good night."

Liz stuck her face into her pillow to stifle her laughter. Dante, suppressing a laugh as well, kissed the top of her head and wished her a good night.

She slept, then, a dreamless sleep, which lasted unbroken until dawn. She awoke, warm in her bag, and gazed at the tent ceiling, a few feet away, as it slowly changed from dark amber to yellow. Outside, a chipmunk, or a squirrel, sprinted in hesitant bouts: feet scuttling, silence, more scuttling, silence.

Yesterday had been revelatory—twice. In the wee hours, with the howling wind as her orchestra, she had screamed her confession to Dante, and survived. She supposed she'd always known she would survive it—that was simply rational—but had feared the emotional fallout from exposing her secrets. She had been a coward. The way she had chosen to move forward, to live her life, was to push away her culpability and guilt. Until yesterday, she had chosen to be a fraud and hide behind the unassailable veneer of a tragically dead husband.

But everything that keeps you comfortable keeps you from being known. And Dante said he wanted to know her. Finally, she wanted that, too, for better or for worse. He was struggling to understand what had happened in her marriage, as was she. He would judge her according to whatever principles he chose to apply. She had no control over it.

Indeed, her shame burned hotter reflected in Dante's eyes. And the disappointment in his voice when she revealed her affair—she hadn't figured on the pain from that. Maybe in telling the truth she had only traded one variety of emotional anguish for another. Time would tell. Or it wouldn't.

At least Dante still loved her enough to stay by her side on this journey. And on this September morning, at the bottom of a canyon, sunk deep in the stony wilderness, that was enough.

The other source of revelation occurred below Muir Pass when she entered the landscape as she had entered paintings years before. The experience didn't leave her more connected with the mountains and the sky. Their scale and impassiveness prohibited it. Rather, Liz came away more rooted in herself. These discoveries were hers, and defined her even if she couldn't say precisely how. When she was young, naive and unbridled, she had found her love for tinkering and, later, engineering. Her upbringing may have left her in the dark about relationships, but she never shied from her instincts (what else did she have, as a child?) nor relied on others unnecessarily. To be alone, curious and calm, is to be free. Even while she ached with feelings she could not name for the socially enmeshed lives of others, she understood they came at a cost.

Gabriel, she now suspected, had arrived at college with the hope of experiencing a modicum of the freedom she had routinely enjoyed, and suffered under. To him, she was the kite already loose in the sky, and he was enthralled. But after college, the routines of work and marriage bore down on him. Liz pursued her dreams as if she were a child building a tower of blocks on a sunny rug. He took the job he knew he should take and flailed at his dreams in the off hours. Both were employed in their chosen fields, but only Liz had had the clarity to choose wisely, with her heart. Gabriel's family was consumed with doing for others, and doing it together, so he never found his wings, much less spread them. He might have been depressed, but more likely he was frustrated and emotionally unprepared to summon the courage to change his life.

Liz recognized how similar she was to her mother in finding her life's work. Claire might not have been blessed with prodigious talent, but she was committed to her art, and supported her fellow artists. While Liz could have benefitted from more attention, and a larger family life, at least her mother did nothing to discourage her from becoming who she was, which included, ironically, someone who could soothe herself in the imaginative exploration of a painting.

The morning after Gabriel had died, Liz had been awakened from her sleep in the chair by a knock at the door. She was surprised to find her mother on the doorstep.

"Look at you," Claire said, laying a hand on her daughter's cheek. "The things life does."

In a single stroke, Liz's troubled marriage, her adultery and her husband's death had been swept into a generic box. That day, she was grateful for her mother's nonchalance.

Claire walked past her, heading for the kitchen. "Gabriel's mother called me, if you're wondering." There was no resentment in her voice for not receiving a direct call from her daughter.

Liz found her mother pulling mugs from the cabinet. "I don't know how your coffee works. Just start and I'll take over while you shower." She looked at Liz, who hadn't moved. "Come on, now. Coffee and a shower. One foot in front of the other." She took her daughter by the shoulders. "Talking about this sort of thing is useless. You'll be sad no matter what." Before she let go, she squeezed. "So, one foot in front of the other."

And that was how it would be with Dante on this hike. She had more to tell him, worse than what he'd already heard, but there was no way around it. It was a boulder in the middle of the trail. Where in the trail, she couldn't say, but they would get there, one foot in front of the other. And, if they were able, they'd continue on to the other side.

Chapter Twenty

After breakfast, Dante headed to the ranger station for a weather forecast. Liz picked her way through the trees to the stream to rinse the dishes. Squatting on a sandy patch, she swirled water into the cups and flung it into the bushes behind her. Breaking twigs drew her attention to the far bank, clogged with willow. The sounds proceeded upstream. She stood, slowly, in case it was an animal, and placed a foot on a half-submerged rock to improve her view. The willows shook like a cheerleader's pompom. The branches parted and Payton Root appeared, fixing his eyes on her. Liz gasped. Her foot slid off the rock and hit the water with a splash. Wheeling her arms to keep her balance, she stumbled, knocking the metal dishes onto the rocks.

He was in front of her, unsmiling. "Good morning." His beard had grown in since she'd last seen him three days before. Somehow, he appeared even larger.

She glanced toward the campsites, but they lay invisible beyond the steep bank.

He came half a step closer. "Surprised to see me?"

She stepped back. "I thought your brother was hurt."

"Well, he was. And now he's better. He's small, but he's tough."

Rodell wasn't small. He was as tall as Dante, but Payton dwarfed them both.

She said, "And yet a knee injury is so unlikely to heal in—what?—half a day. Must be some genetic peculiarity."

"You got a sharp tongue, don't you? Like a rattlesnake." He showed his teeth in a parody of a smile. "Don't get me wrong. I prefer feisty."

Her stomach clenched. She wanted to leave, but picking up the dishes would make her too vulnerable. Instead, she met his eyes. "And with your charm and debonair ways, I'm sure you have your choice."

"Hey!" Rodell appeared from the direction of her campsite. "How're you doing?"

She used the distraction to scoop up her dishes. "Great." Rodell blocked the path "If you'll excuse me . . ."

He ignored her. "I just saw Dante on his way to the ranger's."

"That's great. Now, Rodell, I need to get going."

"Aren't you going to ask about my leg?"

"I can see it's fine. Miraculously so." She regretted her comment immediately.

The younger brother, usually cheerful, jerked his shoulders into place. Pointing a finger at her, he questioned his brother. "You still fancy this one?"

Payton narrowed his eyes and ran his tongue slowly across his lips. "More all the time."

She clasped the dishes against her and took a giant step onto a tall boulder, allowing the momentum to carry her to another stone farther up the bank. She caught hold of a branch and swung herself up the rest of the way. The brothers laughed.

At the top of the bank, in sight of the McCartneys, she paused to arrange the dishes to carry them more comfortably.

"Oh, Liz," Payton called. "I forgot to give you this. Found it on the trail."

She turned and spotted a narrow object in the air as it caught the light before falling to the ground behind her.

A red tent stake.

They laughed again, and Rodell let out a snort.

Dante hadn't returned from the ranger station, but Liz was relieved to see he'd stowed his gear and would soon be ready to leave. She wanted to get the hell away from the Roots. She pulled a pair of used, but dry, socks from her pack and changed into them. There was nothing she could do about her wet boot. She packed the dishes, tucking them in with her clothes so they wouldn't rattle, and secured the toggle closing her pack.

Brensen's campsite was empty, so he must have been feeling well enough. Paul and Linda seemed to be getting a late start, probably with the intention of putting distance between themselves and Brensen. She was about to walk over and tell them about her encounter with the Roots when Dante came up behind her.

"Good news! The ranger says the weather should be fine for the next couple of days."

"That's a relief." She pulled the top of her pack closed. "Dante, you won't believe it, but I just ran into Payton and Rodell at the river."

"I thought Rodell was injured."

"I know. Listen." She told Dante about her encounters with Payton: the time at Purple Lake when she'd been trapped between him and the stream, and today. He listened without interrupting.

"So," she said, "I might not be a social genius, but I can't ignore the fact that every time Payton opens his mouth I feel like I need a shower—or a bodyguard."

"He's definitely strange. Both of them are. But dangerous? Maybe he just likes to get a raise out of women. Maybe he considers that kind of talk flirting."

"I think you mean 'get a rise' out of them. Provoke them."

"Yes. Maybe if you refused to respond, it wouldn't be fun for him anymore."

So, it's me? Liz thought. The nerd who blew her first marriage and was about to blow this relationship needed the behavioral adjustment.

Well, he had a point. She hadn't tried ignoring Payton. But her instincts—and recent events—said it wouldn't work. "And what about the tent stakes? And the fuel? And that little present in our cabin?"

"We can explain those in other ways."

"How? That we're just incredibly careless and unlucky?"

He shrugged.

Liz didn't want to press any further. "Let's just get out of here, okay?"

They applied sunscreen and lip balm, drank water and put on their packs. Liz scanned the site one last time and led the way to the trail.

She wanted to mention the Roots' reappearance to Paul and Linda, but although their gear was still at their campsite, the couple was nowhere to be seen. Liz figured they were upstream collecting water or perhaps had gone to a nearby clearing to take in the view.

They crossed the bridge and continued south on a gentle descent along the Kings River. After less than a mile Dante called to Liz. She heard him stop, so she leaned on her poles and regarded him over her shoulder. He removed his sunglasses and turned to the sky, as if for guidance. Then he looked at her squarely. "I'm sorry I didn't under-stand before how much the Roots bothered you If you want to stay away from them, that's fine. We don't have to talk to them."

"Okay, thanks."

"What do you think they want from you?"

"I have no idea."

"Well, don't worry about it. We'll avoid them, okay?"

"We can try."

As they resumed hiking, she wondered if it would prove possible to avoid the Roots; it certainly hadn't been thus far. The Sierras encompassed a vast area, but in certain ways, not vast enough. For the rest of the trip, it would be harder to avoid other hikers. The passes were about a day's walk apart. Most hikers preferred to cross them in the morning, when their legs were strong, which meant camping on the north side of the passes. To shake the Roots, they would have to go over two passes in a single day, and not get caught in an afternoon storm on the second pass. Some hikers managed this, even covering the entire two hundred twenty miles in a week or less, but it was too difficult for most, including her and Dante.

Today's hike was a case in point. Mather Pass (the highest yet at twelve thousand one hundred feet) was fourteen and a half miles away. The map showed a massive basin on the far side. After the pass, a hiker might have to continue for a few more miles to find a protected site. But, a mile or two shy of this side of the pass were the Palisade Lakes, tucked into a partially forested canyon with ample shelter. She expected to see familiar (if not welcome) faces there.

In an hour they reached Grouse Meadows, where the river spread wide and smooth. Mist clung to the tall grasses, waiting for the sun to gain strength and unravel it into the sky. Here the abundance of water had helped the wildflowers stretch their summer into fall. Periwinkle blue lupine, red Indian paintbrush and creamy yarrow bordered the trail. Liz pointed out a mariposa lily, a delicate tulip-shaped blossom on a slender stalk, the inside of its three white petals touched at their base with a dab of maroon. As they returned their attention to the trail, a deer crossed not fifteen feet in front of them, unhurried.

Liz caught Dante's eye and smiled. If only they could be alone this way for the whole trip, sharing these simple, exquisite moments. She considered suggesting they follow a different route, forget the JMT and leave the Roots (and Brensen and the McCartneys) to wonder where they'd gone. But in her heart she held out hope they could finish the trek as planned, and experience it on their terms. They'd just keep their distance from the brothers as much as they could.

At the next trail junction, they turned east into the Palisade Creek valley. The trail climbed more steeply, and soon they left the pine forest behind and emerged onto a rocky slope. Quaking aspen bordered the creek and spread as high up the mountainsides as they dared. It was the largest stand of aspen they'd seen—a field of green and gold trembling in the morning breeze. Out in the open, the sun roasted them. Sweat broke out on their backs and foreheads. They climbed ever higher, and the temperature moved into the low eighties. By early afternoon they arrived at the base of the Golden Staircase, the last section of the JMT to be built.

"I'm guessing they didn't save the easiest for last," Dante said, craning to make out the route.

"Fifteen hundred feet, straight up." The cragged wall rose before her like a medieval skyscraper. Stare as she might, she couldn't make out the trail.

They rested frequently to drink in gasping gulps and take in the view. Palisade Creek, from this perspective a strip of dark green, took the direct route to the valley from which rose the Black Divide. Instead of the typical silver granite, these peaks were carved of charcoal and ebony, accentuating their contrast with the sky they thrust upward to meet.

The mostly dry and rocky trail was interrupted by rivulets flowing from unseen waters above, creating patches where grasses and wildflowers took hold—miniature oases amidst rock slabs and talus chunks. Halfway up, the switchbacks began. Liz took off her pack and Dante followed suit. He pointed downslope.

"Two people coming up. Paul and Linda?"

"I think so. Boy, they've made up some time on us."

"Good thing they're not the ones we're trying to avoid. They're rabbits."

She thought, not for the first time today, that Payton and Rodell were fast hikers as well, having arrived at Le Conte Canyon before anyone. Then she realized they may not even have slept at Muir Ranch. While everyone assumed the Roots were headed for a doctor, they could have been en route to Evolution Valley. As for today, they might be behind or ahead, and it worried her not to know which.

They admired the view for a few minutes more, and continued upward, crossing the headwall from one side to the other like a shoelace being guided through a tall boot. Looking toward the top, Liz could discern perhaps two switchbacks above her, but beyond them the scramble of rocks yielded no clues.

Dante paused at a corner, a sheer wall forty feet high looming behind him. "How much farther do you think?"

She stared downhill. "Maybe another third?" Paul was taking a photograph several switchbacks below. Linda was beside him. She tipped her head back, drinking deeply from an orange Nalgene.

A scraping sound came from above. Liz, in the center of a switchback, oriented to it, searching for movement. A boulder the size of a basketball tumbled over a ledge some thirty feet up, and bounced with a crash, sending smaller rocks cascading toward her. She scurried backward as the boulder flew by, missing her by a foot before hitting below the trail and dislodging more rocks.

"Look out!" she shouted.

The boulder headed straight for Paul and Linda. Paul, eyes huge, jumped back. Linda did the same, but her backpack was propped against a rock behind her. As she threw herself backward, her heel hit the pack and she fell onto it, legs in the air. The boulder careened off a ledge above her, and grazed her leg. She screamed. The boulder plunged out of sight, but the crush of rock upon rock echoed up to them.

Dante, plastered against the wall, stared at Liz in shock.

She quickly undid her pack and threw it to the ground. "I'm going down."

Without a pack and traveling downhill, she flew. In two minutes she was there. Paul bent over his wife's leg. Tears were flowing down her cheeks, and she bit her lip to stop from sobbing. Her calf was covered in blood, oozing from a four-inch gash. The skin on either side was deeply abraded.

"How bad is it?" Liz asked. Dante appeared at her side and placed a hand on the small of her back.

"It's not out of alignment and when I pushed on her heel, she didn't scream, so I doubt it's broken."

He turned, nodding at the pack behind her. "In my pack, on the left hand side, there's a medical kit."

She opened the pack, pushed aside some clothing and found the Ziploc bag. A quick scan told her the contents were similar to hers: adhesive tape, antibiotic cream, alcohol wipes, gauze, ACE bandage.

Paul went on. "And on the other side is a bag with emergency stuff. I need the tent repair kit in there."

"Paul," Linda said, her voice shaking. "I'm not a goddamn tent."

"The bleeding's not going to stop until I stitch it. Just a few will do the trick."

"Oh God," said Dante, as he crossed himself. His cheeks were pale.

Paul poured water over his hands and swabbed them with an alcohol pad. "One more thing, Liz. There's a silver bottle in my bear can. Tequila."

"You guys have tequila?" Dante asked.

"A couple ounces each evening," Paul said, threading the needle with the coarse thread. "Humped it all the way from Yosemite Valley."

His wife said, "So is what you're using for my leg your portion or mine?"

Paul laughed lightly. "That's my girl." He looked up at Liz. "Please hand me the antibiotic ointment and a couple of squares of gauze." He held the wound open. It filled with blood. He dabbed it clean and squeezed a line of ointment inside.

Dante sat down and put his head between his knees.

Liz watched as Paul pierced the skin with the needle. Linda cried out.

"Sorry, darling," he said. "Only a couple more." He pushed the needle through the other side and tied it off deftly. "Shit. Anyone have a knife? Mine's in my pocket and I can't let go."

Liz reached hers across. "You've done this before, I take it."

"Yes, but not on my wife. Nor a human being, come to think of it. But skin's skin."

Paul tied up the last stitch and blotted the wound gingerly with tequila, glancing at his wife as he did it. Her breath came in gasps as she bore down on the pain. "That's it." He reached for her hand and squeezed it hard. "My brave girl."

Dante had yet to lift his head. "So very brave."

Liz choked back tears, and wondered what brought them on: anxiety over the injury and switchback surgery, or the complete trust Linda had in Paul.

He wiped the needle on a clean edge of gauze and returned it to the bag, along with the thread. He gathered the bloody gauze and stood. A little unsteady, he looked around as if just realizing where they were. Liz fished an empty bag from her pocket. "Here, Paul, put those in here."

He handed them over, and stared up the headwall. "We were bloody lucky. Can you imagine if that boulder had scored a direct hit?"

His wife sat up and examined the neat row of stitches in her leg. "I'd rather not, if you don't mind."

Dante followed Paul's gaze. "How does a rock that size just come loose?"

"It was probably Brensen. The guy is such a klutz."

"Or the Root brothers," Liz said.

"You've seen them?" Linda said.

She nodded. "This morning."

Paul's face darkened. "Are they ahead of us?"

"They're everywhere."

Chapter Twenty-One

Paul dressed Linda's leg as best he could and gave her three ibuprofen. Liz and Dante offered to carry some of her belongings. At first Paul objected, but when Linda said they were in no position to refuse help on account of pride, he relented. They arranged to make camp near one another to facilitate returning Linda's gear. And Liz suspected they all felt as she did: until they found out what, if anything, was causing all these mishaps, it wasn't a bad idea to stick together.

At the top of the Golden Staircase, the terrain

leveled out. The trail bent eastward along the base of the lofty peaks forming the Palisade Range, Disappointment Peak among them. Liz and the others crawled up and over a series of small rises, water crashing down a steep chute on their right. More than usual, she scanned the area ahead and above her. Her vigilant anxiety marred the beauty of the surroundings—the white noise of the river, the sweet smell of pine in the pure air, the unbroken sky of That Color—but she gave silent thanks that it appeared they would not have a storm to cope with that evening.

Lower Palisade Lake, like so many others she'd approached, came upon her all at once. The aquamarine surface stretched from her feet to a low saddle a half mile away, above which lay its twin: Upper Palisade Lake. Beyond it were the mountains containing Mather Pass, over twelve thousand feet. On her side of the lake, a slope comprised of ledges dotted with pines met the water gracefully. But the opposite side was a near vertical wall. Liz's eyes followed its trajectory into the water. It was a deep, deep lake.

Dante had already abandoned his pack to search for a place to camp. She could tell Linda's injury had shocked him, and he was undoubtedly eager to become absorbed in the duties of making camp, of creating shelter. She had the same impulse and wondered if this was the reason she felt energized once she'd pitched the tent each evening. Being on the move invited uncertainty. She never knew what was around the next corner, or over the next rise. She believed in her strength but could never be certain it would get her over these monumental passes. Walking multiplied the degrees of freedom, additional rolls of the dice that might engender a change of fate. A stream to cross (and perhaps fall in), a rock to misjudge (and perhaps twist an ankle), a willow grove to push through (and perhaps startle a bear). A set of switchbacks to climb (and perhaps succumb to falling rock).

Simply by stopping, the degrees of potentially dangerous freedom were reduced. When she lowered her pack to the ground at the end of the day, she knew where she would be for the next fifteen hours or so. Sure, the physical relief from throwing a thirty-pound monkey off her back was considerable, and certainly she looked forward to getting clean, eating and, finally, lying prone. But as she stood on the shore of Palisade Lake, she felt what she supposed was an ancient feeling: knowing she would not be wandering in the wilderness when night fell.

Dante waved to her from atop a ledge twenty feet above the lake, near its outlet. She joined him and he proudly showed her the site on the other side. Two flat areas for tents were separated by a stand of pines, the entire site nestled between the ledge and another wall of boulders.

"Good scouting, Tonto," she said, then had to explain about *The Lone Ranger*.

After organizing the camp, they sat on the ledge where they could spot anyone coming along the trail. Liz took a handful of cashews and passed him the bag.

"What Paul did down there was pretty amazing," she said. "The tent repair kit!"

"No kidding. He reminds me a lot of you."

"Me?"

"Yes. Very focused and calm. Resourceful. Injurious."

"Injurious? The boulder was injurious. Do you mean 'ingenious'?"

"Yes, my little genius."

"Does that mean I'm free to perform surgery on you if necessary?"

"Absolutely." He turned to her, suddenly serious. "I trust you."

Her chest tightened. She wanted to ask him what he meant, but couldn't form the words.

He answered her anyway. "I trust you, *carina*. Absolutely."

She moved closer to him. They sat, shoulder to shoulder, staring at the majestic landscape before them, in a silence as deep as the lake.

The moment would have been perfect, but for the secrets she yet held from him. She wanted to believe if he could push aside one misstep, he could push aside others—he loved her that much.

But an affair during an unhappy marriage, while serious, was much more forgivable than getting pregnant, not telling the father (with whom you lived), and doing away with the child—his child. And Dante had said he always wanted a family. Of course this made her all the more reluctant to tell him. He would, she was sure, have wanted the child. And they would have had to get married. Right away. Liz, who had barely come to terms with her decision to move in with him, could not contemplate, much less embrace, this chain of events. Dante's reaction to her confession concerning Gabriel was more accepting than she expected. Had she known that, had she trusted him enough to tell him before she had gotten pregnant, she might have been able to be honest with him about it at the time. They might have had a conversation, or several conversations. They might never have agreed about starting a family, and she might have chosen to have an abortion anyway, but at least they would have walked through it and considered their options. Together.

But that wasn't how it happened and nothing could change it, or the fact that, as a devout Catholic, Dante would take particular exception to the way she had handled her pregnancy, and its termination.

She was tempted, now, to keep the secret. He loved her, she loved him. She'd opened up to him about her failed marriage, about her guilt in precipitating Gabriel's death. He hadn't been overjoyed by the news but neither had he rejected her. If she said nothing more, they had a chance to be happy together.

But as soon as the thought ran through her mind she saw it for the deceit it was. Dante may never know, but she would. The lie would be with her, a pebble in her shoe, every step of the way.

If Dante excommunicated her (as she fully expected), she would be alone. Not as in alone-for-a-decent-period, but alone. Until she turned twenty, she'd never pictured herself married. Gabriel had altered that, but after he died she'd reset her expectations to the default position. Now she was living with Dante, a tribute to his charm and persistence. But he would soon pay for his efforts, and she was sorry. It was for the best. Her mother had chosen to live alone, and had raised her without guidance of how to live otherwise. Liz didn't fear the prospect of a lifetime without a mate, but it did make her sad. The moments when she felt she belonged to someone—to Dante—were magical. What a shame she was incapable of making them last.

The only thing Liz would never do was set out to raise a child alone. She wasn't her mother.

Linda and Paul arrived a half hour later. Dante showed Paul the campsite while Liz helped Linda clean up at the lake. Her wound was encrusted with blood, but wasn't worse otherwise. Liz rinsed out the bloody sock while Linda splashed water onto her face.

"I wish I could dive in," the older woman said. "I don't deal well with the heat."

"Seems to me you're dealing incredibly well with everything. You're so strong."

"Not really. I'm just incredibly stubborn."

The women regarded each other. Linda's curly hair, which had been under a cap all day, was matted to her head. Her face was ruddy from the sun and cold water, and her eyes betrayed a shadow of the pain she'd suffered that day.

She smiled crookedly at Liz, who returned the smile and said, "Enjoying your holiday?"

They burst out laughing and couldn't stop. It was all so ridiculous, putting themselves through this. And yet neither of them was sorry to be there—Liz could see it written all over her friend's face. The absurdity of it, combined with their exhaustion, brought on laughter in endless waves.

"Oh, my God," Linda said, holding her side. "I'm going to need the tent kit again!"

At six o'clock they convened for dinner, though without a fire, as they were well above ten thousand feet. Paul had poured Linda an extra allotment of tequila. She was, as he put it, "feeling no pain."

"Which only proves what a lightweight I've become on this trip," she said.

Dante asked how they had met.

"I was here doing some consulting, minding my own business, when this blond Californian comes out of nowhere and steals my heart. I sold my company, my flat, my car, my motorbike, and moved five thousand miles. Completely besotted, is what I am."

"Don't listen to him. That's not at all what happened. He was mail order. Bargain basement prices for Englishmen. I could have had a twofer."

Everyone laughed.

"Really, though," Linda said, stealing a glance at her husband. "It was love at first sight."

"That's so romantic," Liz said. Dante placed his hand on her knee.

Paul nodded. "But not easily won Second time for both of us."

Linda said, "Sometimes it takes a while to recognize what you've always wanted."

"And by that time," he added with a grin, "you're nearly dead."

Everyone retired early, eager to escape the growing cold and rest their legs. Once Liz and Dante had shed their outerwear and wriggled deep into their sleeping bags, she brought up Paul's immigration.

"That was a big step for him to take all at once."

"Well, half a step would've landed him in the Atlantic."

"You know what I mean. He packed up and left his life, and his country, behind."

"So did I, *carina*."

"It's different, though, with Paul. He only left to be with Linda."

Dante was silent for a moment. "True, I didn't come here for love, but when I didn't return home after college, it broke my mother's heart."

Dante's mother wanted her only son to do his duty, to marry a Mexican woman and build a family close by—plans that meshed perfectly with Señor Espinoza's desire to pass his company to his son. Liz knew Dante had nothing in principle against marrying a compatriot, but was determined to go beyond his father's notion of who he should become. His mother cared little for the disposition of the family business; money was like water from a faucet—it flowed when necessary. But she needed her children around her, and could not help but take Dante's choices personally. Liz's mind leapt to Felicia's resolve in excommunicating her daughter after her affair. Her son could not be shunned—he had not committed a grievous moral error—but he had disappointed her deeply. And Felicia reminded him of it at every opportunity.

"Do you miss Mexico?" Liz almost said "home," but decided the question was loaded enough.

"Occasionally. I miss something: a smell, a

taste, a way of speaking. But this is sentiment, not preference."

"And what about your mother?"

"One cannot always be on the side of the angels."

Chapter Twenty-Two

Gabriel had died on a Wednesday. The next day, Liz's mother stayed with her overnight, then returned to Santa Fe. "See you at the funeral. You can stay with me, if you want." Later it struck Liz she had no choice, other than a hotel—or the Pembertons'.

It was months before she also realized no one had asked her where the funeral should be held. In fact, no one asked her anything during that time, except whether she would care for something to eat or drink. Almost always the answer was no.

She couldn't remember when the Pembertons showed up—had they overlapped with her mother?—or even in which order. They were a tide. She opened the door to them and that was it. She wasn't complaining, not even in retrospect. She had neither the will nor the expertise to manage her own feelings, much less the grieving process and necessary arrangements for the hordes of mourners the Pembertons assured her would arrive.

Their grief was genuine. Liz confronted the enormity and finality of Gabriel's death in their faces and gestures. Gabriel's mother, Eleanor, had worn a slightly contorted expression, even when she was resting or smiling in response to a child, or a joke. Her face was broken, like the twisted metal of the car in the newspaper photograph Claire had not been quick enough to hide, or like Gabriel himself. Liz had to turn away.

She turned away from a lot of things, retreating to her bedroom—their bedroom—to sit on the floor. She couldn't be on the bed. But the bedroom was not safe harbor either. The pastor entered in search of Gabriel's Bible, his sisters came to choose photos from the dresser to display at the service and, worst, his mother searched her out to see if Gabriel's good suit needed cleaning. Liz would never have thought of it.

Unseen hands set the funeral for Sunday. Liz moved with the Pemberton tide, out to the funeral home that would transfer her husband to Santa Fe, back to the house to deal with paperwork, and out to their local church, where pastor consoled pastor with such warmth and candor that she shrunk away in the shame of the weakness of her belief. After, she was ushered home once more, to choose something to wear. Normally she would have balked at the intrusion, but that day she opened her closet to Eleanor, docile. Gabriel's mother had many choices, because Liz favored black and gray. In high school it represented a reaction to her mother's zest for vivid colors, but later she adopted it as her style. She devoted little con-sideration to clothes and nothing went with black like black. Eleanor chose a narrow black skirt, a gray silk T-shirt and a black cardigan, "because sorrow makes us vulnerable to cold." She was right. Outside the August sun baked the houses in the valley like pots in a kiln, and although the air-conditioning was no match for the weather, Liz needed a sweater. Eleanor understood all there was to know about the aftermath of death, as if she'd been rehearsing.

Then there was Gabriel's youngest brother, the one with Down's syndrome. Seventeen now, with a halfhearted moustache and a deepening voice, Daniel mentally hovered near five, and could not grasp Gabriel's passing. He got it in his head it was a joke, a protracted game of hide-and-seek, and searched for his brother tirelessly if not distracted by something else. On Saturday, Liz sat in the chair she never sat in, while all around her Pembertons prepared to escort her, and their dead son, to Santa Fe. Someone mentioned Gabriel by name. Daniel shouted, "I know where he is!" and flung himself at Liz's feet to search under the couch. She let out a scream—her first utterance of the day—and buried her face in her fists.

Everything she did during the run-up to the

funeral—sitting on the floor, refusing food, allowing others to make decisions—was interpreted as grief. It was indeed grief, but mixed in equal parts with guilt and shame. She learned in those few days that either the signs are the same for all three, or the grief of others blinded them. The sympathy flowing over her was a salty sea biting into the wounds she had made in her own flesh.

On the hour-long journey to Santa Fe, she rode in the backseat with Gabriel's youngest sister. Her mother's ancient Land Rover wasn't in the drive when the Pembertons dropped her off. This concerned them, but she said she would be fine. They watched from the car while she approached the wooden burro by the front door, removed a spare key from under the kachina doll sitting on the burrow's back, and let herself in.

The adobe house was the same as always: a colorful, cluttered hodgepodge of Southwestern and Mexican furnishings, mixed with her mother's modernistic artwork. It was like walking into a peyote dream. The house was filled with elaborately painted animals in comic or menacing poses, vividly striped rugs and throws, ivory skulls with dried flowers in the eyes and mouths, giant pots fashioned from grasses and hides, and swirling canvases of orange, green and red— Claire's signature colors. Liz went straight to her room.

She was relieved to find her mother had not repurposed it—not that she would have resented it—but today the simple, tidy room of her childhood was a haven once again. The dark wooden headboard and navy bedspread sharp against the stark white walls and wheat-colored sisal rug were as she had left them. She put down her bag, closed the door and crossed to the window seat. Here was where she had become herself, with the view of the garden and the privacy of her thoughts.

She had no idea how long she stayed at the window, her knees pulled up to her chest. The front door opened once, but no one came to her room. Claire, if nothing else, knew the value of solitude. Liz watched a hummingbird probe among the flowers, then alight on a thorny branch to dart its beak in and out of its wing like a needle through fabric. The sky at the horizon shifted from blue to lilac. She wondered if the hole for Gabriel had already been dug, and whether Daniel's game of hide-and-seek would end when his brother was lowered into it. She closed her eyes and requisitioned Gabriel's face from her memory, but it wouldn't come.

A knock at the door startled her awake. A voice said her name. Valerie. She got up and found her friend in front of her. For a split second, she knew she would tell Valerie everything, right then and there. She had to. She would confess to her unhappy marriage, to adultery, to deviousness, to complicity in Gabriel's death. She would expose the shame burning up through her grief and downward into her soul.

But she noticed changes in Valerie. Her red hair was shoulder-length, and layered—a more sophisticated look than her perennial longer style. And when she pulled Liz into her arms, she smelled of a citrusy perfume. They weren't much, but the changes made Liz hesitate, and the impulse to confess passed like the shadow of a ghost. There would be other similar opportunities in the years to come, but if Liz was honest, this was the only real one. And it passed.

"Your mom brought tamales from Enrico's," Valerie said, her eyes brimming with tears. "Come to the kitchen and watch me eat them all."

She told Liz she was cutting short her internship to take a job near San Francisco. She was heading there from Santa Fe to look at condos, and planned to put deposit money down.

"There are tons of device companies up there, you know," she said. "I checked."

"Tell me you didn't change your plans for me." Valerie looked at her shoes, and Liz was certain her friend had done exactly that.

"Of course not," Valerie said. "How could I know whether you wanted to leave Albuquerque? I just thought, as long as I'm going to be there . . ."

Liz hadn't thought about her plans at all, but

the moment Valerie raised the idea, she knew she wanted to leave everything behind. "Thanks. Can I get back to you on that?"

She gave notice the Monday after the funeral. Her boss, Stacy Stratticon, was surprised to hear from her, having authorized time off when Liz had called the previous week; she wasn't expecting to lose her promising young protégé. She sounded miffed, then shifted gears.

"Sometimes stability is what a person needs after a tragedy," Stratticon said.

Nice try, Strap-it-on. Liz said she'd be in soon to collect her things and say good-bye.

She hadn't seen or contacted Mike since before Gabriel's accident, so he could not have known she'd admitted the affair to Gabriel, and used the past tense when she did. She hadn't consciously decided to arrive at her workplace at lunchtime. Mike was on his way outside and stopped short when he saw her. He motioned to the bench where they had often sat together. Liz nodded and followed him. Her limbs felt suspended on strings, like a marionette.

"I wanted to call," he said.

"It's okay."

"You look like shit, Liz."

She met his gaze and held it. "I am shit."

The words hit him hard, and he winced. "What can I say that would help?"

"It's not a situation for words. It's a situation for get-the-hell-out."

He nodded. He wasn't going to bullshit her, and she was grateful. A pang of regret, in anticipation of missing him, shot through her, and was immediately and convincingly clobbered by a barrage of guilt.

He said, "Knowing you, you don't want to hear this—"

"I hate speeches that start that way."

"But I might not get another chance. Or I might get one and not take it, so please listen."

"Okay."

His expression held her fast. "Don't give up. Promise me you won't give up."

She stared at the ground and shook her head.

"You're not going to promise? Then try this. Promise me you will remember that I asked you not to give up." He leaned down to see her face. "Can you do that?"

"Yes," she whispered. "I promise."

Valerie wanted to share her two-bedroom condo in Mountain View, but Liz declined in favor of a one-bedroom rental in the same complex. Her friend was right about the prevalence of medical device companies in the area. Liz applied for five openings and was offered three. She decided on Paradynamics because it afforded the best chance to develop her skills and improve the lives of amputees. Several months in, a pharmaceutical giant gobbled up the company. Liz began spending more time in meetings than at the bench, so she moved to Kinesia Labs, where she headed up her own research unit.

She'd been working there a year before she met Dante. Over the next eighteen months, they went from regular weekend dates to seeing each other three times a week. She left a few things at Dante's house, as a practicality. In January, shortly after they returned from Oaxaca and the radish festival, the owner of Liz's condo put it on the market. Before she could decide whether to rent or buy, Dante asked her to move in. He had plenty of room, he said, holding her hand in his. Too much for one person. He must have seen fear flash across her face, because he added, "And I love you very much." Her hand jerked from his grasp, then paused in midair. She remembered her promise to Mike.

Chapter Twenty-Three

At Palisade Lake frost coated the tent and a skin of ice had formed on the water bottles they'd left outside. Liz hopped from one foot to the other waiting for the water to boil. The rustle of nylon against nylon from the tent told her Dante was awake and getting dressed.

Paul came from behind the stand of trees dividing the campsite. "Knock, knock."

She waved him over. He informed Liz that he and Linda would be continuing on at least as far as the junction with the trail to Kearsarge Pass, two days from here. Another trail led out of the Sierra before the Kearsarge trail, he said, but it was very steep and not well maintained, and ended at an obscure trailhead. If Linda couldn't complete the trip, they'd go over Kearsarge and catch a ride into Independence.

"It's sad to think you might not finish," she said.

"We promised each other when we started that we wouldn't endanger ourselves. It's the journey, right?"

"Absolutely."

Liz and Dante left first, having told the McCartneys they'd meet at Lake Marjorie, just shy of Pinchot Pass, if not before. Dante led. The trail followed the shape of the lake, on a high traverse. Liz's legs were chilled, and stiff from yesterday's ascent of the Golden Staircase. She thought of Linda, imagined her stitches would pull as she walked, but doubted it would slow her down much. Was there something in Linda's history that had made her so determined? And in Paul's, to be so daring in his love for her? Perhaps it was simply their personalities, and not life that had sculpted the McCartneys along the way. Who was to say she herself would have turned out differently if she'd been blessed with a doting mother, a devoted father and a houseful of siblings? At nearly thirty, she wasn't sure the answer mattered. Whatever the admixture of nature and nurture, it was her life, and her mess. She could bemoan the lack of scaffolding she'd been provided in building her life, but it was immaterial. She focused her attention on the trail at her feet.

Before long, Upper Palisade Lake was in sight. As they climbed toward the pass, they could finally see the entire Palisade Range that had loomed over their campsite. The massive peaks, all over fourteen thousand feet, dwarfed everything in the vicinity. The lakes were puddles, and Linda and Paul, now visible along the margin of the lower lake, were ants.

Liz and Dante came over a rise, and he stopped short, pointing with his pole at two figures resting on a boulder a hundred yards ahead. The Root brothers. "We'll just go past them, okay, Liz?"

She chewed on her lip and said nothing.

The Roots watched them approach. She had the feeling they'd been waiting for them.

"Good morning," Rodell said, lifting a piece of jerky in the air.

Dante offered a muted hello. Liz nodded.

Payton got up, blocking the trail. "Chilly this morning, isn't it?"

Dante said, "Not too bad once you're moving."

"Well, you're not moving now, are you, *hombre*?"

Dante stood straighter. "What is your motivation, Payton? Do you and your brother find sport in coming to this beautiful place"—he gestured at the mountains and sky—"with the goal of bothering people?"

The large man shook his head slowly. "Now, I really did like you. You're cute. Like those little dogs. What do you call them, Rodell?"

"Chihuahuas."

"Yeah, them. But maybe I'm changing my mind."

Liz felt Dante tense beside her. Her eyes fell to one of the Roots' backpacks. A string of clawed feet, with dried blood and tufts of fur, hung from a strap. She examined what Rodell was holding at his side. It wasn't jerky at all, but a small charred leg. Her stomach turned and bile rose at the back of her throat. She scanned for a detour around these men, but the slope was steep and clogged with large boulders.

"Let's drop it," she said. "We don't need to like one another. It's a big place."

Payton grinned at her and ran a palm along his thigh. A shiver skittered down her spine. "It's big, all right, but the trail is just a skinny little thing. Doesn't take much to create an inconvenience, as you can see."

"Speaking of which," Dante said, "when were you on the Golden Staircase yesterday?"

"Yesterday? Can't remember. Do you remember, Rodell?"

He rubbed his whiskers theatrically. "No, no, can't say as I do."

"Mr. Hollywood was there, though, wasn't he?"

"Yes, he sure was. Swearing a blue streak the whole way up."

Payton frowned. "Took the Lord's name in vain on multiple occasions."

"We don't approve, do we, Payton?"

"No, we certainly don't."

"Daddy used to swear a blue streak. Even on the Lord's day."

"He did indeed."

"Poor Mama. Every swearword was a knife through her heart." The younger brother pinched the corners of his eyes with dirty fingers. "All that swearing and drinking. And raising a hand to her! Knocked two teeth out once, remember?" Payton rested a hand on his brother's shoulder. Rodell exhaled and shook his head slowly. "Came in the door and there she was. Lying on the floor, bleeding and moaning."

They stood in silent reflection, oblivious to their audience. Liz held her breath. All around, the granite waited.

"That was a good dare," Payton whispered. "We fixed him, didn't we, Rodell?"

Rodell patted his brother's hand and looked up at him. A grin spread like oil across his face.

"There'll be no more swearing from Daddy."

Payton's eyes shone with affection. "That was the best dare you ever gave me."

"So far, Payton. So far."

Payton had moved toward his brother, leaving a narrow gap, but Liz's legs were locked solid. Dante reached for her hand, and their poles, which dangled from their wrists, tapped. The sharp clinking sound in the empty morning released her. She tugged Dante's hand as a signal, then let go and darted forward, squeezing past Payton, brushing his shoulder. Dante was right behind her. Liz hurried up the trail, head down, her breath loud in her ears. She didn't look back until they were nearly at the pass.

As they ascended the switchbacks below Mather Pass, they discussed whether to talk to a ranger about the Roots. The next station was at Bench Lake, about a mile before Lake Marjorie—that evening's destination. The problem lay, they agreed, in what to say. The Roots had made no direct threats, nor had they behaved illegally. Even collecting marmot feet was within the bounds of the law, if outside the bounds of good taste.

"What do you think happened to their father?" Dante said.

Liz pictured a desiccated souvenir—an ear, or a finger—then chased the image from her mind. Her imagination was running ahead of the evidence, and beyond common sense. "They could have scared him off, or turned him in. For some reason, they want us to think the worst."

"It's working."

They removed their packs at the top of the pass and had a quick drink and a snack. Looking north the way they'd come, they were relieved to see the McCartneys a good distance ahead of the Roots who, having run out of passersby, had abandoned their troll-like position on the trail.

Liz said, "Let's camp well off the trail tonight."

"To hide from them?"

"Yes. As a precaution."

"What about Paul and Linda?"

"They'll be fine. The Roots don't seem interested in them."

Dante frowned. "You think that boulder was meant for us?"

"Maybe."

He paused, considering. "I suppose it wouldn't hurt to be cautious." He stashed his water bottle and put on his pack. "Shall we?"

To the south lay a surreal vista. A barren basin spread a thousand feet below, two miles wide and long, dotted with small blue-green lakes and nothing else. Liz and Dante began the descent along switchbacks carved in a vertical wall. With each turn, the desolate floor grew nearer, but no less foreign. A miniature lake, as green as an emerald, appeared at the base of the wall. The angle of the light created sparkles floating above the surface like hovering dragonflies. The scene was stunningly beautiful, but haunting in its lifelessness. Aside from the path, whatever humans had undertaken here had left no trace.

Liz crossed this rocky void, propelled from behind by her memory of the hostile stances and dark whisperings of the Root brothers, and pulled by the empty trail ahead of her, as if a gigantic winch sat atop Mount Whitney, reeling her in, ever southward. She felt the pull in her belly, and lower, as a cramp. An unseen knuckle pressed and twisted, releasing an ache that pulsed like a small beating heart.

She stumbled.

The tip of her pole screeched across a flat rock. Her arm collapsed and her knee hit the ground. The pack slid sideways and she toppled backward onto it.

She regarded the empty sky. That Color.

Dante appeared above her. "You okay?"

She nodded, but wasn't certain. She unclasped her pack and wriggled free. Dante pulled her to standing.

"What happened?" he asked, scanning the area for clues as to how she could have fallen on level terrain.

"A moment's inattention." She brushed off her knees. "Doesn't take long to be careless."

She'd gone to the doctor to confirm the results of the home pregnancy test, but she hadn't thought through what she would say at her appointment. Each day since the home test, she expected her period. She was due to start the John Muir Trail in three weeks. Her plans were set. Her menstrual cycle would resume, she would marvel at her lucky break and walk into the wilderness.

A nurse appeared holding a clipboard and called her name. As Liz set the magazine on the side table, she imagined the doctor watching her for a reaction to the news that was not news, but a denial of her denial. She could not anticipate her own reaction. Either she or the doctor would glance at her ringless hand.

She put on the gown and folded her clothes neatly upon the chair. The nurse returned, took her blood pressure and checked her pulse. The word "procedure" winked on and off in Liz's consciousness, helped along by the tray of metal tools beside the sink and bare stirrups at the end of the exam table. Intellectually she knew the scene was identical whether you welcomed the baby or not, but her history in such rooms (and they were all the same) was only ever about preventing pregnancy and sexual diseases. On the wall to her left, an innocuous painting of a house among windswept dunes evoked nothing.

Naked under thin cotton, she felt more child

than woman. "Mother" she could not imagine. Her own mother came vaguely to mind, then wandered off, distracted.

She could not swell with life. Much of the time she barely managed to blow warmth to the edges of her own existence. She hadn't given up on love—not yet—but neither could she support another life. She would cave.

The doctor knocked and entered. Liz remembered Dante had business in Atlanta the following week. By the time the doctor returned the speculum to the tray and asked her to sit up, she knew what she would do.

Leave no trace.

At Lake Marjorie they searched for twenty minutes before locating a campsite hidden from the trail, a hundred feet above the lake, tucked behind boulders the size of trucks. Their first chore was to fill all their water containers— including the cooking pot—so they wouldn't have to venture down to the exposed shore until they set out the next morning. They worked quickly and in silence, taking turns pumping the filter. They washed their faces and hands in the icy water, and scurried up the slope without bothering to dry off.

While Liz erected the tent, Dante set up the kitchen and inflated the mattresses. Every few minutes he climbed atop the boulders and peered over the edge to scout for Paul and Linda, calling himself Tonto.

"What are you planning to do when you see them?" Liz asked. "There's no space for them to camp up here."

"I want to make sure Linda's all right."

"I've been concerned about her, too. But it's only four o'clock. Even if they don't get here for another two hours, it'll still be light. They'll make camp by the lake."

A half hour later, he waved her up to his perch. "Look who's here."

She flattened her body on the sun-warmed stone. Payton and Rodell strode along the lake margin, heads down. "They don't seem to be looking for a site. Maybe they're going up over the pass."

"Another one? This late in the day?"

"Probably another dare in contention for a Darwin Award."

"They don't know where we are, so you can relax."

A small reprieve.

A while later the evening breeze carried voices from below. The McCartneys had arrived and ditched their packs. Linda sat on a log while Paul inspected the two campsites visible from the trail.

Dante opened his mouth to call to them, but Liz placed a hand on his arm. "The Roots could be within earshot. Paul and Linda seem perfectly fine."

"You're right, *carina*." He slid down the rock, crossed to the kitchen area and bent to stir the soup. "We'll talk to them tomorrow. We could even hike together."

"Safety in numbers?"

"Yes, as you are worried about the Roots."

She noticed he didn't say "we." "Maybe."

Dante put the lid on and turned to her. "Why 'maybe'?"

"I guess I'm still hoping this'll become the hike I imagined."

His face drooped.

"I didn't mean the solo part," she said, laying a hand on his cheek. "I meant the contemplative, serene part. Or, at the very least, the not-creeped-out-by-stalkers part. Or the not-attacked-by-falling-rocks part."

"Or the not-confess-your-most-shameful-moments part?"

"Yeah. That."

She swallowed hard against the lump in her throat and, on the pretense of assembling the bowls and sporks, turned away.

"I want to tell you something, Liz."

She noted his serious tone and lowered herself onto a rock. "What is it?"

"When we were in Mexico with my family, I only shared part of the conversation I had with my parents about my sister. And about Rico's role in the family business." He would not meet her gaze. "I was upset about Emilia. Maybe I was seeing it through your eyes a little. My parents— my father—was judging Emilia without even talking to her, and was taking Rico s side. I told him that just because Rico was his right-hand man—excuse me, *his son*—didn't mean his daughter should count for nothing."

"What did he say?"

"He said his mind was made up and it wasn't my business." He looked at Liz with a pained expression. "I lost my temper."

"Did you say something you didn't mean? Couldn't you simply apologize?"

"That's the problem. I told the truth. I admitted that I never intended to work with him—for him. I knew it before I even left for college. I never told him because he wouldn't have paid for it. I couldn't have gone." He studied her, measuring her reaction.

Six years of full tuition, plus full support in the lifestyle to which Dante had been accustomed. A quarter of a million dollars, or more. No wonder Señor Espinoza was miffed. On the other hand, Dante was determined to make it on his own, and believed an American education was his ticket, despite the fact that lots of people with fewer advantages than he enjoyed succeeded without a free ride to a U.S. college. "I'm not sure what to think."

"You can say it. It was wrong."

"Did you know it at the time?"

"Yes. But I knew what I wanted. I was determined. I felt my father owed me for being so unreasonable about my future."

"What do you think now?"

He let out a sigh and ran a hand through his hair. "I feel guilty. I'm considering paying him back when I can."

"He'd probably respect that."

"Only if I included interest."

Liz could sympathize with Dante's desire for an American education, but was surprised he'd strung his father along for so many years. She wondered whether Dante's actions were fueled as much out of anger at being pushed into the family business as out of determination to earn a premium degree in the land of opportunity. She herself had never put her hand in her pocket for her schooling, and was reticent to judge. And at the moment, it mattered more to her that he had told her.

"Let's hit the tent," she said, putting her arms around him. He returned her embrace, his arms strong and warm against her back. They held each other as the wind whistled low between the peaks and swept the last of the day into the valleys below. In the remaining shreds of light, they tucked their packs and gear under the boughs of a stout pine, climbed into the tent and zipped themselves in.

Early the next morning, the sun cast a pale yellow glow on the peaks above the lake. Dante noticed the McCartneys were up, so he and Liz clambered down the hill and explained why they had kept to themselves last night. Paul and Linda agreed the Roots probably had continued over Pinchot Pass.

"I'd be happy to have seen the last of them," Paul said. "Bloody weird pair."

Liz asked Linda, "How's your leg?"

"Not too bad. When it hurts in the night I just stick it out of the sleeping bag and it goes numb in a few minutes."

The couples separated to break camp, then set off together for the Rae Lakes, sixteen miles away.

No two passes they'd encountered had been the same: a notch sliced in the V between sharp peaks, a flat gravel lot on a broad saddle, or a site for a shelter, such as Muir Hut. Pinchot Pass was the highest thus far, and Liz was surprised to arrive there so easily along a gradual incline. Reaching a pass was usually cause for a small celebration, but not at Pinchot. Though early in the day, the wind howled from the north, swept up the slope and hurled itself over the edge with icy abandon.

"I lived in Wales for a year," Linda said, yanking the collar of her jacket tighter. "They called winds like this 'lazy.' "

"Why?" asked Dante. "Doesn't feel lazy to me."

"Because instead of going around you, it goes straight through."

They turned their backs to the wind and descended. As on Mather Pass, the north side of Pinchot was precipitous. Narrow switchbacks covered in broken stone prompted Liz to watch her step. At the bottom, she paused and craned her neck to see the way they had come, but the rock wall was too steep and she lost the trace of the trail halfway up. She turned her gaze south to admire Mount Cedric Wright, so broad and imposing it might have been a range unto itself. She remembered from the guidebook Cedric Wright had been a mentor and friend to Ansel Adams. Wright's ashes had been scattered on this peak, above which a few small clouds had already gathered. She shivered at the prospect of a change in weather.

After a water break, Dante walked in front, and Liz allowed the gap between them to grow until she could no longer hear the tap of his poles on the rocks or the crunch of his boots on the ground. If she lifted her head, she could see him—the terrain was open, for the most part—but if she gazed into the middle distance and allowed her mind to wander, she was alone.

She wondered if Dante's father would ever forgive his son, and if repaying the debt would matter. She wondered if forgiveness was real. Perhaps it could be, for the one doing the forgiving. But for her there was no possibility of a clear conscience, merely the weak absolution of honesty, of confession. If only she had been raised Catholic—or within another religion that embraced the concept—she might find forgiveness and believe in it. But faith was not part of her fiber. She could not buy into the cycle of sin and penance, of death and resurrection. She would always remember what she had done and it would always sting. She would not be washed clean.

But next to this certainty was another truth: mornings on the trail gave her hope. Hope of what precisely, she couldn't say. Each morning of this journey, even after a terrible night, proposed a new beginning. She crawled out of the tent and started over by breaking camp—undoing what she had constructed the night before. When it was as it had been, save for a few boot marks, she returned to the task of walking. But she did not walk over the same ground—everything was new, in the intricate and fractal sameness of rock, lake and sky.

Perhaps that was why she had confessed, and would confess again. Not because she held out hope for forgiveness—it wasn't in her even if it was in Dante—but because there would always be morning. When she had told Dante everything, their relationship would die. The sadness of the fact sat heavy and full in her heart. But the unfathomable emerald lakes and the towering mountains that cared nothing for the heavens into which they reached, proved the next day would be a new one and she would begin again. Even if it was alone.

Chapter Twenty-Four

By noon they'd covered ten miles and dropped thirty-five hundred feet in elevation. Woods Creek followed them much of the way, a cascading rush of white water pausing briefly in bottle green pools, only to tumble down noisily once more.

The trail veered sharply left. Dante stopped and Liz came alongside to stare at the elaborate suspension bridge before them. Tall wooden towers on either bank anchored steel cables supporting a narrow walkway thirty feet above Woods Creek. Undergrowth blocked Liz's view of the far bank, but she estimated the span to be a hundred feet.

"How weird to find such a fancy structure here," Dante said, not having read the guidebooks.

"How convenient."

The McCartneys arrived and Liz led them, single file, up the dozen wooden steps to the beginning of the span. A sign warned them to cross one at a time.

"Looks like you're first," Linda said to Liz.

The construction inspired confidence, as cables

had been strung horizontally at both waist and knee level, and reinforced vertically every four feet. She placed her hands on the lateral cables and stepped carefully onto the wood slats. The bridge undulated. She concentrated on staying centered and walked with measured steps to minimize sway. Far below, foaming torrents of water exploded against boulders.

"Take your time," Dante called over the roaring current. "I'm in no rush."

Two-thirds of the way across, she spotted a pair of sunglasses lying on the bridge. She crouched slowly to pick them up, aware she was risking losing her balance, but feeling compelled nonetheless. Before her hand touched the glasses, she knew they were Brensen's. He was never without them. She examined them in her hand, and a shadow of apprehension passed through her.

"Liz!" Dante's shout was nearly drowned out. "What's wrong?"

She tucked the glasses into her shirt pocket and, hands on the cables, carefully pulled herself up. As she rose, her attention snagged on an object near the water's edge. Something dark blue, on top of a half-submerged log. An arm. Beyond the log was a boulder. A hiking boot, toe pointed to the sky, protruded from behind.

Her stomach rolled, and she gripped the cables more tightly.

Paul shouted, but the river carried the words away.

Her mouth went dry. She scanned the riverbank ahead, searching for anything out of place. There wasn't much vegetation on this side, and few places to hide. Level with the bridge was a campsite with picnic tables and two bear lockers. Empty.

Dante and the others were calling to her, their voices increasingly frantic. The bridge rocked—someone stepped onto it—and she bent her knees to absorb the wave. It had to be Dante, or maybe Paul, coming to see what the problem was.

"Stop!" she shouted at the top of her lungs, and continued across, keeping her focus on the tower in front of her, and a strong grip on the cables in case the bridge moved again.

She stepped off the bridge onto the landing, checked her surroundings again, and turned, placing a hand on the cable supports to steady herself. Dante was halfway across, his face dark with concern. She avoided glancing at Brensen—if that's who was lying in the river—because she feared she'd alarm Dante and cause him to lose his balance. He stared straight ahead, walking more briskly than she expected, and was soon at her side.

"What's wrong? Why did you bend down?"

Liz led him down the wood planks and onto firm ground. She glanced over his shoulder. Linda was crossing.

She fished the glasses out of her pocket. "Aren't these Brensen's?"

"I think so. But why—"

"I saw something from the bridge."

"What 'something'?"

"Someone. In the river."

"Doing what?"

Her mouth was cottony. She gripped Dante's arm. "Lying there."

"What? We should go help them! Show me!"

Her throat closed and a wave of nausea flooded her. "I think it's too late. I—"

"Too late?" He grabbed her shoulder. "Liz, we must look!"

He was right. All she'd seen was an arm. And a foot. But she didn't want to look. Because she already knew.

Linda appeared behind Dante. "What's the matter?"

Dante undid his hip belt and dropped his pack. "Someone's lying in the river."

Linda gasped and turned to Liz, who pointed downstream. Dante headed off. Liz ditched her pack and jogged to catch up to him. As they picked their way down the boulder-strewn embankment, Liz kept an eye out for movement in the woods to her left.

Liz directed Dante. "A little farther downstream."

They rounded a small stand of pines and stopped short. There was a hiker in a blue shirt, a few yards from shore, face down in the water.

His pack lay twisted off one shoulder, as if it had come off, or been torn off, when he fell. It was a silver-and-red Osprey. Brensen's. Liz's heart raced and she shivered. Brensen's free arm—the one she had seen from the bridge—lay draped over a log, bent at an unnatural angle.

Dante took a step forward. "*Dios mio*! Brensen! Brensen!" The actor lay unmoving. "He looks dead!"

"I know!"

"Should we make certain?"

Liz nodded, then regretted it. Her legs felt encased in hard plastic as she stepped across the rocks and squatted on a flat stone near Brensen's head. She took a deep breath and shook his shoulder. Water splashed over the toe of her boot.

A fly landed on the nape of Brensen's neck and climbed over a fold in his shirt. A white smear of sunscreen coated the edge of his ear. Precaution for the long run.

She balked at turning him over and exposing his face. Instead, she reached for the wrist that lay on the log. The skin was paler than the moon. Her fingers found the spot between wrist bone and tendon, but could not find a pulse. His skin felt cold, but so were her fingers. She closed her eyes and swayed, as if she were on the bridge. Behind her, she heard Linda sobbing.

Paul appeared and knelt beside her. "Jesus Christ. What the hell happened here?"

"He's dead." A hoarse whisper was all she could manage.

"It certainly appears that way. Are you okay?"

She swallowed, afraid if she spoke she would burst into tears.

Paul regarded her steadily, but she could see he was rattled, too. "Let's just get him out of the river, okay?"

She nodded, took a deep breath and steeled herself.

"Here, help me turn him over."

It wasn't that simple.

Paul straddled two rocks and struggled to lift one end of Brensen's pack out of the river, but could only raise it a few inches. "I think his arm is caught on something." He sat back on his haunches. "Dante! Can you give us a hand?"

Dante crossed to them, and he and Liz raised the waterlogged pack. Paul, grimacing, pulled on Brensen's shoulder with one hand, and reached underneath to free the arm, the frigid water rising to his armpit. Liz glimpsed Brensen's face. A rough gash sliced diagonally across his forehead, the edges ragged. His nose was broken and bruised, his lips bloodless. She looked away.

The arm broke free and flipped out of the water, hitting Paul in the face. Paul stumbled, splashing water everywhere, then regained his balance. Liz and Dante yanked the pack out of the way, and dragged it to shore.

Paul crouched with Brensen's torso propped against his knee. The dead man's chin had fallen onto his chest, as if he were napping on a bus. Paul stared at Linda, his jaw set. "I don't suppose we can leave the poor bastard where he is."

She wiped her nose with her sleeve and shook her head.

"He's soaked. It'll take all of us."

Her face crumpled. "Paul, I don't know if I can."

"Darling, you can. I know you can."

The men lifted Brensen by the shoulders and each woman hoisted a leg. Even with four of them, they had trouble negotiating the slick rocks and rushing current. Dante refused to look at the corpse and tripped twice, bringing everyone to a halt. They finally deposited Brensen on the sparse grass between the river and the trail. Liz's breath hitched in her chest as she went to Brensen's pack, unsnapped his towel and laid it across his face. They stood over him without speaking for a moment. Linda was hunched, crying. Paul pulled her to him and led her away to where they had left their packs. Dante dropped to his knees next to Brensen, clasped his hands to his chest and murmured a prayer. The sight of this simple, honest gesture overwhelmed Liz, but she couldn't leave. Instead she gazed ahead at the bridge and the river, the image swimming before her. The rushing of the water droned in her head.

Dante wavered as he got to his feet. He took her

hand and they joined the McCartneys at a picnic table. It was past lunchtime but no one got out their food. Linda slumped over the table, head on her arms. Paul rested a hand on her back. Away from the dead body, Liz's head cleared a little. She studied the bridge and the woods, intent.

Dante handed her a water bottle. "What are you looking for?"

"Our friends the Roots."

"You think they did this?"

"It's possible. They didn't exactly take a shine to Mr. Hollywood. He broke the code."

Dante nodded.

Paul glanced downstream. "Of course, where we found him is also consistent with falling off the bridge."

Liz pointed at the structure. "I know it sways, but it'd be hard to fall off without help."

Linda raised her head. The creases in her face had deepened since the morning "Remember, Brensen had a concussion not three days ago. He was falling over his own feet."

"What about his forehead?" Dante said, squinting to shut out the image. "Could that have happened when he fell?"

"Sure," Paul said.

Liz shrugged. Paul's hypothesis was as valid as hers and she was too upset to debate it. They couldn't establish cause of death sitting there, but they did need a plan.

Hands trembling, she pulled the map out of her pocket, spread it on the table and pointed to their current location. "We're fifteen point four miles from Roads End, where I think there's a permit station, which may or may not be open. Cedar Grove is another six miles."

"So at least another day's hiking in that direction," Paul said.

"Right. But the Rae Lakes ranger station is seven miles this way." She indicated south on the JMT.

"Isn't that where we were going anyway?" Dante said.

"Yes."

"But the ranger may not be there."

"They're not innkeepers," Paul said. "They patrol the trail."

"They pick up trash," Linda added. "And help hikers in trouble." Her voice caught.

Paul gave her a sympathetic look. "How much farther from Rae Lakes to civilization?"

Liz added up the mileage for each segment. "Exactly twelve miles to the Onion Valley trailhead. Then we could hitch a ride into Independence."

"So, that's our plan. But you and Dante don't have to hike out. Two people are more than enough to report a dead body."

That depends on how you think it got that way, Liz thought.

Dante turned to Liz. "Paul's right. We haven't got far to go."

"True." She held his gaze, acknowledging his commitment to finish the hike. "Let's see what happens at Rae Lakes, okay?"

Paul pulled the towel off Brensen's head and took a photo to show the authorities. Liz opened the actor's waterlogged pack and removed a tent.

"What do you want that for?" Dante said.

"To wrap him up. A winding sheet."

"We're going to bury him?"

"No. We're discouraging the animals."

Dante blanched and sat heavily on a rock. "Don't tell me anything else."

She slipped the tent from its sack and positioned the orange rectangle next to Brensen. The four of them lifted him onto it, everyone looking somewhere other than at his face. Liz shook out the fly and draped it over the body. Linda retrieved the guy lines from a small pouch that had fallen to the ground. Paul hoisted the head end of the bundle, then the foot end so the women could loop the lengths of cord around it in four sections, tucking the fly under the body. A wave of nausea rolled through Liz each time her hands contacted the solidity of Brensen's flesh beneath his sodden clothing. She drew the last length of cord around his ankles and crawled away to a rock where she hugged her knees to her chest. Paul tied the knots while everyone looked on. Dante closed Brensen's pack, propped it against a tree and stood back from the others.

Brensen lay encased in his orange nylon shroud. They'd done everything they could. But despite her desire to leave this tragedy behind, Liz was reluctant to leave. It seemed wrong to abandon him here where it would soon be dark and cold. She choked back tears and chewed her lip. It made no sense to be troubled by the vulnerability of the dead.

Chapter Twenty-Five

She hadn't noticed the sky. Lost in thought about Brensen and alert for the possibility of encountering the Root brothers, she hadn't registered the gradual loss of blue until an hour and a half after they left the bridge, and Brensen's body, behind. Hunger had overcome the shock of his death, and the four of them stopped to eat in the shade. Liz tipped her head back while taking a drink and saw the clouds, already tall and thick, blocking the sun.

"Is it me, or is it getting humid?" Dante said, plucking his shirt away from his body.

"It's sticky, all right. Could turn into a storm."

Dante nodded at the McCartneys, resting nearby. Linda was lying on her back with her arms across her face. Paul was studying a map. "Are we waiting for them?"

"It makes sense to talk to the ranger about Brensen together."

Linda unfolded her arms and rose with labored movements. She noticed Liz and Dane watching her and managed a weak smile. "You kids ready to rock?"

The trail insisted they make up all the elevation gain they'd lost that morning. Up they went, through the heat of the afternoon, pausing only to filter and drink water. They came to Arrowhead Lake, clogged with algae and sedge around its margin, the water an unnaturally vivid green. Liz doubted it would have been safe to drink even after filtration. They continued past the lake without a word, bearing the heat and grief individually.

In the late afternoon, they arrived at the first of the Rae Lakes. The dark clouds rendered it a deep aquamarine, the water so clear Liz could perceive sharp edges of submerged rocks thirty feet out. The bizarre curved peak of Fin Dome rose from the lake's distant shore.

A mile farther they reached the turnoff for the ranger station, and minutes later approached a log cabin set upon a stone foundation. Liz didn't bother to remove her pack before ascending the steps to the narrow porch. She felt the emptiness of the cabin even before she called hello. When no one answered, she knocked.

Dante came up beside her. "They're gone?"

"And there's no note. They're supposed to let hikers know when they'll be back."

Liz gave a thumbs-down signal to Paul and Linda, who were waiting a short distance away, and wondered whether she ought to add the ranger to the list of people she was concerned about.

She suggested camping at the cabin, in case the ranger returned, leaving unsaid how much safer she would feel next to this sturdy building in a thunderstorm. But there was room only for two to sleep on the porch and no patch of ground in the vicinity flat enough to accommodate a tent.

They broke up in pairs to search for campsites. After a half an hour, the women found a small secluded site, well away from the lake edge and the trail, partially protected by a stand of white-bark pines.

Linda leaned against a tree trunk. "Do you mind if we take this one? I'm not feeling so great."

Liz laid her hand on the woman's forehead. "You've got a fever."

Linda sat on a log and straightened her injured leg. Liz rolled up the pant leg. The flesh around the wound was swollen and red. Droplets of white pus oozed from between the stitches.

"It started itching this morning. I should've said something to Paul, but I was hoping it'd just go away. He'd have been so worried. Then the whole thing with Brensen—"

Liz touched the inflamed skin and Linda flinched. Liz put her hand over her friend's. A fat raindrop landed on her knuckle. "I'll go find Paul."

The men had located a site fifty yards away, on the other side of a rocky knoll, wedged between a cluster of boulders and a shoulder-high granite bench. After learning of Linda's condition, Paul agreed they would sleep there, as it promised better protection from the elements. Liz led the way to the other campsite.

Once the three of them rejoined Linda, Paul knelt in front of her. "Let's have a look, darling." He inspected the wound and gently rolled down his wife's pant leg. "Tequila and acetaminophen this evening, and then, I think, an early start. Twelve quick miles, some antibiotics and a pizza, and you'll be as fit as a fiddle."

"You're fretting, Paul. Don't. I'll be fine."

Liz said, "Do you want us to go with you? Just in case?"

Linda and Paul spoke at the same time. "We'll be fine." They laughed lightly. Linda added, "If our situations were reversed, we'd keep going. It's only a few more days." Paul nodded.

Liz said, "We haven't really had a chance to talk about it." And her own thoughts on the subject had been muddled. She scuffed her boots in the dirt. It seemed wrong to be concerned with finishing a hike when someone had died, although nothing anyone did or didn't do would bring

Brensen back. Yet the decision was before them. Maybe all she needed was distance from it. A night's sleep. A new morning, a fresh section of trail. It sounded simple, suddenly, to leave what had happened behind them, to continue as before. Even the specter of the Root brothers had become oddly familiar, as if they were an integral part of the JMT experience, and she might find their names ("Root, Payton; Root, Rodell") in the index of the guidebook. She didn't mention them again, however. They seemed to haunt only her.

Raindrops fell, widely spaced, splatting on the ground. The air grew dense.

Paul said, "We'd best get our tents up."

Dante pulled his wallet from the top of his pack, handed Paul a business card and shook his hand. "In case we don't see you in the morning. You know where to find us in the meantime."

"Thanks, mate. We'll expect a photo of you two on the summit."

Dante bent to kiss Linda on both cheeks. "I'll text you if I've got reception."

The image of their summit selfie flashed in Liz's mind, and the edges of her spirits lifted. The rain began to fall in earnest. She gave Paul a quick hug, then embraced Linda. "Take good care."

"You, too."

It was after six o'clock and Liz and Dante were rushing to set up camp. The rain fell from the sky in sheets and the wind off the lake hurled freezing water at them. Liz's numb hands fumbled with the guy lines, and twice a gust snatched the fly and tore it from her. She shouted at Dante to stop rummaging in his pack and hold down the fly so she could stake it. Once the tent was secure, they pulled rain covers over their packs and took refuge inside.

They jostled each other as they blew up the mattresses and arranged the sleeping bags, too exhausted to care about manners. As they changed into their sleeping outfits, their clothes stuck to their skin, and the tinny smell of ozone mixed with the odor of wet wool and mud. Liz was on the verge of bursting into tears, but fought it off. If she started she would not be able to stop. The shock of Brensen's death—and worry about its cause—on top of sixteen miles of strenuous hiking had left her shattered. Lifting each leg and reaching forward to put on her leggings was almost more than she could handle.

A crack of thunder made her jump. She lost her grip on the leggings and fell backward onto her bed. Another boom of thunder, farther off, rolled into the distance. Rain pelted the tent. She swiped her wet bangs from her forehead and reminded herself she was safe and on her way to being warm and dry.

Unlike Brensen. Accidentally or by foul play, either way he died a violent death, and a premature one. And for all his kvetching, he'd pulled himself together and accepted, if not embraced, the hike. He would've been able to reach for those experiences when he made the film. It might have been his best performance ever, not that she'd seen all his movies. She wondered if the movie would be canned, or if they'd cast someone else. It didn't matter. Brensen lay in the dark of the woods, encased in his tent. She shuddered.

Dante exhaled loudly as he lay down and cinched the bag around his shoulders. "Can you feel your feet?"

"Not yet." At last she succeeded in putting on her leggings. She slipped on her socks and hat, and snuggled deep into the bag, facing Dante. Only his eyes peered out between his hat and his cocoon.

"You okay?" he said.

"Probably not. But I'm so beat I can't be sure how I feel."

"I know what you mean. Maybe food will help." He extracted an arm from his bag and selected an energy bar from the pile of snacks between them—their dinner. Too much rain and too little enthusiasm for a cooked meal. He unwrapped the bar, handed it to her, and picked another for himself.

Her mouth flooded with saliva at the first taste of chocolate and berries. She chewed as if it were something she'd never done. Her mouth filled with sweetness. She took several more bites, chewing each with care. "Does yours taste unbelievably good?"

"I never thought I'd say this about a bar, but yes."

They ate and listened to the rain drumming the fly.

After a few minutes, Dante propped himself on an elbow and drank some water. "What's our plan, *carina*? Are we continuing toward Whitney?"

She'd posed this question to herself countless times over the seven miles since the bridge. All the logical answers had been the same: there was no reason not to continue. She'd come a long way —over a hundred eighty miles—and following the McCartneys over Kearsarge Pass to civilization would serve no purpose. Unless she simply wanted to quit. Unless the threat of stormy weather—both outside the tent and within her— had proven unbearable. Unless she believed the Root brothers posed a true threat to her safety.

"Liz?"

The amber glow through the tent fabric was fading fast. She could barely make out his face. The merest glint of diffused light was caught in the dark pools of his eyes.

"You want to, don't you, Dante?"

"I do. God help me."

Words formed on her lips. They may have arisen from an atypical impulse to follow instead of lead. Dante wanted to finish, and so should she. Days ago he promised her he would and was \ready to keep his word, despite everything. (Well, perhaps not everything. He didn't know everything.)

Her answer might have signaled resignation to her fate. She had never believed in fate, nor understood its attraction. But so little of what had happened on this hike seemed within her control; she may have to alter her view. At the very least, she could throw away her map and her compass. The trail, and all the forces it represented, were leading her inexorably south.

Really her answer was straightforward. It was what she had planned. What she had wanted. And it was certainly the rational choice.

"Me, too."

Chapter Twenty-Six

She zigzagged between wakefulness and sleep, falling into dreams that transmuted into nightmares. She'd jolt awake, or claw her way out of the dream, but snippets hung in her consciousness like spiderwebs, forestalling both relief and rest. The nightmares told no story. Kaleidoscopes of crumbling mountains, poisonous water, falling bodies (hers? or perhaps her mother's?), storms that made rivers run red and the earth beneath her feet alive with sparks, maps that could not be read and trails that wound in circles or led to the collapsing edge of a bottomless void. Within the arena of her dreaming mind, she had no agency and no hope, only fear. She was pure soulless adrenaline.

After each nightmare, her heart pounded and sweat ran off her forehead. She shivered in the dark of the tent until the hum of Dante's breathing gradually restored her and she fell into another dream. Finally, after what seemed like hours, her exhausted body prevailed and the cycle ended. From then until morning, she slept as if her fuse had been yanked out.

She awoke to brilliant light and shielded her eyes with her hand. The veils of sleep lifted from her mind and she realized it was so bright inside the tent because the fly was gone. She sat up, confused, and noticed Dante and his sleeping bag had also disappeared. Anxiety nudged her wider awake and she recalled, vaguely, having had nightmares. She pulled off her hat—why was it so hot?—shucked off her bag and knelt at the door, her fingers on the zipper. She smelled coffee and released the breath she'd been holding. Crises in the wilderness were never served with coffee.

"Dante?"

He stuck his head into the vestibule. "Good morning! You slept in. It's nearly eight thirty."

"You're kidding."

"I spread the fly out in the sun. It's almost dry. You want your coffee in there?"

"No, I'm coming."

She crawled out of the tent and crossed to a clump of trees a dozen yards away to pee. When she returned, she found Dante poring over the map. She kissed the top of his head and retrieved her coffee from a rock where he had set out bowls of granola and milk. The coffee was lukewarm but after two sips her mind began to clear. She looked out across the lake, mirror-still but for the rings of feeding trout. The mountains were bathed in sunlight, the pines in sharp silhouette, everything scoured clean by the rain. Above, the sky was a vault of blue. Nothing broke the stillness.

"Beautiful morning," she said.

"It is."

"Did you see Paul and Linda go by?"

"No, but I'm sure they are over Glen Pass by now." He looked up from the map. "What do you think? Should we camp close to Forester Pass tonight?"

"Forester already?" As soon as she said it, she knew it had to be. This morning, Glen Pass. Forester, the highest pass before the ascent to Whitney's summit, was next. After that, a night near Wallace Creek, then the last campsite before the final climb to Whitney. Three more nights. It hadn't registered before how near they were. "I think there are a couple spots next to a tarn"—

she moved behind him and pointed it out on the map—"there. At the origin of Bubbs Creek." Bubbs Creek. Woods Creek. The Woods Creek bridge. Brensen. She clasped her cup in both hands and lowered herself onto a log.

Dante regarded her. "Are you all right?"

"Just thinking about Brensen. I'd forgotten until now."

"Yes, I've been thinking of him, too." He folded the map and handed it to her. "Do you know if he had children?"

Her fingers paused for a beat on the smooth, plasticized paper before taking it from him. "No. I mean, I don't know."

"It'd be especially sad if he did."

"Yes, it would." She stood and tucked the map into her pocket. "Thanks for getting everything ready, Dante. And I'm sorry I'm so late. Let's eat, okay?"

They broke camp as quickly as they could and set off. The Rae Lakes sat at ten thousand five hundred feet and Glen Pass, two miles ahead, was a few feet shy of twelve thousand. They climbed steadily across talus slopes and wide granite slabs, pausing only to admire the changing view of the lakes below. More lakes appeared, tucked into the folds of mountains' cloaks, bottle green remnants of last winter's snow. Liz pictured everything around her blanketed in drifts of snow and wondered how anyone, or anything, could find its way through a boundless nowhere of white upon white. Perhaps the peaks and, at night, the stars above, were enough.

The pass was a knife edge. Talus tumbled precipitously down either side. The wind howled up the north side and over the gap. Liz and Dante stopped a moment for one last look behind them, then continued down switchbacks winding through rough scree until they found a windbreak. They shared a liter of water and some trail mix, and resumed their descent.

Below the tree line, the trail softened. They walked together through sparse lodgepole forest on a gentle downhill course. They had become so accustomed to their packs, it felt like a day hike. In a few hours, they might return to the trailhead parking lot and discuss what they should have for dinner on the ride home. Liz allowed this illusion to infuse her, and something akin to happiness lightened her step further.

They had lunch at an intersection. To the left was the trail the McCartneys would have taken earlier toward Kearsarge Pass and the Onion Valley trailhead. To the right was the way down to Charlotte Lake and another ranger station. As they ate, they talked about where Paul and Linda might be at that moment and whether there was any point whatsoever in seeking out the ranger.

"I've come to the conclusion they are mythical creatures," Dante said. "Like the Yeti."

"What about the one at Lyell Canyon?"

"A clever avatar, perhaps. Or a mirage."

"Maybe they're all together at a party. A ranger rave."

"Yes. Drinking home-brewed beer and swapping stories about ignorant hikers."

"And the worst thing they ever found at a campsite."

He grimaced and put a hand on his belly. "Stop right there."

Liz laughed for the first time in days, and Dante joined in, his tanned skin crinkling around his eyes. Their laughter died down, then stopped abruptly. Liz was thinking of a ranger finding Brensen wrapped in his tent, and she could see Dante was, too.

She bent her head as a swirl of emotion moved through her. "The authorities in Independence will know about him by the end of the day. I say we stick to the trail."

"Agreed." He reached for her hand. "And I'm so sorry, *carina*, that your trip has not been as you dreamed."

She smiled at his kindness, and at the notion that this trip was ever about fulfilling a dream. She'd sought clarity, solitude, escape and, under duress, the purge of confession. It was hardly the stuff of dreams.

They finished lunch and continued their descent on a south-facing slope toward Center Basin, a broad, sloping valley between the towers of East and West Vidette peaks. The afternoon sun bore down on them and they stopped at the crossing of Bubbs Creek to refresh their water bottles and themselves. The creek stayed on their right for most of the day, at times so close they felt spray from the cascades, other times so far below the trail Liz wondered if they might run short of drinking water. On the western slope, the aspens burned gold in the sun, quivering in wisps of breeze. The pines shaded the trail until late afternoon when Liz and Dante emerged onto a boulder-strewn plateau. The heat climbed onto their backs, and wrapped itself around them like swaddling cloth.

They spoke little. Liz concentrated on the trail in front of her, or on the sky, a blue as deep as a lake. The business of walking, and of ignoring the heat and her growing exhaustion, occupied her completely. They stopped to talk with the handful of hikers they passed. None were going past the Woods Creek bridge, so neither Liz nor Dante mentioned Brensen. They'd agreed earlier there was no point in casting a pall on someone's hike without reason. By now Liz thought it likely Brensen's death was accidental, and that she'd suspected the Roots only because of their interest in her. Nevertheless, she found herself rounding blind corners with a measure of caution and was relieved whenever the trail ahead of her was empty. The last time they'd seen Payton and Rodell was two days before at Lake Marjorie—a lifetime ago—and she hoped their paths would not cross again.

The pines thinned, the temperature soared and the twelve miles that had promised to be an easy day on paper were getting longer by the minute. Dante hiked behind Liz in silence, the click of their poles and the intermittent squawking of nutcrackers the only sound. Bubbs Creek dropped away from the trail and hid in the willows, running narrow and muffled at the bottom of a steep incline to their right. When they found its source, they could stop. Junction Peak stood in front of them, a monument of granite. The campsite was somewhere at its base, but not near enough.

It was past five o'clock when the terrain abruptly leveled and they came upon a circle of trees enclosing a campsite. Liz walked a hundred yards farther to ascertain that a narrow verdant channel contained running water. She lowered her pack onto the moss, took off her boots and socks and stuck her feet into the icy flow. Dante joined her, and they lay side by side, numbing their sore feet, eyes closed.

"How high are we?" Dante said.

"Eleven thousand, two hundred."

"Is that what Lake Marjorie was?"

"Uh-huh. And Rae Lakes was only seven hundred feet lower."

"But we climbed, what, thirty-five hundred feet today?"

"Give or take."

"And about the same the day before?"

"Yup."

He paused. "Has anyone ever told you the story of Sisyphus?"

They snacked on salami and trail mix, and made camp. Liz grabbed her towel and went to clean up in the stream while Dante began heating lentil soup for dinner. When she returned, he took his turn to bathe. The sun had dropped behind the peaks and a stiff wind blew down from the pass, so Liz donned her fleece jacket and hat. The skin on her face and arms was taut and raw from sun, wind and cold water. She blew on her hands to warm them and squatted on her haunches and stirred the soup, wincing at the pull in her Achilles tendons and lower back. She thought she really ought to do some stretches— she had kinks everywhere—but was too tired. Instead, she turned the flame down, moved to a rock and pulled her knees to her chest. Her legs felt like bags loaded with lead shot. Wasn't she supposed to be stronger each day? She tucked her head into her arms and allowed the weight of her exhaustion to sink through her, into the ground. If she could have summoned the energy, she'd have crawled into the tent and forgotten about dinner.

Dante nudged her from her fugue. "You okay? We should eat."

"I'm fine. Tired."

He handed her a steaming bowl and a spork and sat on a log facing her. She placed the bowl on her knees and cupped her hands over it, warming them. Dante stirred his soup and lifted a sporkful to examine it.

"Why is it," he said, "that everything we eat resembles baby food?"

"What?" Liz's knees wobbled and she gripped the edge of the bowl to stop its slide.

"Baby food. Oatmeal, mashed potatoes, pureed soup . . ."

Liz's breath caught in her chest. She let out a small cry before her throat snapped shut.

Dante stared at her. "What's wrong?"

She opened her mouth but it filled with cotton. Lies of cotton. Spun and stuffed full. Suffocating on cotton, clean and white. A white cotton gown. Cotton sponges to make it dry. Cotton gauze to soak up blood. She gripped the bowl tighter, ignoring the searing heat. An iron fist squeezed her lungs.

Dante was in front of her, on his knees. He took the soup from her. Held her hands. "You're shaking. What's wrong?" His eyes skipped across her face, trying to catch sight of the cause of her distress.

A broad ache searched through her, a dark,

roiling river. She heard herself moan. Dante's face became hazy. She blinked. Her face grew cold but he was no clearer.

He asked her again, more insistent. "What's wrong?"

She pushed the word against the cotton in her mouth. "Baby."

"What?"

"Baby." She'd never noticed how sad the word was. How delicate. Two tiny syllables ringing, the sound of glass wind chimes, set in motion by a breath. Baby baby baby baby baby. Two beats that could go on forever.

Not like death. Death was a hiss. You said it only once.

"Baby? Baby what?"

He uttered the words and they pierced her, blooming into a throbbing pain behind her eyes. She pulled her hand from his and pinched the bone between her eyes as hard as she could. The pain shrunk back. He lifted her chin but she dipped her head, avoiding his gaze. "Liz, what do you mean? Why are you crying?"

Was she? And what did she mean? There was a baby and now there was not. Was that the story? How could she not know? After all of this, how was it possible not to understand? What was perfectly clear at that moment, and in all the moments before, was that she was afraid to tell him. Afraid because he would no longer love her. Afraid because of the anguish she would cause. Afraid because of the person she would reveal herself to be. Her fear was a mountain so tall it had no summit, and so wide she could not circumvent it. It was unconquerable and inescapable, looming over her, casting a chilling shadow wherever she turned. She'd taken refuge there, alone. It was her place, bitter and cramped. She'd had enough of it. And Dante was begging her to relinquish the lie.

She raised her head to look out across the valley where the shadows of the peaks lay in great triangles upon the eastern slopes. She and Dante, alone in the middle of nowhere, with the truth.

She swallowed with effort, and spoke to the mountains. "A baby. There was a baby."

"What?"

She finally turned toward him. He waited, tension strung tight across his features.

"A month ago, I learned I was pregnant."

"You're pregnant?" He leaned closer, amazed. "Now?"

"No."

A long pause. The moments fell away until he spoke, his voice hushed. "What happened?"

"I had an abortion."

"What?"

"An abortion. I'm so sorry, Dante."

He blinked several times, then removed his hat and smoothed his hand over his still-damp hair.

He turned the hat over in his hands and put it back on. He shook his head, his lips pursed. "I don't believe it."

"But it's true."

"You're saying you were pregnant? And you didn't tell me?"

She nodded. "I was afraid to tell you. I should have. I'm sorry."

He shook his head again. "I'm not believing you, Liz. That you would do such a thing. That you would do it and not tell me. That you live with me, share a life with me, and then you would do this . . ." His voice trailed off and he hung his head.

Liz stared at the top of his hat where the stitching came together at the crown. She wanted to lay her hand on his head but did not dare. She was suddenly uncertain of him, and of herself. They were different now, on the other side of a divide, where a random drop might run in a different direction. Like the moment she told Gabriel about Mike. Her world, and Gabriel's, had pivoted, and tilted sharply, throwing him off, throwing him and his car into oblivion. The change in her was definite. Emptied of her lie, she was carved out, hollow as a cave.

She watched Dante now, her skin prickling, terrified of what she had set in motion, but unable to look away. He exhaled loudly and returned to sit on the log, hunched over, elbows on his knees.

He stared at her, his brow furrowed, his eyes begging her to tell him none of this was true. She looked away, shivering. It was getting dark, and cold.

After a few moments, he spoke in a whisper. "Was it mine?"

The question should not have surprised her. How much incrementally greater a sin was infidelity? Would it be easier for him if it had not been his? It didn't matter. She could not lie now, even for the right reason. "Yes." She choked on the lump in her throat. "Of course. Yes."

He rubbed his hand roughly across his face as if wiping away cobwebs. His lips drew tight. She opened her mouth to say more, to apologize again, but his eyes had turned hard and glassy.

"I would never have thought—" He stood abruptly, his arms stiff at his sides. "Remember two days ago I said I trusted you? What a mistake!" He spun away and stooped to pick up a stout branch. He ran three steps, smashed it against a tree and cried out—a sound of agony and fury that echoed back to them. A piece of branch landed near his foot and he kicked it, swearing. Pine needles scattered in a cloud of dust. Liz got up, without knowing why. He strode away several paces, his fists balled, then wheeled around and came to stand in front of her. His eyes were wild with pain. She wanted to flee or at least close her eyes, shut him out, but forced herself to absorb the fallout.

"How could you do this?"

She had no answer.

"A child is a gift from God! A gift!" He cupped his hands to show her. A cradle. "You may not believe this, but you know that I do. Don't you?" She nodded. He leaned closer, searching her face for someone he once knew. Dissatisfied with what he saw, his anger shifted an inch and became betrayal. "You, Elizabeth. The one I love with all my heart." Tears filled his eyes. "How could you?"

He stood there for an unbearably long time, waiting for an explanation she could not summon and that would never suffice. Finally, he picked up a water bottle and his bowl of soup, left the campsite, crossed the trail and disappeared behind an outcropping.

The cold had tunneled in to lie along her bones. She hugged herself, teeth chattering, staring at the spot where he had vanished.

He wouldn't go far, Liz knew. He couldn't. There was nowhere for either of them to go.

Chapter Twenty-Seven

For the second morning in a row, she awoke alone. The light was soft; it was dawn. The sound of rustling nylon and boots scratching on gravel came from outside. She put on her warm clothes and climbed out of the tent, dragging her sleeping bag and mattress behind her. Dante was stuffing gear into his pack, which rested against a pine. A half-finished bowl of granola was balanced on a nearby rock.

"Hi," Liz said.

"Hi." His voice was flat.

They'd not spoken the night before. Or, rather, she had said, "I'm sorry," several times and he had either put up his hand to stop her saying more, or ignored her. Between bouts of crying, self-recrimination and restless sleep, she'd spent the night thinking of what else to say. But if he wasn't ready to talk, her speeches were irrelevant. She'd have to be patient.

Her clean coffee cup stood next to his dirty one. She checked for water in the pot and lit the burner. "You want more coffee?"

"No, thanks."

Her stomach growled. She hadn't eaten last night. She poured granola, dehydrated blueberries and milk into her bowl and ate it standing up. When the water was ready, she stirred it into the coffee and chocolate mixture in her cup.

Dante cinched the top of his pack closed and applied sunscreen to his face and neck. His posture betrayed weariness, but he nevertheless appeared stronger than she'd ever seen him. She could discern the outline of his shoulder muscles under his shirt, and his calves were lean and brown. He had been hers. Pride rose in her before she could stifle it. But her shame was close at hand, and sickened her. Dante was too good for her. What goodness she might hold in her heart had been overshadowed by her actions, again and again. She wasn't a bad person, but she might as well be. She sipped her coffee to stem her tears.

He was ready to go. He swept his hand to indicate the tent and remaining gear. "You got all this?"

"Yes. But, Dante, we should talk."

"I'm sure you're right." He hoisted his pack onto his back and clicked the hip belt. "But I don't feel like it, Liz. I'm going to walk." He pointed at the sky. "It's a clear day, so you won't need me to hold your hand during a storm."

She winced. It wasn't like him to be mean. She had hurt him and he was biting back. "I'll see you at Wallace Creek, then, if not earlier."

He nodded, in acknowledgment if not in agreement. He slipped his hands through the loops of his poles, turned on his heels and left her and the empty tent behind.

She finished her coffee and packed everything, working deliberately. There was no reason to rush. She wasn't chasing Dante. If he needed to— or wanted to—he could camp on his own, without the tent. It'd be cold, but feasible. He had food in his bear can and she was pretty sure he had the water purification tablets. She had the map, but it was nearly impossible to get lost. When it came down to it, they didn't need each other.

She stowed all the gear in her pack and carried it to the small tarn east of the campsite. The surface was a sheet of steel. The mountains stood mute. Wisps of fog clung to the peaks, claiming them.

The trail to the pass lay to the right but she faced, instead, the way she had come. She couldn't see far down the trail—not more than a hundred yards—because it snaked around a corner, but she knew the way. The way back.

To what? At the moment, she didn't care. Like the winter fox that leaves a foot in a trap, she felt lighter. She'd done what she needed to do. It hurt like hell, but what of it?

She imagined retracing her steps, down where she'd gone up, up where she'd gone down, camping first where she had camped last. Perhaps she should walk at night—she had a headlamp—and sleep during the day. Some nights, there would be a moon. She'd enter the tent after dawn and gradually the sun would warm her as she slept. She'd be short of food, but she would need little, light as she was.

John Muir had crossed these mountains again and again with nothing more than a hunk of bread in his pocket. Of course, he had God with him and, he believed, all around.

She turned her back on the trail she had already walked and headed south, as always. She could not undo anything by retracing her steps, and her legs itched to climb. For two miles and two thousand vertical feet, she hiked without rest across talus, welcoming the ache in her thighs and the stab in her lungs. The tarn fell away behind her and the fog on the peaks evaporated. A trio of men in their early twenties passed her halfway up. She said hello and carried on. A few times she tried to discern where the trail found the pass, but as before it remained a mystery. Only the increasing proportion of sky to rock—and the decreasing availability of oxygen—told her she was near.

She came at last to a small level area surrounded by a scramble of boulders and marked with a sign: ENTERING SEQUOIA NATIONAL PARK. FORESTER PASS, ELEVATION 13,200 FEET. Liz felt light-headed and glanced at her watch. Quarter to ten. She considered stopping for a snack but a frigid wind pushed at her chest. As from so many other passes, the southern vista was striking, if barren. To her left, a massive wedge— Diamond Mesa—spilled from the back side of Junction Peak. Two royal blue lakes lay at its base. Framing the scene to the right was the Great Western Divide, a wall of mountains that appeared to be a world unto itself. In between the Mesa and the Divide was a wide plain, broken only by low rock ledges. The tree line was miles away.

Liz started down and wondered how the trail

engineers could possibly have chosen this route. The switchbacks were tight and rock-strewn, some cut into solid granite and others built atop stone walls. One foot in front of the other. A pole, a foot, a pole, a foot, as she had done for so many miles. She braced herself with her poles to relieve the stress on her legs, and caused her shoulders to ache. Somewhere soon she would rest.

A falcon appeared, tracing an arc against a dark cliff. She stopped to see where it would go, what it could possibly desire here where there was nothing. She lost it in the shadow of an enormous outcropping, and thought it possible it had flown through the mountain. But then the bird materialized against a white cloud, at a distance farther than she imagined it could have reached. She strained to see it, and tipped sideways, jamming a pole into her armpit. She cried out, and the cliff ricocheted the sound back to her.

She lowered herself onto a stone and slipped off her pack. She pulled her knees to her chest, bent her head and began to cry. She was alone, exhausted and afraid. Earlier in the trip, the overwhelming scale of the wilderness had seemed a blessing; she paled to insignificance. Her secrets and fears and desires could fall upon the hard rock and into the deep blue pools and fly away into the endless sky without notice. But now that she had confessed, she was open, exposed. The indifferent wilderness was now harsh and she longed to be comforted. She thought of Valerie and the ease of their friendship. She thought of Muesli and the simple happiness they shared. Neither her friend nor her cat was enough, but she longed for them, for someone.

After a time, hunger and thirst brought her around. She pulled a bag of almonds from her pack and tossed a handful into her mouth. Four more handfuls and half a liter of water, and she was ready to walk again. Somewhere ahead of her was Dante, or so she hoped.

The switchbacks gave way to open, sandy terrain. Liz headed across the basin, a dot in an empty Euclidean space marked by a single vector, the trail. Over the course of an hour, she passed the twin lakes and the edge of Diamond Mesa. There, to the east, far in the distance, was Mount Whitney. It presented a strange profile, a massive cylinder sliced at an acute angle, and didn't conform to any template for a Sierra mountain that Liz's mind had developed. She'd seen pictures, of course, but was struck anew at how unlikely, how unimpressive it appeared. It was high, no doubt about that, but not magnificent. Still, to see where she was going, to have in her sights the place where the trail ended, moved her. She continued walking—she would have to leave the mountain farther behind in order to approach it—but glanced at it frequently. She wondered if Dante had seen it, if he even knew which peak it was.

Before long the tree line was in sight. She spotted what appeared to be a person a half mile or more ahead, but the shadows from the pines complicated her view. As she neared, she became more and more certain it was Dante. He stood in the trail without his pack, looking her way. At first she was cheered to see him. He had waited for her. She was under no illusion that he would have forgiven her so quickly, but perhaps he was opening the door. His position in the middle of the trail, however, seemed odd. She slowed. Now she could make out his face, and his worried expression.

She lifted her trekking pole in greeting. A strange sound came from her left, a good distance away. At first she guessed the high, undulating cry emanated from an injured animal, but then realized it was human. Or humanish. And a little bit musical.

She stopped in her tracks and listened for it to repeat. Dante had oriented toward the sound as well. The wind swirled in the treetops. At the top of a pine, a nutcracker squawked twice. The cry came again, pitches rapidly alternating between low shouts and falsetto. Someone was yodeling.

It was ludicrous.

From a different location, perhaps nearer, an answering call. She tried to pinpoint its source, but the steep slopes around her played with the sounds, sending notes across the valley and back again, until the cry seemed to come from every-where.

Her pulse quickened and she hurried along the trail to Dante.

"What was that noise?" he said.

"Sounded like yodeling."

"Like in *The Sound of Music*? You're right. You think they're doing it for fun?"

She shrugged. "It was used originally to communicate."

"Communicate what? Mental problems?"

"Position. Maybe identity. I'm just guessing."

Dante nodded, then frowned. "I stopped because I found something very disturbing." He turned to indicate the trail behind him. "Someone put a marmot, a dead one, on a sign just ahead."

"What?" Dread swam to the surface of her consciousness like a feeding fish. "Show me."

"I took it off and threw it as far as I could. It was disgusting. But I'll show you where it was."

A dead marmot. Liz immediately thought of the Roots. She scanned the sparse woods around them for movement or a flash of color. Nothing. Had that been the Roots yodeling? She unbuckled her hip belt, slid her pack to the ground and followed Dante.

He led her a short distance to where the trail dipped behind a rocky ledge. A sign, similar to those they'd seen everywhere on the trip, marked an intersection. It was waist-high, constructed of metal, with the place names and mileages drilled through the metal plate, like a stencil. This one said, LAKE SOUTH AMERICA 2.8 with an arrow pointing to the right. The rusted metal was stained with blood, still wet in places. She had imagined the marmot draped over the sign, intact. A chill spread down her arms.

"Dante, what exactly did you find?"

"You really want to know?" It was a challenge as much as a question. He waited until she nodded. "Okay. The belly was split open and the head was bent over the top of the sign." He reached into his pocket. "And whoever did it used these to hold it in place."

Liz stared at his open palm, unbelieving. Two red tent stakes.

"I washed them in the stream."

"I don't understand. Hold it how?"

He hesitated, deliberating how to answer. "The stakes were driven through each paw and into the letters." He pointed at two places either side of the central post.

She pictured the marmot's head in the middle, the forelimbs splayed. Her stomach rolled and her palms became damp. "A crucifixion."

His eyes widened. "Yes, I suppose it was. I didn't think of that. I wanted to get rid of it before anyone else had to see it. Without touching it, of course. I used my poles." He ran a hand through his hair. "Disgusting."

Out of habit, she reached for his hand to comfort him and to thank him for removing the carcass before she got there, but he moved away and headed back to where they'd left their packs. A thick ache of sorrow passed through her as she realized he was avoiding her touch and might never accept it again. Everything had played out exactly as she had feared. She had broken his heart, and her own.

Another thought pushed to the front of her mind. She returned to where Dante stood with his pack.

"How long do you think it had been there?"

"The marmot? How could I possibly know?"

His anger was palpable, but she had to pursue the questioning. "Well, the blood hadn't dried, for one thing." She thought for a minute. "Did you pass three guys earlier?"

"Yes. Maybe a half hour or forty-five minutes before I got here."

"They would've mentioned the marmot."

"Of course. So, it wasn't here very long."

She stepped closer. "The Roots saw you coming, Dante." A shadow of worry passed over his face. "And the yodeling happened as I arrived. They've seen me, too." She reached out her hand, and noticed it trembling.

He ignored it. "So you want to stick together, is that it?" His expression hardened. "Do you think just because some twisted creeps are trying to scare us that everything is fine between us? Because it isn't." He pointed a finger at her. "Remember, Liz, the Roots are only guilty of killing a marmot."

Her heart beat faster and blood rushed to her face. She stepped back, shock morphing into a flash of indignation. "You're right! I know what I did, and I know we're not even close to fine. But you might think about the fact that I didn't get pregnant by myself. We were at Etta's wedding, remember? In Santa Fe? You knew I was drunk. You didn't care about birth control that night any more than I did. Most of this is on me, Dante. I admit it. But not all of it."

His eyebrows shot up. He spun away and strode several paces, and stared into the distance. Liz inhaled deeply to calm herself. She waited, hoping Dante would not run off and leave her. He was right. She couldn't imagine facing the rest of the journey by herself, with the Roots stalking and threatening them. And, practically speaking, she and Dante had so little between them that could be used to defend themselves. It made sense to try to work together—if Dante could stomach it. He turned to her. "As we are here, it seems foolish not to continue together. And at night it's too cold without a tent." He moved to his pack. "I'm having lunch now."

Liz watched him for a moment, relieved, then dug some cheese and dried fruit from her pack.

As she ate, she searched the woods for signs of movement and the skies for signs of a storm.

After eating, they descended through foxtail pines, crossed Tyndall Creek and climbed away from the Kern River drainage toward Bighorn Plateau. The mountains of the Great Western Divide stayed beside them, increasing in grandeur as the trail ran parallel to the range. In the middle of the afternoon, they arrived on the plateau— two miles across, level as a pool table and framed on three sides by granite peaks. A deer bent to drink at the rim of a small, round lake. There was not a breath of wind.

Dante, in the lead, stopped and pivoted to take in the view. Liz pulled a water bottle from his pack and gave it to him, as only a contortionist could reach a bottle on his own pack. When Dante finished drinking, he handed it back.

She drank the rest and inserted it in the pouch. "I've still got a half liter, which should last until Wallace Creek."

The deer lifted its head. They marched on, accompanied by the grinding of their boots on the ground and the click of their poles.

The path led across the plateau and down sharply to Wright Creek, one of several wild threads that rushed off the precipitous eastern slopes to spill into the Kern River. They crossed on half-submerged boulders, using their poles for balance, a performance now second nature to both of them. A mile farther along, they encountered Wallace Creek and a large campsite in a stand of trees thirty yards from the riverbank.

They agreed on the placement of the tent and proceeded to set up camp, all with a minimum of conversation. Liz inflated the air mattresses and fluffed the sleeping bags (thinking all the while it didn't feel as much like nest building as it had in the past) and prepared to head for the river. She picked up her sleeping outfit, stacked her towel and comb on top and stepped into the meadow separating the campsite from the water. She stopped short. An undulating call—a bout of yodeling—originating from somewhere upriver. Dante had been organizing his clothing on a rock ledge and froze at the sound. They looked at each other, waiting. Another call, similar to the first, filled the valley.

"Shit," Dante said.

"Shit is right." Liz hugged her clothes tighter to her chest and retreated into the cover of pines.

"If we only knew what the hell they wanted."

"The calls sounded like they came from the same place, so they weren't communicating with each other. That was for us."

He clenched his jaw. "There must be something we can do."

She put down her clothes and approached him. "We have to try. I don't think I could sleep knowing they might be planning something."

He considered her. His face softened a notch. "Where do we start?"

"With seeing what we've got to work with."

They took inventory, taking pains to regard the familiar objects they'd carried with them for two weeks with fresh eyes. Other than Dante's slingshot and a single flare, nothing could reasonably be categorized as a weapon.

Dante said, "We could move our camp to someplace less obvious."

"We could. But it's getting late and we'd be just as likely to be moving closer to them instead of farther away."

Dante picked up the bundle of nylon cord. "Can we do anything with this?"

Liz glanced at the position of the tent, then scanned the entire area. "I've got an idea."

They moved the tent to the edge of the site where it was bordered on two sides by ten-foot-high boulders crammed against a steep hill. Using trees as anchors, and tent stakes when necessary, they strung cord along a twenty-foot perimeter, eight inches off the ground, hoping it would be invisible at night. It wouldn't stop the Roots from getting to the tent, but at least there might be a warning.

They ate dinner, washed the dishes and got ready for bed, taking care to step over the trip lines. Dante gathered stones in a pile outside the tent door and practiced a few times with the slingshot. Clouds appeared, and coalesced, turning magenta, violet and turquoise with the setting sun. Liz wondered if it might rain, or even storm during the night, and decided she didn't care. In fact, if a storm would keep the Root brothers at bay, she'd welcome it.

At dusk she and Dante entered the tent. The temperature had dropped rapidly and they hurried into their sleeping bags. For a long while, they lay on their backs listening to the wind sweep up the valley and stir the branches overhead. Liz wasn't confident she could sleep, both because of a possible threat from the Roots, and because she was lying next to a man whom she loved dearly but who was in all likelihood no longer hers. She wouldn't cry—she was spent. She would simply close her eyes and await the morning.

Dante rolled over to face her, although the dark was absolute. "You were right to say it was partly my fault you became pregnant. I wish we'd both been more responsible."

His tone was sincere—when was he not sincere? —but guarded, as if a bigger truth was on the way. "Thanks. So do I."

"But I can't see how that changes what you did, and how you hid everything from me."

"No, it doesn't change it. Nothing will. But, Dante, I knew that you would want to keep the baby, and get married."

"Is that so awful, Liz?"

"I wish you wouldn't put it that way."

"How would you put it?"

She sat up, agitated. "That if pregnancy automatically means marriage and a family, then people who can't remember to use birth control should probably not be having sex!"

He was quiet for a moment. "So what is it you regret? Moving in with me? Ever having slept with me?"

She felt pinpricks behind her eyes. Her mind was awash with emotion. She couldn't think straight. With pain running like acid through her veins, she did regret those things. She regretted everything.

She lay down and he went on. "Now that I think about it, you only moved in with me because you lost your condo."

"That was the impetus, yes," she said weakly. "But I wanted to."

He ignored the last part. "And sleeping with me in the first place? Or dating me, for that matter? Or having a drink with me at Freddie's? What was the impetus, as you say, for that, since you seemed to know you would come to regret it all?"

The feeling came to her with the certainty of a sunrise. "Hope. Foolish hope."

They gave up on talking and retreated into separate, broken worlds. In those parallel landscapes, Liz on her inflated rectangle and Dante on his, they each found sleep.

Chapter Twenty-Eight

She was half awake and contemplating whether she needed to go outside to pee or whether she could wait until morning. They'd gone to bed so early she guessed it was now not even midnight. She was summoning the motivation to brave the cold when the sharp snap of a branch alerted her. She pushed her hat away from her ears and rose on one elbow. Rustling sounds, or maybe the wind.

She placed her hand on Dante's cheek. He stirred and she moved a finger to his lips. He touched her arm in acknowledgment and rolled to his side.

More rustling. A faint light winked, or maybe she imagined it.

"An animal?" Dante whispered.

A loud thud. "Oof!"

Liz sat upright, her heart racing. Dante shucked off his bag and fumbled for the zipper on the door.

Outside, "Darn it!" Rodell. "Don't move, Payton. There's a friggin' wire!"

Dante crouched in the vestibule. Liz's hands darted around her, searching for the flashlight. She found it in the corner near her feet, pushed the button and shone it toward him. The beam shook and she used both hands to steady it. Rodell swore again and she could hear one of them move through the undergrowth. Dante loaded the slingshot and scuttled sideways out of the vestibule, determination and fear written on his face. Liz crawled to his side and pointed the light to the location of the sound. Rodell was framed in the beam, scrabbling for the flashlight that had been knocked out of his hand in the fall.

"Get out of here!" Dante shouted.

Her hand shaking, Liz swung the beam to the right. Her heart stopped. Payton, framed between two trees, exactly as she'd seen him that night during the storm. His feet were planted wide, his shoulders broad and squared. She shone the light directly at his face. He didn't squint. He tucked his chin and glowered at her. She gasped.

Dante grunted and released the stone from the slingshot. Payton ducked behind a tree and the stone flew past, narrowly missing him. Liz spied Rodell's light moving and jerked her own back to him. He was retreating, cutting through the meadow with a limp.

Payton shouted, "If he's hurt, you two are gonna pay!"

Dante had reloaded and was aiming in the direction of Payton's voice. She searched for Payton with the light but saw only tree trunks and shadows. Dry leaves crunched underfoot. A twig snapped. Liz held her breath. More rustling, now farther away. She was shaking badly now, from cold and fear, but kept scanning with the beam.

Beside her, Dante lowered the slingshot and exhaled. "*Dios mio.*"

Her breath came in shallow gasps. She shone the light all around, again and again.

Dante said, "Let's go inside."

Liz wasn't convinced the Roots had gone—how could they know?—but crawled into the tent anyway. She tried to zip her bag closed but her numb fingers couldn't grip the tab. Then she realized she still had to pee. She clambered over Dante with the flashlight, apologizing, and crept a few yards away, in the opposite direction of the Roots. As she returned to the tent she swept the beam across the trees and meadow, but saw nothing unusual.

Her teeth were chattering as she blew into her hands. She managed to open the zipper and slipped into her bag again. Her voice wavered as she spoke. "That was exactly what Payton looked like the night he scared the crap out of me at Shadow Creek."

"You were right about them all along. I don't know why I didn't see it."

"They didn't want you to. Until now, they've saved their best for me."

"But I should have believed you. Thank God we put up the cord."

"Yeah, it actually worked." Liz shuddered, thinking about what the brothers had intended to do, and anticipating they might be back. "We should take turns keeping watch for them."

"Okay. I'll go first. Just let me warm up." He paused. "Do you think they really did kill Brensen?"

"I don't know. It's all fun and games with them. Hard to tell where they'd draw the line."

"If they wanted him dead, they could've shot him."

"Assuming they really have a gun. I'm not sure what I saw."

"And this way it's less clear how he died."

A wave of fear pulsed through her at the cold-blooded premeditation this suggested. She wished Dante would go out and stand watch. She tightened the drawstring on the hood of the sleeping bag and rubbed her feet together to warm them. "Paul and Linda would've told the police about Brensen yesterday, or the night before. Do you think they've already come to get him?"

"Probably. Are you thinking about an autopsy?"

"Yes. But then again, as Paul said, a fall and a push might look pretty much the same."

"So we can't count on anyone coming after the Roots."

"I don't think we can count on anything." Her words hung in the air.

They lay still, striving not to disrupt the pockets of warmth their body heat had created. After a few minutes, Dante sighed and crawled out of the tent. A light crossed the ceiling, then swung away. She listened as Dante's footsteps receded toward the meadow. She willed him not to go far. The beam lit the tent again as he approached. He made several small circuits within the trip lines before returning inside. She smelled the cold on him as he wriggled into his bag.

"The wind's increased." His voice quaked. "It's unbelievably cold."

"I'll go in a sec." She pulled her knees into the fetal position, gathering heat and resolve. She didn't want to leave the tent, but neither did she want to be ambushed. She wanted peace, and sleep. She closed her eyes, but her brain was in overdrive, rifling through images of the Roots: Payton looming over her at the creek, Rodell acting out the dare at the pass during the storm, the two of them folding their tarp like house-wives. Even that quotidian act disturbed her in retrospect. She pictured them lurking in the woods beyond the tent and sat up. "I'd better go."

"Stay near the tent."

"I will."

She climbed out and stood, directing her flashlight into the forest, sweeping the beam back and forth. She hugged herself with her free arm and stomped her feet as the icy breeze stole her body heat. Crouching into a ball, she returned to the question that had been eating away at her since she first felt Payton Root's peculiar attention:

Why her? Finally, she believed she understood. Stripped of her shell of lies and deceits, she could see herself as Payton did: a woman strong enough to be worth conquering, and fragile enough to break. It terrified her to know he was pursuing her, threatening her, with his brother in collusion. And as much as she wanted Dante by her side, Payton didn't consider him a deterrent. She could only hope she and Dante could hold off the Roots until they encountered other people, or until someone realized they were in trouble and sent help.

The cold found its way to her bones. She scanned the trees one last time, unzipped the fly and crawled inside. Dante shifted as she climbed over him and settled into her bag. They didn't speak, but his breathing told her he was as alert as she was, despite their exhaustion. Morning could not come soon enough.

Several times over the next hour, Dante crawled partway out of the tent and scanned for signs of the Roots. Liz's eyelids would not stay open, and she struggled to listen for sounds above the whistling of the wind. She slid briefly into unconsciousness, but her jangled nerves prevented her from finding real sleep.

Dante clamped his hand on her arm. "Liz!"

She pushed herself up, disoriented, and rubbed her nose. A smell. A barbecue? Dante was scrambling out of his bag, grabbing his jacket, jamming his hat on.

"What—"

"A fire! We need to get out!"

Her stomach dropped. "Where?"

He opened the door and stuck his head out. "All I can see is smoke!"

Her mind racing, she tried to unzip her bag. It caught. She cursed and wriggled out. She threw on her jacket and stuffed whatever clothes and gear she could find quickly into her sleeping bag. Dante climbed outside, cramming his feet in his boots as he went.

Liz shouted, "Get the packs first!"

She crawled out, dragging the sleeping bags behind her. Her heart beat in her throat as she stood. Smoke everywhere, illuminated faint orange on the far side of the campsite, toward the trail. Too much smoke to see how large the fire might be. The wind was blowing toward them. She waved smoke from her face, the acrid smell stinging her nose. Where was her flashlight? She dropped the sleeping bags. Hands trembling, she fumbled in one pocket, then the other and found it. She clicked it on and spun around to find Dante hoisting both packs. He ran away from the blaze toward the meadow.

"To the river!" he shouted over his shoulder.

She scanned around her with the beam, holding her arm over her nose. Her legs wouldn't move. Panic swamped her brain. Think. What was vital? She stuck the flashlight in her mouth, and shoved on her boots, tying them roughly. Stuffing one sleeping bag inside the other, she tossed them over her shoulder and crossed to the cooking area, waving smoke away as she did. She threw the stove and lighter inside the cook pot, grabbed two water bottles and hugged everything against her with one arm, and took the flashlight from her mouth with the other. Coughing, she sprinted after Dante. Her foot hit the nylon trip line, and she flew forward, twisting sideways as she fell. Her left arm hit the ground, the blow cushioned by the sleeping bags. She pushed herself upright, scooped up the water bottles she'd dropped and raced ahead.

Dante was running toward her. "The bear cans!"

"Oh, shit!" They'd left them somewhere between the tent and trail, close to where the fire seemed to be. She abandoned everything except the flashlight. The beam jumped up and down as she ran back to the campsite. The wind parted the smoke for a moment, revealing flames licking the stunted trees, a dozen yards away. Dante was near the tent, smoke billowing around him. Where had they put the cans? An image appeared in her mind. A large rock. She swung the light to Dante's left where she thought they might be.

"Over there!"

He moved quickly, waving smoke away, coughing. She was nearly at the tent, searching for the cans with the light. The smoke was densest near the ground. There! Dante's hands were already on them. He picked them up and was enveloped by smoke. She shone the light in his direction to help him, but he was already gone.

She started after him, but turned back. If she could rescue the tent, she should. They had nothing else to protect them in severe weather. She cast the light into the thickest part of the smoke, trying to see how close the flames were, but it was impossible. Flashlight in her mouth, she grabbed a corner of the tent and jerked it upward, pulling the stake out of the ground, freeing the ground sheet, tent and fly. She palmed the stake and she moved around the tent, yanking stakes from the ground and pushing aside the rocks she had used as anchors. Smoke stung her eyes and twice she had to remove the flashlight from her mouth during a coughing fit. She cursed herself for not having the headlamp handy. The last stake refused to budge. She recalled struggling to drive it into the ground earlier. She pulled with both hands, her heart pounding and hands slick with sweat. The stake flew out, disappearing into the smoke. Liz grabbed the tent and dragged it toward the meadow. Nearly blinded by smoke, the flashlight useless, she kicked each foot in front| of her, searching for the trip line. Her foot hit the cord. She stepped over it, lifting the tent clear. Dante appeared and together they carried the tent to the stream edge.

Liz bent over, hands on her knees, coughing. She swallowed, the taste of sour charcoal burning her throat. As she got up, Dante pulled her into a hug. She put her arms around him and he exhaled as if he'd been holding his breath a long time. His jacket smelled of ash, and she could feel the warmth of his body through it. He stepped back and held her by the shoulders. The flashlight lay in the grass. She couldn't see his face.

"Are you all right?" His voice was gravelly from the smoke.

She nodded.

He pulled her close again. "I could have lost you."

She held him tighter and bit her lip to quell the surge of relief rushing through her—for being alive, and for that meaning something to him. Fear and fatigue had shredded her, so however much he cared, at that moment it seemed enough.

"Dante, I'm so sorry I hurt you."

He nodded, brushing his face against her hair. "I wish I could say it doesn't matter. But I can't."

A tide of sadness and regret rolled through her. The apology she'd already offered many times came to her lips but she didn't utter it.

He let go of her and cast his eyes at the gear strewn around them. "We should take care of this stuff." He picked up the flashlight and handed it to her. "You hold the light and I'll carry everything across."

The creek was shallow and only a dozen feet

wide, so the task was finished in minutes. Liz joined him on the far side. He picked up the water bottles and handed her one. She drank, the cool liquid easing her raw throat.

He said, "This was the Roots, wasn't it?"

"Had to be. No lightning and no campfire. I can't think of anything else."

"They could've killed us."

"I know." She drank more water. This time it made her shiver. "We should put on some more clothes before we get chilled."

They located their clothes amid the sleeping bags and collapsed tent. Dante was missing a sock but found a dirty one in his backpack. They sat on their backpacks, facing the campsite, and drew their sleeping bags around their shoulders.

Liz was almost breathing normally again. She checked the time. Five thirty. She tried to remember how far they had to go today. Not too far, she thought. She pictured the map but the miles along each segment kept sliding off. She gave up.

Across the meadow were a few scattered flames, all at ground level. In the beam of the flashlight, smoke still billowed in the same direction but, it seemed, with less force.

Dante said, "Should we be doing anything about the fire?"

She shrugged, which made her cough. She wiped her eyes with her sleeve. "We could dump water on it with the cook pot, but I'm not thrilled about doing it in the dark. Too easy to fall. Besides, the wind seems to be dropping."

"The fire doesn't look that big."

"The smoke was bad enough. And you can never tell with fire. If we had been asleep—" Her voice was blocked by a lump in her throat.

He put a hand on her shoulder, left it there a minute, then took it back. He pointed at the eastern sky. "First light."

"New day," she said, without conviction.

As soon as light permitted, they carried water from the river in bottles and the cook pot and dumped it on the hot spots. The closest was a few yards from where the tent had been. The wind had died down completely, and the smoke became a low fog.

There was a lot to do. Their belongings were scattered. Soot coated everything and had to be washed or shaken off. Liz and Dante attended to their tasks in silence. Liz felt dizzy and untethered from lack of sleep and too much adrenaline. She fumbled the dishes as she rinsed them in the creek and had to run downstream after a cup that floated away from her. Several times she thought she heard someone approaching from the woods, and her heart leapt into her throat, but it turned out to be a squirrel, or nothing. As she returned to camp, she noticed Dante kept looking up from what he was doing and peering into the trees. What would they do if the Roots came after them again, other than run? They were, in truth, defenseless. The best they could hope for was to find other people, and soon. She said so to Dante.

He nodded, but didn't say more. His shoulders were slumped and he moved with deliberation. She'd never seen him so beaten. He was tired, scared and sad.

"I'll make coffee," she said.

"Good idea."

She filled the pot, lit the stove and placed the pot on it. A memory flashed so vividly she thought she was hallucinating and lowered herself onto a rock. Her mother stood before her, asking Liz to show her where the coffee was. Gabriel was dead. Her mother steered her toward the shower. One foot in front of the other. Coffee, shower, food. Normalcy, routine, sanity.

Liz shook her head to dispel the image and scooped coffee into the first cup. The tremor in her hand rattled the spork against the edge. She breathed deep into her lungs, forcing her hand to be still. There wasn't enough coffee to waste.

She sat waiting for the water to boil, and thought of her mother at home in Santa Fe, standing in front of her easel, surrounded by color and light. The image calmed her—Claire was content—but Liz was also struck by the irony that her lesson in the comfort of routine should come from Claire, whose thirst for freedom through art trumped schedules of any kind. Maybe in times of crisis everyone, even the highest-flying kite, returns to

Earth and the complacency of time and order. Either that or go mad. Liz poured water in the cups and stirred.

"Coffee's ready," she said.

Dante was folding his clothes and sniffed his sleep shirt. "I'm going to throw everything away when I get home."

Liz held her cup in both hands. She stared at him a moment, then got up and walked to the edge of the meadow, unable to guess whether "home" included her. A knot formed in her belly. She wished she could be alone, to think about what she wanted to say, what she wanted to do. She wished she could start this trip again. But why stop there? Why not rewind the clock further? To before the abortion, or before Etta's wedding. Or before Gabriel's death. Before Gabriel. She laughed at herself. She might run out of life before she ran out of regret.

Dante appeared beside her with his coffee. "What's funny?"

"Nothing."

Chapter Twenty-Nine

After they ate and packed, Liz and Dante consulted the map. The John Muir Trail continued south from Wallace Creek another four miles to an intersection, then veered due east six and a half miles to the Whitney Trail junction. There, the north fork led in two miles to the summit of Mount Whitney. The south fork led in a half mile to Trail Crest, a pass of 13,650 feet, then continued another nine miles to Whitney Portal, a trailhead with a campground, store and small restaurant. Most hikers, Liz informed Dante, camped near Guitar Lake their last night, eight miles from where they were sitting.

"How hard is the last day?" Dante said.

"Hard. Two to the Whitney Trail junction, where, if we were going to the summit, we'd drop our packs. The round-trip to the top from there is four miles."

"But we're skipping that."

"Right. Another nine to the Portal, so eleven in all, with twenty-five hundred feet up and over five thousand down."

He frowned and shook his head. The stress of the last few days told on his face. "But the Roots will be following us, or waiting for us."

Liz's chest constricted. Thousands of miles of wilderness, and they were trapped.

Dante bent over the map. "Is there another way out?"

Liz pointed to trails leading out of the Kern drainage. "We could go out this way, but it's a lot longer. Also, the way we're headed is the popular route. Even though it's late in the season, tons of people go up Whitney every day."

"How many?"

"More than a hundred. You get a permit through a lottery. Except if you go the long way, like we are. But most people are day-tripping from the Portal."

Dante looked hopeful. "So the trail to the top will be crowded."

She nodded. "If we can make it to Guitar Lake today, there should be some hikers coming up from the Portal this morning, bagging Whitney, and stopping at the lake on their way someplace else."

"Let's hope so."

Her logic was sound, but even to her own ears she was less than convincing. It was as though the Roots controlled the entire wilderness, that they'd staged Brensen's fall to appear accidental, directed a wind to blow the fire their way, and would empty the trails of hikers. Liz was frightened and tired enough to almost believe they had the power. She glanced at the sky, a washed-out blue. Perhaps they could summon the clouds, too.

They donned their packs and left the charred campsite behind, Dante in the lead. Liz turned to look at the site as approaching hikers would. The damage didn't appear to be the result of anything more than an out-of-control campfire, not significant enough for anyone passing by to report to a ranger.

They climbed out of the watershed onto the broad shoulder between Kern Canyon and the Whitney massif. The terrain opened, and the mountains of the Great Divide came into view. After three miles they reached Sandy Meadow. A mile farther, they left the main trail and turned east. It seemed impossible Whitney was less than ten miles away. Liz noticed clouds had formed above the peaks in the distance, although it was not yet noon. Not an encouraging sign.

She pushed her concerns about the weather to the back of her mind and divided her attention between the rocky trail and the possibility of the Roots approaching from behind. She was especially vigilant in wooded areas where she and Dante could be ambushed. She glanced behind her frequently and noticed Dante looking around more than usual. They spoke little. Dante was undoubtedly as tired as she was but didn't com-plain.

They ate lunch near a stream running through a pink granite gorge from where they had a clear view of the trail in both directions. The clouds had stitched themselves together above their heads, and darkened. As they finished eating, the first drops fell. They frowned at each other and put on their rain jackets and, as a precaution, slipped rain covers over their packs.

The storm was quick to gather momentum. They'd covered less than a mile before intermittent drops became continuous rain. At Timberline Lake they lost the protection of the trees, and the rain became a downpour. Piercing drops roiled the lake surface. A steep hill, mostly granite and dotted with a few pines, rose behind the far side of the lake. At the top would be Guitar Lake, sitting at the foot of Whitney, but they couldn't see even the lower slopes of the mountain because of the rain.

The trail traced the crease between the hill and the near-vertical face of Mount Young to the left. Halfway up a set of switchbacks, they paused to catch their breath. Water ran off the bill of Dante's cap, which stuck out of the hood of his jacket.

He pulled Liz's rain cover aside, retrieved a water bottle and offered it to her. "I thought there were supposed to be people camping at Guitar Lake, but we haven't seen anyone."

"Maybe they read the forecast."

"Maybe."

"But it is weird." She thought a moment. "Maybe if they were heading south, they'd have cut the corner near Crabtree, so we wouldn't have passed them."

"But would everyone be heading south?"

"Doesn't seem likely."

The absence of hikers disturbed her. Whatever courage and moxie she had found when facing the Roots in the past had evaporated, and the thought of another encounter terrified her. As it was, she was so exhausted she could barely manage hiking. The hope that they'd find friendly faces at Guitar Lake was the only breath of encouragement she could find.

They continued upward, a hard, slow slog. They came over a rise and Guitar Lake appeared before them, gunmetal gray and dull. The area around the lake was empty—no tents, no people—and barren, devoid of trees and large boulders for shelter, or cover.

Dante jammed his pole into the ground in frustration. "Where the hell is everyone?"

Liz swiped the rain and sweat from her forehead and fought back tears. "I have no idea." She hadn't realized how much she'd been counting on seeing other people, and the disappointment sat heavily on her. She turned and scoured the trail behind them, trying to discern color or movement in the driving rain. She didn't see anything, but that did nothing to allay her fear.

Dante was scowling, and his voice was sharp-edged. "So we go higher, find a place to hide?"

"We have to. If we stay here, we're sitting ducks."

"We *are* sitting ducks, Liz! That's exactly what we are."

Before she could speak, he turned up the trail. She hurried after him, certain his anger and frustration did not stem solely from the threat of the Root brothers. The wounds from her actions and her deceit were deep and fresh, and the feelings they evoked would not be subjugated. She understood this well, because although the malevolence of the Roots was close upon her like a pall of smoke, the fear of losing Dante gripped her heart.

The next level terrain lay three-quarters of a mile away—nothing compared to the miles and mountains they left behind—but Liz struggled. Her pack was as light as it had ever been, but seemed filled with stone. Her legs and lungs burned. Several times she stopped, to rest or to quit, she wasn't sure which; but Dante climbed on, so she did, too.

The switchbacks ended and a traverse brought them to the top of the hill behind Guitar Lake. An acre-sized tarn appeared on the right. The terrain from there to two lakes at the base of Mount Hitchcock sloped slightly downhill, away from the trail. Unlike Guitar Lake, there were numerous outcroppings and slabs.

Liz stood beside Dante. "This looks promising."

Dante exhaled and squinted into the rain, searching. "Somewhere hidden from the trail."

She pointed toward Hitchcock Lakes. "And also from this gulley."

They stashed their packs and began searching together. The rain fell in torrents. Twice they broke off their search and went to the edge of the shelf from which they could survey the lower trail and most of Guitar Lake but saw no one.

After forty minutes, they discovered a tiny patch of crushed gravel wedged between a sloped bank and a slab of granite the size of a garage. They returned for their packs and confirmed the location was invisible from the main trail. Someone at the lower Hitchcock Lake might detect them, but the chance the Roots would come this far was slim, especially in bad weather.

Once they were secure in the campsite, Liz and Dante relaxed a little. The rain let up. Dante fished the salami from a bear can and divided what remained between them. Liz sat on a rock, bit off a large chunk and chewed, allowing the pleasure of salt and fat to overrun her.

They pitched the tent and Liz placed the mattresses and sleeping bags inside. Everything smelled of smoke, an insistent reminder of last night's close call. She finished setting up the beds in haste, eager to return to the fresh air.

Although it was not yet four o'clock, they were desperate for more food, so Dante began to prepare dinner: vermicelli with pesto from a tube. Liz carried the filtration kit and the water bottles to the nearer lake, taking a long look up the gulley before she hurried to the shore. She crouched behind a boulder and pumped water into the bottle between her feet, recalling the first time she'd done so on this trip, high above Yosemite Valley, chatting to Dante about how the water from every stream tasted different. They'd sampled dozens of creeks, rivers and lakes during the last seventeen days, often too distracted, too tired, too scared or simply too thirsty to taste it. She pumped three more times. The bottle was full. She pulled the adapter out and took a long drink. Cold. Flinty. A little salty. Sweet.

She filled the other bottles, tucked the filter into its pouch and looked at the sky. Above the craggy summit of Mount Hitchcock, banks of clouds were piled high like whipped cream on a sundae. A sudden wind blew up from the Kern and set the clouds in motion over her head. The billows flew by and parted. Blue sky. Sunlight angled through the gaps, searchlight beams of yellow-white touching down upon the lake, the granite, her. A shaft of light, a passing moment of warmth. The beams sped along the earth until the wind relented and the edges of the clouds met and joined, trapping the sun again.

She retraced her steps to the campsite, keeping watch for movement in the direction of the trail. She wondered whether Dante had seen the sunbeams and the patch of blue sky, too. Then she remembered such shared moments were probably a thing of the past, and felt anew the ache that had taken up residence in her chest. This was their last campsite, probably forever. Even in this stony wilderness, twelve thousand feet above the sea, unchanged for millennia, forever was a heartbreakingly long time. She found the campsite and said nothing to Dante about the taste of the water or the beauty of the sky.

They wolfed down the pasta and discussed the next day's plan. Dante set his watch alarm for five o'clock. They'd have coffee, maybe two servings each, and break camp, stashing energy bars and trail mix in the top of their packs to eat on the way up, or at the top. Despite their acclimation, the extreme altitude was a concern. Liz had read it was better to face the ascent on an empty stomach. They could eat as much as they wished on the way down and that evening in Lone Pine. There was no point in discussing what they'd do if the Roots confronted them, as it would depend on where they were. If by some miracle they were left unmolested, they'd arrive at Whitney Portal in the early afternoon.

"For a burger," Dante said.

"And fries."

"And maybe a second burger."

"And more fries."

They were silent a moment, lost in a reverie less about food and more about normality, and safety. Dante turned to her. Exhaustion had left fine wrinkles in the corners of his eyes and around his mouth, but his gaze was level. She waited for him to speak. He had said so little since she'd confessed to him, but knew he must be thinking about her, and about them. He rubbed his fingers across his chin and pursed his lips, as if moving his thoughts around into spaces where they might fit. She would not press him.

He pushed his hands against his knees and stood. "Ready for bed?"

The sun faded into the clouds at the horizon, blurring the sky with wash upon wash of pastel. Liz crawled into the tent and shed her outer layer, folding her fleece jacket into a square pillow. Dante followed suit. They lay there for a long time, alone with their thoughts, watching the fabric of the tent change from yellow to amber to brown. A breeze luffed the fly from time to time, reminding them of the outside world, huge and empty all around them.

The last ember of twilight lingered. Liz could just make out the half circle of the screen door.

Dante said, "I've been wondering about something since you told me." She held her breath. He went on. "When you knew you were pregnant and were deciding what to do, did you think about me at all?"

"Yes. I felt awful for you right away. And ever since."

"Because you knew you wanted an abortion."

"I didn't want it at all. And I didn't think in a logical way." She searched for the right words. The true ones. "I panicked."

He exhaled sharply in disbelief. "I was around you, Liz. Almost the whole time, except for that short trip. I didn't see you panicking."

"No. You wouldn't have. I don't realize it myself sometimes."

"You could have told me that. Exactly that. 'I'm pregnant and I'm panicking.' It would have been a start."

"Followed closely by the end." She rolled on her side to face him in the darkness. "If I had managed to say that, it wouldn't have changed what you wanted to do."

"But it was my decision, too." His voice was hushed. "It was also my child."

"I know. You deserved to know. But can you honestly say we would have discussed anything other than my impending motherhood?"

He lay very still. "Probably not. I would have done everything I could to have that child with you."

Tears pooled in her eyes. She let them fall. "Can't you see, Dante? You're entrenched in your beliefs. And I'm entrenched, too. In, I don't know—my fear. There's no place for us to work it out. There's no middle ground."

"Fear? It seems more like independence to me. You do things your way and do them alone. Keeping things to yourself. You were brought up that way and nothing's changed. All those secrets in your marriage, then having an abortion and not telling me, or anyone." He paused. "Did you tell anyone, Liz?"

"No."

"Not even Valerie?"

"No."

"Because you were ashamed?"

"Because I couldn't tell you first. Because I knew it would come to this." She turned away and chewed her lip. Each breath snagged in her throat. She strove to calm her breathing, to clear her mind. She wiped her eyes with her sleeve. "I'm trying to do the right thing now, Dante. I realize it will never be enough, but I'm trying."

"I wish you had come to me. Or that you felt you could." His voice grew hoarse. "I don't want to become my father, who stands with his beliefs like a king with his army."

Liz reached across to stroke his cheek. His beard was so much softer than it looked. "Maybe the world is simpler for him."

He took her hand in his. "He's skilled at trimming the pieces that don't fit without bothering about the reason."

She knew he was thinking of his sister, Emilia, and himself. "That doesn't sound like you."

Dante held her hand against his chest and tucked the sleeping bag around it. "We should sleep. Good night, Liz."

"Goodnight, Dante." She wanted to say "*Te amo*" but could not. What if he said nothing in response? In that moment, she could have poured herself into him. But a splinter of doubt, hard and sharp as glass, remained. He might not want her.

"I'm sorry," she said.

"I know."

She closed her eyes, having said everything her heart knew to say, and wandered along the border of consciousness. She pictured their tent as viewed from far above, the regularity of the dome the only hint it did not belong to the jumble of granite chunks and slabs surrounding it. Somewhere, perhaps near Guitar Lake, was the wedge of the Roots' tarp. The brothers were under it, like cockroaches. She willed them to remain.

Chapter Thirty

Liz lay awake, expecting the alarm at any moment or, rather, dreading it. The exposed part of her face was numb. It had to be the coldest morning so far. She burrowed deeper into her sleeping bag.

The alarm sounded. The trumpeting of reveille, over and over. She sat up, her back stiff.

Dante silenced the trumpets. "You sleep well?"

"Yes, finally. You?"

"Yes. It was heaven."

"It's freezing. I'm hiking in my leggings until it warms up."

"I'm hiking in everything."

They turned on their flashlights, dressed, stuffed the sleeping bags in their sacks and deflated the mattresses.

Dante climbed out. *"Dios mio!* It's cold!"

Liz handed him their belongings, then joined him. Except for the flashlight beams, the darkness was complete. Only the shimmering stars betrayed where the mountains became sky.

They'd left their wet rain jackets outside and now shook the frost off and put them on. Dante prepared coffee while Liz took down the tent, snapping the frozen condensation off the fly and stopping frequently to blow her hands warm. The bear cans held only a little leftover food and Ziploc bags stuffed with trash, so she added an empty fuel can, the stove, dirty socks, cups and bowls and whatever else they wouldn't need again.

As they finished stowing the gear and clothing in their packs, dawn arrived. With Whitney standing over them, however, the sun wouldn't find their campsite until long after they'd gone. Liz squinted at the enormous wall they would climb. Somewhere on it was the trail. She strained to see moving dots—hikers—creeping along a switchback, but saw nothing except rocks of every imaginable size.

They hoisted their packs and grabbed their poles.

"Let's go find the sun," Dante said.

They picked their way down to the gulley and bore right toward the wall. They were halfway to the trail when Dante stopped short and pointed ahead and to the right. Two hikers, about a quarter-mile away, ascending the trail.

A wave of panic shot through Liz. "Shit."

Dante turned to her, eyes wide, "Is it them?"

In the dim light, she couldn't make out the color of the hikers' backpacks, but the one in the front was tall. Her mouth went dry. "I don't know," she whispered, conscious of sounds carrying in the still of the morning. She'd felt secure in their campsite, tucked away. Now it was as if a searchlight had been trained on them. Instinctively, she crouched down, her heart thudding in her chest. One of her poles bounced off a rock. She winced at the sharp ringing sound and glanced up at the hikers. They hadn't paused, but that didn't mean she and Dante hadn't been spotted.

Dante squatted beside her, his agitation reverberating in the space between them. He nodded to the right, where a tall boulder stood. "How about over there?"

"Okay." She fought against the impulse to dash for cover. She rose slowly, the muscles in her legs thick with adrenaline, and moved across the gulley, holding her poles in one hand. Dante followed. They reached the boulder and slipped behind it. Liz leaned against the granite, resting one hand on the stone, rough and night-cold.

Next to the boulder was a five-foot-high ledge. They removed their packs and rested them against it.

Dante peered over the edge. "They're still walking. Maybe they didn't see us."

"They might when they get higher."

He shook his head in frustration. "I wish we knew if it was them."

"We haven't seen anyone else for two days."

"Perhaps we should stay where we are."

"We can't hole up here, Dante. We don't have the food. Plus, if that really was Payton and Rodell, they might wait us out. And they're happy to eat marmots." She thought of the one crucified on the trail sign. Her stomach turned.

"So what do we do? Let them get ahead, keep our distance?"

"That's all we've got. Plus, there'll be day hikers up there." It was less of a logical statement than a prayer. She looked west across the valley through which they'd come. A strip of clouds hung over the peaks of the Great Divide. "We don't want to be up at Trail Crest too late."

Dante nodded. "Weather. So, long enough for them to get to the junction? Because they could be waiting partway up."

"True. We need to give them time to get to the junction or over Trail Crest. They won't want to be up there late, either, especially if they're going to the summit." She glanced at her watch. Quarter to seven. "We might be able to see them going up. But why don't we figure on two hours?"

"Two hours it is."

They broke out the cooking gear, made a second cup of coffee and ate breakfast. The coffee warmed them for a time, but soon they were stamping their feet and rubbing their arms. Periodically, one of them peered over the ledge to monitor the progress of the hikers, who crept steadily up the hulking west face of Whitney. About an hour after Liz and Dante had first spotted them, they vanished, too far away to see.

Dante consulted the map. "I'm guessing in another half hour they'll be at the junction."

"Sounds about right."

He proposed that, instead of sitting there freezing, they could start the ascent and hike slowly, leaving the same distance between themselves and the putative Roots. Liz agreed, and twenty minutes later they were on the trail.

She led the way and focused on her surroundings to quell her anxiety over a potential encounter with the Root brothers. She noticed the granite here was lighter than elsewhere and studded with pink rectangles of feldspar crystals. The terrain was austere and only a few low, stoic plants squeezed life from between the rocks.

The sun caught the tip of Mount Hitchcock, painting it orange. Liz and Dante climbed, the sun climbing with them. The shadow of Whitney slid down Hitchcock until the entire mountain was aglow, the changing pattern reflected in the lakes at its feet. How Guitar Lake had earned its name hadn't been clear when they skirted its shore during yesterday's downpour, but now it was obvious—as obvious as the increasing cloud cover. What had been an innocuous band of white over the Great Divide was now a mass of tall, cumulus formations. In the last ten minutes, several small puffs had materialized over Mount Hitchcock. She wasn't worried, though. It wasn't even ten.

They stopped to remove a layer of clothing and drink water. They could still see their breath in the frosty air, but the effort of the climb had warmed them.

A low buzz came from the valley. Liz tried to pinpoint it, but failed.

"There." Dante pointed beyond Guitar Lake. "A helicopter."

Liz spotted it, flying low. It banked above the lake and flew southwest toward Crabtree Meadow. The buzz faded and the helicopter disappeared. "I wonder what that's about? They use them for supplying ranger stations, but why would one be up here? Because of Brensen?"

He shrugged. "I thought they would have picked him up a couple days ago." He looked across to Hitchcock, judging their elevation relative to the peak. "Shouldn't be much farther, right?"

"No, we've done most of it."

The final approach to the Whitney Trail junction was a long traverse. Liz felt sure they should be able to see hikers above them heading toward the summit, or returning from it, but there was only talus. She could make out sections of the trail now and all of it was empty. A knot formed in her stomach. Dante was leading and she asked him to stop, then traced with her trekking pole where she believed the Whitney Trail led. Frowning, he searched the slope and shook his head. Not a soul.

The air was noticeably thinner and they took small deliberate steps. Ahead and to the left was a tall spire with a trail cut into its side. To the right the trail disappeared around a corner. Liz saw a sign. The junction. Where all the packs should be. She sped up, her heart beating in her ears. Dante was right behind her.

They were a dozen yards away. The knot in her stomach tightened. Where were the packs? Sixty through-hikers and not one on the summit trail right now? Divide it in half—it was late in the season—and still someone would be going to Whitney midmorning. And what about the day hikers? A quota of a hundred and no one in sight.

She reached the junction, an open area of broken shale fifteen feet across, bordered by the spire on one side and a shoulder-high slab on the other. Beyond the slab was a two-thousand-foot sheer drop. Liz halted in the middle of the junction. Dante came up next to her, his mouth tight. "No packs? Why aren't there any packs?"

"I don't know." She looked past him along the

Whitney Trail, which wound around rock formations and towering pinnacles of granite. She could see only pieces of it, but every strip was empty. "There's no one here." She swallowed, her mouth parched. She stared at Dante. "Why is no one here?"

"Let's rest a moment and think it through."

Liz unclasped her hip belt and a shadow passed over her. Startled, she jerked her head up. A cloud. She lowered her pack and stood it against the wall next to Dante's. A stiff breeze funneled up from the valley. They dug out their jackets and put them on, then crossed to the slab and found places to sit. Dante scanned the slope they'd ascended. "No one coming up behind us."

Liz's attention was on the sky. The clouds above the Kaweahs and the surrounding peaks to the west had formed a solid shroud, slate-colored at the bottom. Mount Hitchcock, too, was almost entirely in shadow, the lakes below iron gray. She twisted to see the sky above them. A few innocent puffs.

Dante followed her gaze. "Are you worried about a storm?"

"The clouds over Hitchcock moved in really quickly."

"Maybe the weather is keeping people away."

"It might discourage a few, but honestly, it's so unpredictable that most people with a permit would go for it anyway."

"Trail Crest is only a little farther. We could see if anyone's coming up."

"Good idea."

They set off for the pass, a half mile farther. The narrow trail followed the jagged contours of the mountain, making it impossible to see more than a dozen yards ahead. Liz held her breath as they approached each corner, hoping to see a friendly hiker and expecting Payton Root. Fear coupled with the altitude soured her stomach, and she stopped twice thinking she might vomit.

They came around a tight bend. Ahead was a sign indicating the pass. The wind rushed through the gap, blowing tears from the corners of Liz's eyes. They paused for a moment, then Dante led them down the other side a short distance to where they could see the trail coming up from Trail Camp and Whitney Portal. From where they stood, the trail veered to the right across a stretch of ice and snow. Steel cables had been installed on the downhill side to prevent hikers from tumbling fifteen hundred feet to their deaths. Past the cable section were the famous ninety-nine switchbacks, winding back and forth across the precipitous face.

Liz stared in disbelief. No one. A chill ran up her spine. "I don't like this, Dante."

"Neither do I. Do you think they closed the trail?"

"They must have. But there's no fire. Maybe some other emergency—"

Dante clamped a hand on her arm. She glanced at him and followed his stare. She gasped. Rodell Root, standing on a slab above them, a stone's throw away. He waved, grinning.

Dante said, "Come on, Liz!" and stepped forward, making a break for the switchbacks. They had a chance to get there before Rodell could intercept them. Liz dashed after him, slipping her poles off as she went, ready to grab the cables. Every tendon in her body felt spring-loaded and alarms were sounding in her head. The drop-off to her left was too steep to be nearly running. Dante stopped abruptly and she braked just in time, bracing her arm against his pack to avoid a collision.

Payton Root stood in the trail a dozen steps away. He interlaced his fingers and stretched his arms in front of him. "Better watch out, *hombre*. First step's a doozy." From the ledge above them, Rodell let out his pig snort laugh. Payton's lips stretched into a grin, but the rest of his face was as hard as the stone at his feet.

A voice inside Liz's head screamed at her to flee, but her feet would not obey.

Dante grabbed her shoulder, spun her on the narrow trail and gave her a nudge to set her in motion.

She ran up the trail as fast as she could, not daring to peer over her shoulder to see if the brothers were in pursuit. Her lungs were on fire.

She focused only on the ground in front of her, heard only her own gasping breath. She crested the pass with Dante on her heels and scurried down toward the Whitney Trail junction.

She shouted without turning or slowing. "What do we do?"

"They're following us! Either we go down the way we came or try to lose them on the way to the summit."

The spire at the junction came into view. They scrambled down the rough trail.

Liz said, "The way down is too open. We have to hide and hope they pass by. Then we can turn back and get the hell out of here." They arrived at the junction and veered right along the summit path. Liz's heart beat in her throat as she navigated the jumble of broken rock and angular boulders where landslides had occurred, interspersed with sections of smooth gravel. The trail snaked between gigantic pinnacles and stacked rectangles of stone, creating shadow patterns that fooled Liz's eye and made her stumble again and again. She pressed on, the menace behind like a hot breath on her neck. She could find no rhythm. The trail opened up for a stretch, a yard-wide strip between the sloping talus on her right and a sheer drop of two thousand feet on her left, then wended amid the granite formations again, where she was forced to career from rock to rock. Her lungs squeezed painfully, begging for oxygen. Her temples pounded.

She paused to lean against a boulder, panting. "Are they still following us?"

Dante's face was twisted with effort. "A minute ago they were." He scanned around them. "I thought there'd be places to hide."

"We can't stop. We have to keep going." She heard her voice, shrill with distress. She pushed off the boulder and sped up the trail, fighting to control her breathing, searching for a cadence. The footing improved and she took her eyes off the ground to check the sky. Fear stabbed her insides. Gigantic thunderclouds filled the space between Mount Hitchcock and the Whitney massif, blocking the top third of the Hitchcock range. The clouds bore huge mushroom caps. And the wind was blowing them their way.

She shuddered as she placed her right foot onto a large rock. It tilted sharply under her weight, throwing her off balance. Her right pole skidded across a slab, and her pack swung sideways, toppling her. Her elbow smashed into the slab. A searing volt of pain shot up her arm. Her shoulder collapsed and her head hit the ground with a thump.

"Liz!" Dante squatted beside her. "Are you hurt?" She opened her eyes. Dante's boots. He was touching her head. "Your head's bleeding. Not too much."

She shifted to push herself up. A stab of pain from her elbow froze her. She stretched out her other arm. "Can you help me up?"

He grasped her arm in one hand and her shoulder strap with the other and pulled her to standing. She touched her forehead. A lump. Her fingers came away slick with blood. She moved to straighten her right arm and cried out.

"Oh, *carina*." He turned to search the trail behind them, but only a short stretch was visible. He placed his fingers under her chin. "We're going to find a place for you to rest, okay?"

She nodded.

"Can you carry your pack?"

"I think so."

He took one of her poles from her. "Okay, follow me. And watch your feet."

She hugged her injured arm to her belly and stepped where Dante stepped. One foot in front of the other. She bit down hard on her lip to take her mind off her throbbing elbow and planted her pole with care. She didn't monitor the clouds or look behind her. She knew all too well what she would see.

Chapter Thirty-One

Dante stepped from behind a block of granite and motioned to her. She climbed up to him and slid past into a space the size of a closet. He helped her remove her pack. She squatted in the far corner and cradled her arm. Now that she'd stopped, the pain was worse. She struggled not to cry. Dante handed her a water bottle and she drank deeply, realizing how thirsty she was.

"How's your arm?"

"Not good."

He untied the top of her pack. "Ibuprofen. And I can make a sling out of something."

"That would help a lot. But Dante, I'm really worried it's going to storm." Her voice broke.She closed her eyes, tried to focus, but she couldn't dispel the image of looming thunderheads.

He opened the bottle of pills, tapped four into his palm and gave them to her. "I agree we need to get off this mountain, but the Roots are between us and the exit." He pointed to the opening. "They'll find us here. There are so few places to hide."

She could see he was thinking the same thing she was: they should have retraced their route to Guitar Lake, gone out the long way through the Kern. Hindsight. He frowned, and fished the map out of the top compartment of her pack and unfolded it.

"What?" she said.

"I just want to look." He pored over the map. He looked up at her, excitement lighting up his face. "There's another trail." He turned the map so she could see and pointed at a dotted line to the east of the Whitney summit.

For a split second she believed a new way off

the mountain had magically appeared. Then her heart sank as it hit her what the dotted line represented. "It's dotted because it's not a regular trail."

"What sort of trail is it?"

"A mountaineering trail."

"What the difference?"

She'd read about the route in her book on Whitney. "It's steep—climbing, not walking. For most of the year, you need an ice ax and crampons for the top section."

"And the rest of the year?"

"Dante, we don't have the gear."

"People use ropes?"

"Some."

"So, it's possible without anything special?"

"Yes, but—"

He squatted in front of her and brushed her hair from her forehead. "We can't stay here. We can't go back. The Roots are waiting for us. Looking for us. They might not know about this route. And, even if they do, they won't expect us to take it."

Her mind spun, searching for a better alternative, coming up empty. Despair wrapped her tightly in its grip.

Dante locked eyes with her, his expression determined. "We need to get going, Liz." His eyes softened. "We need to go home."

His words broke into her. "Oh, Dante." Tears clogged her throat. She bent her head, unable to meet his gaze. "Do I even have a home with you?"

He paused. When he spoke, his voice was hushed. "It's what I've always wanted."

She'd been so stupid to doubt him, so blind in not seeing the strength of his devotion. And she'd wounded him in the worst possible way because of it. But did he want her still? She couldn't ask for fear of the answer.

He touched her shoulder. "We can't sit here, Liz. We really can't. Help me figure out what gear we need. Please."

She raised her head and wiped her eyes. "Okay." Moving quickly, he emptied both packs. He consulted with Liz about what they would need in a worst-case scenario, and refilled his pack with the tent, sleeping bags, ready-to-eat food, medical and safety kits, headlamp, knife and Aquamira for purifying water. In anticipation of increasing wind and the likelihood of rain, Dante put on his rain jacket and helped Liz into hers. He fashioned a sling from a shoulder strap, padding it with a rolled-up shirt, and stashed everything else in Liz's pack to be left behind.

Dante scouted to ensure the Roots were not in sight, and they left the hiding spot and resumed their climb toward the summit. The pills had taken the edge off Liz's pain, and she breathed more easily without the burden of a pack. Still, the air was thin and her heart raced. Dante walked behind her and offered encouragement. They left the twisting path behind and moved into the open. To the left, the face fell away steeply into the valley. To the right, a line of subpeaks of the Whitney massif came into view. At the far end was Whitney itself, a wedge of talus jutting into space. A hut stood near the lip, a tiny square set on a sloping plane of staggering proportions. The mountain's size was matched by thunderheads above, towering anvils with black undersides, changing Whitney's white granite to lead. The scope of the scene horrified her. The mountain was too vast, the clouds too dark and piled too high. She would be swallowed whole. Liz hiked faster, deaf to the ache in her muscles and her chest.

Dante called to her to stop. His grim expression told her everything. He pointed with his pole to a section of trail behind them, less than a half mile away. Two dark figures, one seated. The seated one rose and both set off toward Liz and Dante at a brisk pace.

"They've seen us," Dante said.

And there was nowhere to hide.

Liz smelled the sharp tang of ozone. She swallowed hard. A raindrop hit her boot. More drops fell noisily, dark splotches on stone. A low boom of thunder rolled in from the west. The skin on her arms prickled and dread filled her body with an ache like flu. She pulled up her hood and tightened the toggle. Dante gave her a wan smile and she turned from him and walked on toward the summit.

With every step they took, the sky darkened. Thunder rumbled, nearer and nearer each time. Out of the corner of her eye, Liz saw a flash of lightning. She turned to witness a series of strikes —five, six, seven—above Mount Hitchcock and closer, each followed by a roar of thunder, each igniting a paroxysm of distress in her. Her pace slowed. The trail led higher, and higher was not where she wanted to be.

They passed a gap between the eastern wall of peaks, windows through which they could see mountains and lakes and snowfields, and far beyond, the Owens Valley, where Lone Pine, and safety, lay. A few steps farther and the windows were behind them.

A deafening crack, resounding so close it trembled through the ground and up through the soles of Liz's boots. She dropped into a crouch and her knee hit her right arm. She screamed and squeezed her eyes shut. The hair on the nape of her neck tingled. Fear bloomed inside her, spreading out to her limbs.

This is it, she thought.

Dante was next to her, his arm around her. "It's okay, Liz."

She shook her head, her eyes still closed.

"We need to keep going. We're pretty close."

"I can't."

She made herself smaller, lower. If it weren't for her arm, she'd flatten herself against the earth. So flat, the lightning would never find her. So flat, the Roots would never see her. She would meld into rock, become stone. Become hard, unbreakable, impervious. Insensate. Unable to be hurt, to be lost. Payton Root could do nothing to stone. Stone could do nothing to Dante.

Thunder roared and her mind skipped. She glanced around her in jerking movements, taking in the trail, the slope, the dark sky. A realization hit her. Flat was wrong. Her best chance was the least contact with the ground. She scooted onto a flat rock balanced on sharp points.

Dante followed her. "What if we go to the hut?"

"The hut? No! It's not safe! Nowhere's safe. Lightning spreads. It hits and it spreads. You have to stay small!"

A rumble like a freight train overhead. Liz whimpered, bracing for the strike.

Dante knelt, their knees touching. He bent to see her face. "We can make it to the trail. You said it starts below the summit. We'll find it and go down. Then we'll be okay, Liz."

"You go. I can't do it. Not with a broken arm."

"You can. I'll help you."

She shook her head.

"Liz, no one's going to rescue us. They can't fly helicopters in a storm, not this high."

"I'll stay here. Leave me a sleeping bag and the fly."

"You can't sleep here! What about the Roots?"

She couldn't explain it to him, but the Roots and the storm were the same thing. She couldn't control them, couldn't evade them. She had faced them and been beaten back. They had it in for her. It was ridiculous to think that of a storm, but that's how it was. Like her, the Root brothers lacked moral structure (as did thunderstorms, of course) but they, at least, had power.

"Liz, listen to me. You have to walk. It's not far."

She shook her head again. Her cheeks were wet with tears. Her head pounded and arrows of pain shot down from her elbow. She could not, would not, move.

Dante didn't want her. He did before, but not anymore. She'd fucked that up. He was trying to get her off the mountain, but he'd do that for anyone. He'd do it for a cat.

A lightning flash so bright she saw it through her eyelids. She rocked and moaned, waiting for the jolt, the end. The sound of a tree splitting apart. Thunder so near she was sure the mountain would shatter, the ground beneath her crack wide open. Engulf her.

Dante said, "The lightning was in the sky. It didn't hit the ground. None of them are."

The storm was toying with her. Cat and mouse, like the Roots.

"Liz." He cupped her chin. "Open your eyes. Look at me."

She wouldn't. There was nothing to see except the pain she had caused. She had nothing to show him except regret.

"Elizabeth. I beg you." His voice had thickened. "Look at me."

She did. His beautiful brown eyes, awash in tears.

He said, "I'm going to help you get off this mountain. I'm not leaving you."

She breathed into the small space that opened in her chest. Afraid, she looked away. He lifted her chin with his fingertips, and kissed her softly. Her lips trembled against his. He pulled back and his eyes met hers, asking her to believe. "I'm not leaving you. Not now. Not ever."

"But—" A sob choked off her voice. She bit her lip and stared at him, waiting for him to take it back. She wanted nothing more than for him to love her again, but, with the yawning chasm between her fear and mistrust and his principles, her hope was so thin as to be transparent. She wanted to believe in love, to believe in them, but it wasn't something she could do alone.

Dante's eyes sparkled like sunlight on a river. She saw he meant what he said. The corners of his mouth lifted and he kissed her again. A sweet warmth flowed through her. She smiled and traced the curve of his cheekbone with her fingers, wiping away a tear.

"*Te amo*, Dante."

"*Te amo, carina.*"

Liz walked in front of Dante as rapidly as the altitude and terrain would allow. Each boom of thunder rattled her, but she kept on. Twice, the sharp scent of ozone alerted her. She dropped into a low crouch on a loose stone with her feet together and hands off the ground. Dante did the same. As she had explained to him, the posture reduced the chance an electrical charge would hit them and pass through their vital organs.

They passed another window, offering up a view to the sun-soaked valley, and approached Keeler Needle, the last peak before Whitney itself. The rain began to fall more heavily. This would have cheered Liz, as lightning strikes were less likely, but she knew rain would make the descent more hazardous. After Keeler Needle, the trail swung downhill before veering east for the final push to the top. Somewhere before the summit, along the north ridge, was the mountaineers' route.

A half hour later they stood on the broad summit slope. The roof of the hut was visible two hundred yards uphill. Dante asked her to stop. "So how do we find the trail?"

She'd been wracking her brain to recall what

she'd read a month ago, when she had no idea their lives would depend on it, but lack of oxygen and the threatening storm conspired against her. Thinking was like moving blocks in her head.

"All I remember is the route splits near the top. One is steeper and closer to the hut. The other is a longer traverse farther up the ridge." She pointed in front of them, where the rocky plane curved away and disappeared.

"Which do we want? The traverse?"

"I think so. If we can find it."

The air crackled. Dante grabbed hold of her good arm and pulled her into a crouch. She screamed as a bolt of lightning struck between them and the hut, puncturing the air with sharp white light. Liz concentrated on Dante's touch, binding them, a force equal to that of lightning. A thunderclap sounded above their heads and echoed off the distant peaks. She steadied her breathing, and stayed small.

After a few moments, Dante stood, lifting Liz with him. "Let's be mountaineers."

They moved slowly up the main trail, searching for side paths to the right. The first two they followed fizzled out before nearing the edge. The third was more distinct and angled to the west, a direct shot to the summit for climbers coming up the traverse. Liz and Dante increased their pace as they neared the lip.

Dante pointed ahead. "Look! Isn't that a carn?"

Liz saw the pile of stones and smiled. "A cairn, *amigo*. Yes, it's a cairn."

They reached the cairn and peered over the edge. A rough path through scree, a foot wide, ran diagonally across the face. The way off the mountain. Patches of snow and ice clung to shadows under the overhangs.

"Doesn't look too bad," Dante said, convincing himself. "I should go first."

Liz heard the unspoken clause. In case you fall.

She watched as Dante began the descent, the wind whistling up the face behind her, throwing rain against her back. He hadn't made it ten steps before his boot slipped a few inches, sending a cascade of stones down the slope. She tensed, stock-still. He paused a moment, and started again, with smaller steps. She was relieved to see the technique seemed to be working better. She exhaled and followed him. Her pole on the downhill side proved useless, as the scree was too loose to offer any support. She was desperate to make progress and her mincing steps frustrated her, but one look at the alarming distance she might fall kept her steps short.

The traverse ended a half hour later at a small level area, perched at the top of a three-hundred-foot cliff. A lake lay two thousand feet below. Liz stepped back, overcome with vertigo. She waited for the feeling to subside, then examined the narrow chute above them. The other way down.

No way she'd have managed it. The sky above the chute was black as coal. The Root brothers were somewhere up there, perhaps searching for this trail. The cold hand of fear moved inside her again. She stood anchored to the spot.

Dante was putting away his poles, knowing they'd soon have to use their hands to descend. He reached for her poles to stow in his pack, but she gripped them tightly.

"Liz? They'll get in your way." He saw her distress and placed his hand on top of hers. "Trust me." Her grip loosened. He took the poles and handed her the water. She drank, the cool liquid erasing the metallic taste of fear.

They headed down to a scree-filled gully to the north, the only obvious route. Dante cut across to stable rock at the edge, but soon returned to the center, as the rock was dangerously slick. They placed each foot with care, but nevertheless set off landslides, which sent Liz's heart racing. A person could tumble to the bottom as easily. When she followed the flying stones with her eyes, it induced vertigo, so she turned away. Her thighs and calves ached from the effort of positioning each foot before putting weight on it, and from bracing herself when she slid. The strain of the descent showed on Dante's face. Sweat beaded on his forehead and his mouth was taut with concen-tration. He stopped frequently and watched her progress with concern.

Finally, the edge of a lake came into view. Halfway down the gully, they could see the entire circle of the lake carved in barren rock. Two shapes—orange and yellow—huddled near the north edge.

Dante said, "Are those tents?"

"Looks like it."

He grinned at her. "Don't run, okay?"

She'd never been so glad to see signs of other people. She wanted to fly down to the lake. "I won't. It's a long way." Liz knew they had about four thousand feet more to descend when they reached the lake. But the sight of the tents lifted her spirits, as did the increasing likelihood they had finally escaped the Roots.

They crept down the scree and talus, periodically trying the more solid rock at the edge. The rain began to ease. Liz's knees ached from the strain of the pitch, and her elbow hurt whenever she moved her arm, as she was forced to do several times when she skidded. Three sections required actual climbing where being short a limb terrified her. Dante gripped the rock face directly below her, showing her the footholds, or moving her foot into position. Once he was the foothold. Unable to move to the right because of her arm, she couldn't reach the jutting rock Dante had used. He braced himself and she placed her foot on his shoulder to attain the next hold. She thought about being stranded on the steep face of Whitney alone and her throat pinched shut.

They stopped for a brief rest and ate some trail mix. From here they could see most of the route above them. No one was there. Dante gave Liz two more ibuprofen and took three for himself. "A poor substitute for beer," he said.

"As much beer as you want tonight." Tears stung her nose at the thought of sitting with him, having a drink, being together, with no secrets waiting in the shadows.

"It doesn't seem possible."

"I know."

Two hours after they left the rim of Whitney, the gulley ended and they hiked along a solid path to the lake. The rain had nearly stopped. Liz had to resist the urge to run. As they neared the tents, a bearded man wearing a red beanie crawled out of the nearest one. He waved.

Dante reached for Liz's hand. She spun to face him. The furrows in his brow were gone. He looked like a little boy. She laughed and threw her good arm around him. They kissed, smiling as they did. Liz no longer felt afraid or exhausted or forsaken. The cramping in her chest, the tightness in her throat had gone. In its place, exhilaration. She was grinning like a fool and couldn't care less.

Chapter Thirty-Two

The man was Joe from Boulder, here to make a bid for the north face of Keeler Needle. He and his girlfriend had been playing Yahtzee, waiting out the rain. "You two look like you been in the Whitney blender."

In their relief, Liz and Dante quickly told Joe about the Roots, and Brensen. Liz explained her arm was probably broken, and that they didn't know the way back to the Portal.

Joe frowned. "Holy crap." He cast his gaze at the trail leading up the gulley. "You think those two followed you down?"

Dante said, "We haven't seen them since the top, but it's possible."

"Holy crap."

Liz said, "We haven't run into anyone else in two days and thought the trails might be closed. But you're here, so . . ."

Joe looked at his feet. "We've been here two nights, but didn't bother with a permit. Figured we'd bag the Needle and be out of here before anyone noticed. This late in the season we didn't think it'd be an issue since they don't patrol up here much."

A woman wearing French braids crawled out

of the tent and joined them. She introduced herself as Trina.

She listened intently as Joe filled her in. "We heard a chopper this morning. Remember, Joe? Thought it was kinda late for resupplying a ranger station."

"We saw it fly over Guitar Lake," Dante said. "Low."

Joe said, "Someone's looking for those creeps, that's for sure. The weather's clearing up, so they might decide to come down this way. If I were running, that's what I'd do."

Liz exchanged looks with Dante. "We hadn't thought about it that way."

Trina nodded toward the second tent. "I'll wake up Marshall. We should pack up and get out of here, just in case."

Liz and Dante found seats where they could monitor the trail while the climbers broke camp. Trina spoke with Marshall through his tent door. A moment later he popped out like a spider darting onto its web. A wiry man sporting black-rimmed glasses, he moved with breathless efficiency. He stowed his sparse gear in his pack in minutes, then helped Trina and Joe with theirs.

Joe hoisted his pack and waved to Keeler Needle, its tip buried in cloud. "Next time, big guy."

Marshall was familiar with the trail and led the way, followed by Trina, Liz and Dante. Joe took up the rear. Marshall hiked well ahead of the group, but Trina set a moderate pace. Liz shadowed her, step for step, allowing herself to relax a little. Simply hiking with four people instead of one made her feel less vulnerable. Marshall waited at difficult junctures for the others to catch up, and he and Joe assisted Dante in helping Liz down tricky sections. In several places the route was indistinct or, to Liz's eye, completely invisible. If she and Dante had been alone, they could easily have lost their way. As they descended, the air thickened and Liz took full breaths for the first time that day. The knots in her shoulders and neck began to loosen. The way was steep, but the footing was stable—at least compared to the gulley.

They passed Lower Boy Scout Lake and arrived at the edge of a vast granite face. Liz scanned for the route but saw nothing but dead ends.

"Ebersbacher Ledges," Trina informed them. "Lots of people get tangled up here." They navigated the steep, circuitous route, and dropped to a streambed where the path was choked with willows. After fighting their way through for a half mile, they came upon a stream crossing. A rustle on the far bank startled them. Marshall paused midstream. Liz clamped her hand on Dante's arm, her heart in her throat. The willows parted and a woman in uniform appeared—a ranger. She moved onto a flat rock and a policeman pushed through the growth and stood beside her. Dante turned to Liz, his eyes sparkling. Relief coursed through her limbs. "At last," she whispered to Dante, "saved by a ranger." He stifled a laugh.

The hikers picked their way across the stream and assembled on the bank. The ranger extracted a notepad and pen from her pocket and asked for their names.

"Elizabeth and Dante, we've been expecting you, though not coming this way. But I don't have any record of the other three."

"Yeah, sorry about that," Joe said. "We were flying under the wire."

The policeman, a trim man in his forties, spoke. "We have a bit of a situation here. We've asked the Park Service to close the trails, due to an interdepartmental manhunt."

"Which is one reason," the ranger said, staring pointedly at the climbers, "we like to know where folks are."

Joe lifted his hands in apology. Marshall stared off downstream, impatient to continue.

The policeman pointed at Liz's arm. "Are you injured?"

Liz nodded. "You're looking for Payton and Rodell Root, right?"

"We sure are. Where'd you last see them?"

"They were less than a mile from the summit," Dante said.

"And that was when?"

Dante consulted Liz. "Maybe noon?"

The policeman gestured to the trail behind him. "Let's take this conversation someplace more comfortable. It's not far."

The ranger and the policeman led them to the main Whitney Trail and down to the Portal, about a mile. As they walked along a narrow paved road toward the parking lot, several official vehicles, including an ambulance, came into view. More than a dozen police officers, rangers and other personnel stood in small groups. A tall, beefy man in a black nylon jacket met them as they approached, introduced himself as FBI Agent Gutierrez and took their names. When he found out the climbers had no contact with the Roots, he let them go.

He spoke to Liz. "You need someone to look at your arm right away, or can I ask a few questions first?"

"I'm okay. But can we sit down?"

They moved to a picnic table a short distance down the road. A map of the area was spread across it. Someone brought them each a sports drink, which they quickly emptied. Gutierrez explained the Root brothers were wanted on a number of drug charges, and in relation to the suspicious death of their father.

"What about Matthew Brensen?" Dante said.

"That, too." He gestured at the map. "Now, I

want to hear the whole story, but first show me where and when you last saw them."

Dante located the spot on the Whitney Summit trail. "Around noon, they were about here."

"And they were heading toward you?"

"We thought so. The storm was terrible, so we couldn't really tell. We only wanted to get off the mountain."

Gutierrez called over two men from the Sheriff's Department and relayed the information. The men left and Dante related their encounters with the Roots, pointing out the locations on the map. Gutierrez asked Liz a few questions, but otherwise she let Dante talk. Told all at once, the magnitude of their ordeal struck Liz anew. She could feel Dante's eyes on her from time to time, but she kept her gaze on the map. He was telling their story, and it was in the past tense, but the terror she experienced on the summit was very much alive inside her. She leaned against Dante's shoulder and fell silent. Her arm throbbed and a tide of exhaustion rose within her. She closed her eyes.

"That should do it for now," Gutierrez said. "An officer can take you to the hospital in town, get that arm taken care of." He shook their hands, thanked them and handed them his card. The policeman whom they'd met on the trail approached and asked about their car. Dante explained they'd left it in Yosemite Valley and had planned to take a bus back.

"It's a little late in the day for that. If it's all right with you, I'll call down to the Sierra View Motel and set you folks up with a room. Won't be anything fancy, mind you."

"Sounds like heaven," Dante said.

He accompanied Liz to the hospital, then left to buy clothes for them while Liz received treatment. She had been waiting in the lobby a few minutes when he returned, fresh from a shower, wearing tan cargo shorts and a navy T-shirt. She looked down at her elbow cast, brilliant white in contrast with her tanned skin and dirty, soot-stained clothing.

"Oh, Liz. Your poor arm!"

"It's okay. Only six weeks to go." She stood and placed her hand on his cheek. "I'm glad you haven't shaved your beard."

He smiled. "We can discuss its future over dinner at the steakhouse."

"I hope I'm not too tired to eat."

"Don't even think that, *carina*."

They walked the three blocks to the hotel. The late-afternoon heat rose from the sidewalks, dulling her senses. They crossed the main street to the hotel and climbed the exterior stairs to the second-floor rooms. Liz stopped halfway. Her legs, encased in stone, balked at the command to climb higher. After a rest, she managed the last steps. Dante opened the door to their room and ushered her inside. It was basic, but clean, and contained everything Liz needed: running water, a real bed and Dante.

She collapsed onto the edge of the bed. A pair of gray capris and a blue-and-white striped T-shirt lay beside her. "Thanks for getting these."

"They didn't have much of a selection."

"Yeah, but I bet every single piece was clean."

"Good point. I'll start a bath."

She considered lying down but feared she'd never be able to get up again. Her eyes went to the window, and the open curtains, and the door. She rose with effort, peered out at the parking lot and pulled the curtains shut. She hung the chain across the door and threw the deadlock, exhaling deeply as the bolt slid home.

They ate dinner at the steakhouse, choosing a table at the back. The food was delicious, but neither of them could manage more than half of their steaks. "My stomach has shrunk," Dante said. "How sad."

By the time the check arrived, Liz felt she was melting into the booth. They left the restaurant, crossed the parking lot, climbed the stairs and locked the door behind them. Liz undressed and slid between the sheets, so smooth against her skin, raw and taut from sun and wind and cheap soap. Dante climbed in and encircled her in his arms. She laid her head on his chest.

She said, "It's not rational—I know we're

safe—but I'll feel so much better when they arrest them."

"I know, *carina*. So will I."

They fell silent then, and Liz soon fell asleep, Dante's heartbeat a metronome of solace.

The next morning they had breakfast at the Lone Pine Diner, feasting on eggs, bacon, pancakes, home fries and a side of waffles. Liz watched Dante transfer another pancake from the stack to his plate.

"You should be proud of your stomach. Such a quick recovery."

He nodded and returned his attention to his plate. His phone vibrated on the table. He tapped the icon and put the phone to his ear. "Hello? Yes, speaking. Good morning, Agent Gutierrez."

Liz put down her fork.

"Yes, I see. Yes, Liz is fine."

Her mouth was parched. She sipped her water. Dante was listening and nodding. She raised her eyebrows at him, hoping for a signal, but he didn't notice.

"Thank you very much. Yes, you, too." He said good-bye and tapped the screen closed. He reached across the table and took Liz's hand. It was trembling. "It's over, Liz. They captured the Root brothers in the lower Kern Valley. He couldn't give me any details, but wanted us to know they're in custody."

"Thank God." She let out a long breath, one

she felt she'd been holding for a week, and imagined Payton in handcuffs, staring defiantly out of the rear window of a police cruiser. "The agent couldn't tell you anything?"

"No, because of the ongoing investigation. The same as on TV."

"I guess we'll read about them in the paper."

"I might prefer to forget about them."

She nodded, suddenly unable to speak. Dante squeezed her hand and she let the tears fall.

They finished eating and went back to the room. The sunlight filtered through the curtains as it had through their tent, a dim amber glow. They returned to bed and made love, their every breath a whisper of tenderness, and faith.

Chapter Thirty-Three

Liz pulled her phone from the hip pocket of her jeans with her left hand, an awkward move even after two weeks. A missed call, probably as she'd gone through airport security. She slid the icon to the right.

"Hey, Liz. It's Russ. Your dad. Yeah, so I was talking to your mom and she mentioned your hiking trip. Anyway, if you've got a minute . . ." His voice trailed off and the message ended. She'd not heard from him in two years, and then only because he had business in San Jose. She checked the time—her flight for Albuquerque wasn't boarding for a half hour—found his number and called.

"Russ here. Tell me you're not selling me something."

"I'm not selling you anything. It's Liz."

"You don't say! This time of day all I get are salespeople."

"You're a salesperson."

"You got me there, kiddo." He took a swig of something and smacked his lips. "You pick up my message?"

"Yes."

"Well, I thought I'd give you a jingle. Sounds like one helluva camping trip."

She couldn't help but laugh.

"Read about those guys in the paper." He whistled. "Blew up their dad with a rigged door, then ran off with the goods from the family pot farm, plus the other stuff. What's it called?"

"Meth."

"Yeah, meth. That's it. Boosted a truck, too. With a gun in it, naturally. Maybe killed that actor. Bronson?"

"Matthew Brensen."

"He's the one. Anyhoo, that's a considerable amount of wrongdoing. Lucky you didn't get hurt."

"Only a little."

"What? Oh, right. Your arm. Your mother

mentioned a fellow. A Mexican guy. He your boyfriend?"

"He's more than that," she said.

"You don't say. Well, that's nice. It's not healthy to be alone."

Relationship advice from her father. The world was officially upside down.

He cleared his throat. "Your mother and I went camping a lot, even a couple of backpacking trips. Had some great times."

This was more information than she'd ever received about her parents. "Where did you go?"

"Bandelier, the Pecos, Sedona, around Flagstaff. All those places I took you. Used to go there to dry out from Seattle."

And she had thought her camping trips with her father had been about economizing, not connecting her to his past.

He went on. "And it looks like you got the hiking bug. That's nice."

"I do love the mountains."

"Remember that time in Bandelier? You aren't still afraid of thunderstorms, are you?"

"I'm working on it."

"That's good. I wouldn't like to think anything happened on my watch that scarred you for life." He chuckled at the idea.

"I think you would have had to try harder. There weren't many watches."

"I suppose not." His tone signaled increasing boredom. "Well, it's bedtime out here, and the grandkids are coming over tomorrow."

She wondered which one of the half siblings she'd never met had had children. She tried to conjure an image of Russ holding a baby, and failed. "I won't keep you. Thanks for calling."

"No problem. You take care. Maybe I'll be out there one of these days."

"Maybe you will."

"If my back isn't a mess, maybe we could even go for a little hike somewhere."

"I'd like that, Russ."

She rented a car in Albuquerque and drove north, arriving at Claire's house in the late afternoon. Claire hugged her at the door and ushered her inside. Her mother had made unusual flourishes of hospitality: takeout from Enrico's in the fridge, a jar of chrysanthemums on her nightstand and a pair of fuzzy slippers by the bed. When Liz thanked her, she shrugged. "It's so little, really. And the tile floors do get chilly this time of year." They drank tea and shared a scone at the chipped blue table. Her mother slurped her tea and chewed gracelessly, the inevitable consequence of too many solitary meals. She spoke of the recent death of a close friend, and of the stoicism of another battling cancer.

"She's my age," she said, squinting beyond the bare branches at the window, as if she might see what lay in store for her. Without looking down, she swept the crumbs to the floor.

The next day they walked along the river and across to the plaza. Liz slowed her pace to match her mother's. She had never been conscious of Claire's age before; her mother had always been colorful, inviolable and ageless. They approached the Romanesque cathedral, whose large, square towers, Corinthian columns and rose window contrasted dramatically with the ubiquitous adobe buildings.

Claire said, "I attend mass here from time to time. For the singing."

She pictured her mother at the far end of a pew, but not at the rear—Claire wasn't a lurker—humming and swaying to hymns that were to her only songs. Liz imagined if her mother returned for ten, fifteen years, she might absorb the church's religion the way its stones absorbed the sun's heat. A song could become an anthem.

A man passed by, holding hands with a little girl eating ice cream. Liz remembered what she'd been meaning to ask her mother.

"Russ mentioned the two of you used to hike near here." Claire gave her a questioning look. "He called me."

She nodded. "We were roughly your age. He loved to drag me into the woods. Made it hard for me to wander off on my own, as was my inclination. Is." She stopped short and regarded her daughter. "How long was the backpacking trip you did with Dante?"

"Eighteen days."

"I always thought you were a loner, Elizabeth. Like me."

"So did I. But not anymore."

She brushed the transformation away with her hand. "Either way is fine. You just need to decide what you prefer."

"Don't you get lonely?"

"Of course. But that's the price I pay to get out from under the weight of other people's perceptions, their judgments. I'm not strong enough to bear them."

She pitied her mother then, because Liz knew the things that matter most are not borne because of others, but with them.

Late that afternoon, she called Dante from the boarding area. He picked up on the first ring.

"*Carina*. How is your mother?"

"The same. Older. But fine." She checked her watch. "My flight's on time."

"Good. I've missed you."

"I've missed you, too."

"But Muesli, I'm afraid, feels differently. She has taken up residence on your pillow."

"Two days and you give her squatter's rights?"

"She's persuasive. Especially her claws."

Liz laughed. "See you in a few hours."

"Safe travels, *carina*."

"Te amo."

"Te amo."

She boarded the plane, took her seat at the window and settled in with her book. She looked outside from time to time as they passed over the desert, shadows from the mesas deepening in the canyons. An hour and a half into the flight, Death Valley appeared, glowing like hammered copper. She put down her book. The Sierras came into view, the eastern slopes soaring out of valley, crests dusted white from a recent snow. Row upon row of peaks, stretching northward out of sight. Somewhere below was Mount Whitney. She may have spotted it, but couldn't be sure. From this vantage point, even the highest mountain in the continental U.S. resembled the others. Somewhere below was Wallace Creek, running to the Kern, and Bubbs Creek and Woods Creek and, farther north, out of sight, the Tuolumne. Someone, quite a few intrepid someones, in fact, were stirring dinner over a tiny stove, or lying huddled in their sleeping bags. Nutcrackers were returning to their roosts. Somewhere below the wind was stealing a treasure of aspen leaves and floating them to the ground. And everywhere pine boughs gave in a little to the snow and granite did not.

The foothills flowed, reaching for the sea. The Sierras were behind her now. She was going home.

Author's Note

For the purposes of the story, I suggest the park rangers are largely absent, and perhaps not performing their duties. The rangers I have met while backpacking have been universally competent, serious in their duties and extremely friendly. They perform a tough job in a tough environment, and I hope they forgive my license.

The John Muir Trail described in this novel is as close to the actual trail as I could manage, but those familiar with the area may notice I omitted the Crabtree Ranger Station.

Questions for Discussion

1. How did you feel about Liz when you learned she'd had an abortion and kept it a secret? If your feelings changed over the course of the novel, what caused this change? Did Dante's ultimate compassion and love alter how you saw Liz?

2. At one level, *The Middle of Somewhere* can be understood as an allegory, with life as a wilderness and the trail representing the journey through it. The Root brothers, within this metaphor, represent evil. What other elements of the story (characters, events, and places) have allegorical significance?

3. Liz's marriage to Gabriel began with love and hope and ended in betrayal and disaster. As Dante pointed out, they were very young. Is that the whole story? What is your understanding of what happened between Liz and Gabriel? Do you think Liz has put that behind her?

4. How do you feel about Liz's affair? Did you feel she had "paid" for her infidelity with the death of her husband? More generally, how

do you view Liz in light of her upbringing, her actions (the abortion, the affair, the secrets), and her feelings about herself?

5. Along the trail, Liz and Dante encounter and sometimes befriend other hikers. What role did these characters (Brensen, Paul, and Linda) play in the larger story?

6. The story was told from a single point of view: Liz's. What would have been added, or diminished, by adding other perspectives?

7. The Root brothers became more and more of a threat as the story progressed. Did you see the stress they caused as a mirror of the conflict between Liz and Dante? At what point did you realize just how dangerous the Roots were? The reason the Roots pursued and threatened Liz and Dante was never completely clear. Did this bother you, or did you draw your own conclusions?

8. The barren splendor of the Sierra is central to this book. What did the landscape mean to Liz, and did that change over the course of the hike? Can you imagine this story in a different setting? In other words, how dependent was the unfolding and resolution of Liz and Dante's journey on the physical surroundings, including the weather?

9. If you have been on an outdoor adventure, did that experience cause you to reflect on your life in a new way? In general, does "getting away from everything" or deliberately jumping out of one's comfort zone promote new thinking? Is this something you'd welcome in your life?

10. Why do you think Liz chose to go on the hike? What was she looking to accomplish? Did she succeed?

11. What do you believe happens after the book ends? Do Liz and Dante marry? Do they have children? Does Dante reconnect with his estranged sister, Emilia? Do you foresee any changes between Liz and her parents?

About the Author

Sonja Yoerg grew up in Stowe, Vermont, where she financed her college education by waitressing at the Trapp Family Lodge. She earned her PhD in Biological Psychology from the University of California at Berkeley and published a non-fiction book about animal intelligence, *Clever as a Fox* (Bloomsbury USA, 2001). Sonja, author of the novel *House Broken*, currently lives with her husband in the Shenandoah Valley of Virginia.

Center Point Large Print
600 Brooks Road / PO Box 1
Thorndike, ME 04986-0001 USA

(207) 568-3717

US & Canada:
1 800 929-9108
www.centerpointlargeprint.com